REASON AND THE LOVER

REASON AND THE LOVER

by John V. Fleming

PRINCETON UNIVERSITY PRESS

Copyright © 1984 by Princeton University Press
Published by Princeton University Press, 41 William Street,
Princeton, New Jersey 08540
In the United Kingdom: Princeton University Press, Guildford, Surrey

ALL RIGHTS RESERVED

Library of Congress Cataloging in Publication Data will be
found on the last printed page of this book
ISBN 0-691-06578-0

Publication of this book has been aided by The Whitney Darrow
Fund of Princeton University Press

This book has been composed in Linotron Garamond
Clothbound editions of Princeton University Press books are printed on
acid-free paper, and binding materials are chosen for strength and
durability. Paperbacks, although satisfactory for personal collections, are
not usually suitable for library rebinding.
Printed in the United States of America by Princeton University Press
Princeton, New Jersey

CONTENTS

FOREWORD

This book has its origin in one of the very few facts concerning
the *Roman de la Rose* that lie beyond controversy: the fact that
it is very long. Any poem that by comparison makes *Troilus
and Criseyde* or *Paradise Lost* seem short, if it does nothing else,
challenges the critic who would pretend to give an account of
it at once comprehensive and detailed. No general analysis is
likely to carry more conviction than it gains from the strength
of specific close readings in which it is based; but a close reading
of twenty thousand lines of poetry is hardly the task of a single
book. The problem is exacerbated by the stubborn structure
of the *Roman de la Rose*, which provides the reader with no
convenient subsidiary units that we can analyze, with real or
imagined justification, as exemplary models of the whole. Ver-
gil gives us books, Chaucer tales, Dante cantos; but the *Roman
de la Rose* gives us merely 21,750 lines of continuous verse.

In an earlier book (*The Roman de la Rose: A Study in Allegory
and Iconography*, 1969) I attempted a rather general interpre-
tation of the whole poem. Though I have continued to study
both the work and its criticism intensively since that time,
finding new poetic dimensions and not infrequently modifying
my own previously held views, I remain convinced of the
justness of my general characterization of it. At the same time,
I have become increasingly conscious of the need for the kind
of specific and detailed textual analysis that might offer a
convincing test of my more general findings. For this purpose
I have sought out a tractable and coherent narrative passage,
and I have begun where Jean de Meun himself began, with
what the manuscript rubrics sometimes call the "chappitre de
Reson," the dialogue between Reason and the Lover that oc-
cupies lines 4191 to 7200 of the Lecoy edition.

My purposes in this book are to explore the literary genre

of this dialogue, to examine some of its most important literary relationships, and to analyze some of its more remarkable poetic techniques. My findings suggest that Jean's text demands a good deal of its readers, and certainly more careful study than it has always received. Jean's persistent patterns of Christian classicism, and in particular his intellectual and literary mediation of Cicero, Augustine, and Boethius, have important implications for all the major movements of his poem—the "chapters" of Amis, La Vieille, Nature, and Genius—that I hope perhaps to explore in future studies.

Although the *Roman de la Rose* remains something of a neglected masterpiece, its critical study has increased significantly in the past decade. In rethinking the critical challenges posed by the poem, I have reviewed, with a few negligible exceptions, all the materials listed in the bibliographies of K. A. Ott's *Der Rosenroman* (1980) and Maxwell Luria's *A Reader's Guide to the Roman de la Rose* (1982), the best general guides to study of the poem. For the text I use the recent edition of F. Lecoy, which is now more generally accessible than that of E. Langlois. Much recent work on the *Roman* is illuminating and challenging, and I am deeply indebted to it even when—as with the work of the Ithacans, submitted to critical analysis in my first chapter—I frequently have found myself in sharp disagreement with it. It is my hope that *Reason and the Lover*, founded in the study of the artful dialogue with which Jean de Meun took up his *Roman de la Rose*, can itself contribute to a larger conversation about the whole poem.

As the years go by, I am ever more keenly aware of the privilege of association with a great university, humblingly rich in its scholarly facilities and its intellectual community. I wish that in thanking Marilyn Walden and William Bowen— a departmental secretary who typed my manuscript with her characteristic professional skill and a university president indefatigable in his nurture of the conditions that allow scholarly research to flourish—I might make adequate if token acknowledgment of the numerous remarkable people who have sped my study. But such thanks cannot serve to recognize the wisdom, the courage, and the vision of those vanished generations of our common benefactors who have enabled our shared enterprise. We probably remember them too seldom, but in such a formal moment as an author's adieu to his book they do crowd the mind. Perhaps they peer down from the philosophical detachment of the sphere of the fixed stars and chuckle indulgently at a college professor's extraordinary agitation over the interpretation of a thirteenth-century poem.

Sublunary gratitude is easier to express, though no less heartfelt. No book of mine has made me more cognizant of my continuing debt to my students than has *Reason and the Lover*. Its direct ancestor was a small graduate seminar on Jean de Meun and Geoffrey Chaucer composed of students of rare talent, two of whom—Carolyn Dinshaw and John Longo— have since written important studies bearing on the *Roman*. Seldom can a teacher have taught less or learned more. I owe another substantial debt to many friends and friendly antagonists, some of them known to me only through correspondence and the cordial exchange of offprints, who have helped me in ways not always adequately expressed by footnote citation. I want to mention particularly Nikolaus M. Häring, Thomas D. Hill, David Hult, Douglas Kelley, Maxwell Luria, Karl August Ott, Rupert Pickens, Nancy Freeman Regalado, Eugene Vance, and Winthrop Wetherbee. Several friends and colleagues read and commented upon the manuscript: Charles Dahlberg, Gail Gibson, Seth Lerer, and D. W. Robertson. No good deed goes unpunished, and they are to be held entirely responsible for any infelicities and imperfections remaining in the work. Three people who actually know something about Petrarch—my colleagues Robert B. Hollander and Thomas P. Roche, and Enrico Fenzi in Italy—read my final chapter without quite gagging, and I interpreted this qualified approbation as sufficient license to proceed. Tam Curry has once again proved herself a superbly competent editor, a model both of *rigor and of tact. I acknowledge with thanks Josephine Lee's* valuable help with the proofsheets. Finally, I want to thank Michael Stugrin and Peggy Knapp, who commissioned an earlier version of my second chapter for publication in the inaugural number of *Assays*, which they edit. To the usual folks—Joan, Rich, Katy, and Luke—go the usual thanks for things too small and too great to mention.

Princeton, April 1983

REASON AND THE LOVER

1.

THE LINEAGE OF LADY REASON

I. A Brief Refutation of the Ithacan Heresy

In a book published now more than a decade ago I advanced the argument that Reason alone of all of the Lover's teachers in the *Roman de la Rose* commands the authority to be trusted, that hers is the one voice within the poem to which we can confidently listen for the moral adjudication of the poem's amatory doctrine. Unlike many other views expressed in the same book, this one I did not regard as particularly controversial, and I have been surprised that the question of Reason's credibility has become the specific focal point of more serious discussion of the poem. My views have not been widely accepted, and they have been contradicted by a number of scholars who maintain, on various accounts, that Reason herself is an imperfect, flawed, or limited guide and that we can no more turn to her in confident assurance than we can turn to the god of Love, la Vieille, or Amis in search of wholly reliable doctrine. For such critics, the ironic claims upon the poem are very great indeed, and we are left with no certainty save that we can construct ourselves. As one of them puts it, "Ultimately, no figure emerges to provide an authoritative, valid definition of *amor*, because none can be drawn from this context, from the realm of postlapsarian Nature."[1]

The view that Reason is a "limited" character within the poem, incapable of addressing the Lover's situation or incom-

[1] Michael D. Cherniss, "Irony and Authority: The Ending of the *Roman de la Rose*," *MLQ* 36 (1975): 230.

petent to pass moral judgment upon his behavior, I call the
Ithacan heresy. I find the jocular term "heresy" appropriate
not only because, from my perspective, it denotes a serious
misreading of the *Roman de la Rose* but because many of the
issues involved in its discussion—free will and moral respon-
sibility, for example, or the nature of the sexual appetite—
are precisely those that commanded protracted debate in the
struggle against "heresy" in the high patristic period, and in
particular during the lifetime of St. Augustine. The heresy is
"Ithacan" for the simple reason that its most effective advocates
have written from Ithaca. I use the term in a good-natured
way, and with an awareness that, at least in these matters,
one man's heresy may well be another's orthodoxy. For I, too,
am a heretic, indeed a heresiarch.[2] And of course, I share the
admiration that even St. Augustine on occasion expressed for
his brilliant adversaries, agreeing fully with him that heresy
has the signal utility of making us rethink the points of our
own belief with greater depth and clarity. My own aim in the
following pages is to advance a discussion of the *Roman de la
Rose* focused on careful readings of specific passages of text.
Some theological controversy is but a prolegomenon, if a nec-
essary one, and I shall be brief. The Ithacan heresy is a serious
inconvenience to the understanding of the *Roman* in general,
and absolutely fatal to an understanding of the literary character
of the dialogue between Reason and the Lover with which Jean
begins his poem. Before we can possibly understand what
Reason was for Jean de Meun, we must see why she cannot
be what the Ithacans have made of her. We must defend Lady
Reason from detractors. We must make a brief refutation of
the Ithacan heresy.

[2] My view that its cultural circumstances would make the *Roman de la
Rose* inevitably "Christian" qualifies me for *two* heresies: "the heresy of
philosophical predominance and the heresy of univocal zeitgeist," according
to William Calin, "Defense and Illustration of *Fin' Amor*," in *The Expansion
and Transformation of Courtly Literature*, ed. N. B. Smith and J. T. Snow
(Athens, GA, 1980), 35-36. I can barely pronounce these heresies, let alone
promulgate them effectively; but one does what one can.

Although our debate is about Reason, some discussion of the Lover himself is inevitable since the character Reason may be regarded as a figure of the Lover's rationality or of human reason generally. Thus it is that the first Ithacan error is, strictly speaking, an error concerning Amant's *ability* to follow Reason. In general, the Ithacans insist upon the "postlapsarian" character of the world of the *Roman de la Rose*, and they imply or even state a radical disjunction between the power of rationality as it existed before the fall and as it exists now. Here, for example, is the opinion of Michael Cherniss: "In a postlapsarian world—which Deduit's garden certainly is—Reason does not hold uncontested sway over human emotions."[3] My quarrel is not with this unexceptionably true statement, but with what the statement implies and is meant to imply, namely, that in a prelapsarian world Reason *did* enjoy such power. It should be obvious that if prelapsarian Reason had been invincible, there would have been no lapse. The seduction of our first parents in Paradise was generally taken by medieval scholars as the very type of the triumph of the "human emotions" over the reason. The human capacity for irrational behavior is a fundamental fact of man's primal nature, absolutely dictated by the fact of his free will—just as, on the other hand, is his capacity for rational choice. Man was created "sufficient to have stood, though free to fall."

The argument is already only a short step from denying the freedom of the will, for if fallen man's rationality is radically impaired, he can hardly exercise full rational choice. This is exactly what Winthrop Wetherbee claims about Amant in the *Roman de la Rose*: "What Raison cannot understand, though it is ironically implicit in her speech, is a depravity such as to make man incapable of responding to her love."[4] Wetherbee

[3] Cherniss, "Irony and Authority," 230.

[4] Winthrop Wetherbee, "The Literal and the Allegorical: Jean de Meun and the 'de Planctu Naturae,' " *MS* 33 (1971): 271. In the reworking of this article in Wetherbee's *Platonism and Poetry in the Twelfth Century* (Princeton, 1972), the idea is expressed thus (p. 258): "But like Alain's Nature,

does not say "the Lover" but "man," and he does not say
"unwilling" but "incapable." The only conclusion to be drawn
from this statement that *man* is so depraved as to be *incapable*
of responding to Reason's love is that the race lacks free will
and, hence, moral accountability. This would overthrow Au-
gustine, Boethius, and indeed all of medieval Christian thought
about the nature of man, and I believe *a priori* that from an
historical point of view it is nearly impossible that Jean de
Meun could have espoused such an idea. There is, however,
no need to argue the case at the level of abstraction, since there
is the clearest possible textual evidence that the foolishness of
the individual man Amant is not the inescapable nature of *all*
men. I refer to the pointed contrast made near the end of
Reason's speech between Socrates and Amant. Socrates is an
historical, mortal, postlapsarian man and a "gentile" exempt
from any possible special graces of the Covenant. He is thus
a splendid example of one possible vision of "natural Man,"
and in textbook syllogisms known to every medieval student
of the arts, he is actually used as the representative of all men
in general. Of him Reason says this:

> Por ce fu Socratés itex   6857
> qu'il fu mes amis veritex.
> Le dex d'Amors onc ne cremut
> ne por Fortune ne se mut.
> Por ce veill que tu [*sc.*, Amant] le resembles,
> que tout ton queur au mien assembles . . .

To this the Lover replies, among other nonsense: "Je ne pri-
seroie .iii. chiches / Socratés . . ." (6879-80).

This line of argument is bad enough, but there is worse to
come, as the moral culpability of the Lover is transformed by

---

Raison cannot understand the full implications of human depravity, the
contradiction between the fact of a powerful *Amors* for which the only remedy
is flight, on the one hand, and the necessity of procreation in obedience to
Nature on the other." Wetherbee cites no text in the *Roman de la Rose* to
support this claim. I certainly have not found one.

the Ithacan argument to the spiritual incapacity of Reason. "Like the Nature of the *De planctu*," writes Wetherbee, "Raison cannot think in theological terms."[5] He would refute the exalted station that Robertson and I have claimed for her in the following way: "See line 4373 [Mes je sai bien, pas nou devin], where Raison introduces her speech on procreation with what seems to me a pun on *deviner*, meaning 'guess,' 'prognosticate' or 'engage in theological speculation,' and her repeated references to the will of Nature, her high court of authority."[6] I too admit a pun on *devin* (see line 5071 where *devin* are clearly friars, the "theologians" *par excellence* of Jean's day), but I fail to see how using a word meaning to "engage in theological speculation" speaks to a putative inability to think in theological terms. I read these lines to mean that Reason can know the natural ends of sexuality without recourse to special revelation. I know, without divining it, that sex is linked to reproduction. It seems to me dangerous to conclude from such a statement that "Raison cannot think in theological terms," unless we are willing also to impute the same incapacity to St. Paul, who can make a similar appeal to the powers of the naked reason to know the divine purpose (Rom. 1:20ff.) and for whom the index of disordered thought is likewise disordered sexuality.

If "theological terms" are terms that speak of God and God's relationship to men, I am tempted to say that Reason thinks in practically nothing but them. Her self-identification as the daughter of God, mentioned by Wetherbee, is of course a theological statement, and there are many others during the course of her conversation. Let me cite but one. At line 5089 Reason launches an attack on misers and the avaricious that includes these lines: "Certes Dieu n'aiment ne ne doutent / quant tex deniers en tresor boutent" (5091-92). There is a probable echo here of Matthew 6:19 in *tresor boutent*, and there

---

[5] Wetherbee, *Platonism and Poetry*, 258.
[6] Wetherbee, *Platonism*, 258n.

is *certainly* theological consciousness in the idea of "loving God" and its negation. "Dex le leur savra bien merir" (5096), which speaks of God as the judge of souls, is likewise a theological statement of course; and the idea that God will punish those rich men who are indifferent to the sufferings of the poor probably is drawn from the story of Lazarus (Luke 16). Next Reason cites, without attribution, a well-known saw from the *De contemptu mundi* of Innocent III concerning treasures on earth: that there is great labor in acquiring them, fear in possessing them, and pain in relinquishing them.[7] She continues by saying that "God hates avaricious men . . . and damns them as idolators" (5219-20). The idea that misers are idolators is not one that makes a great deal of sense outside the context of Christian theology. The same passage includes a condemnation of usury based explicitly on a theological perception: usury is contrary to God's order.

What of Reason's "repeated references to the will of Nature, her high court of authority"? Wetherbee does not provide specific instances, and I have not found them in the poem. The first thing we learn about the relationship of Nature and Reason, and the only thing in Guillaume's part of the poem, is that Reason is too beautiful to have been created by Nature: "car Nature ne seüst pas / ovre fere de tel compas" (2971-72). No high court of authority there. During the discourse of Reason in Jean de Meun's poem, an interlude of some three thousand lines, the name of Nature comes up precisely four times. Reason reports to the Lover, as a matter of fact and without discernible obeisance, that all men follow the god of Love, except for those (homosexuals) whom Genius excom-

---

[7] Lines 5167-72. Cf. the *De miseria humanae conditionis*, ed. M. Maccarrone, 1.15, p. 21: "Labor in acquirendo, timor in possidento, dolor in amittendo, mentem eius semper fatigat, sollicitat et affligit: 'Ubi est thesaurus tuus, ibi est cor tuum.' " Jean de Montreuil on avarice puts Jean's French back into Latin as follows: ". . . ait ingeniousus de Magduno: *labor in acquirendo, timor in conservando, et in dimittendo angaria atque displicentia*" (*Epistolario*, ed. E. Ornato [Torino, 1963], 301).

municates because of their crime against Nature (4315). A few lines later, in discussing the natural purpose of sexual love, Reason says that Nature wills the continuation of the species and that she has implanted *delit* in the sexual process in order to encourage the works of procreation (4382ff.). Reason imposes her own independent authority on the discussion by insisting on the dangers of pleasure and, in fact, by interpreting the purpose of sexual pleasure. In this passage Reason is the high court, Nature the appellant. Reason next mentions Nature in an incidental way in a quotation from the *Consolatio Philosophiae*: Fortune cannot give to men those things that Nature made alien to them. A final reference to Nature comes in a discussion of "natural love" (5733), defined as "a natural inclination to wish to preserve one's likeness by a suitable intention, either by engendering or by caring for nourishment." Natural love is a fact of biological creation, and it applies to men and beasts alike. Its operation is morally neutral. Reason ends its discussion with the well-known Augustinian analogy between alimentation and sexual reproduction, an analogy that inevitably brings with it the Augustinian implication that the supernatural graces accessible to human reason are of a higher order than the natural inclinations of the flesh. The Ithacan interpretations of the *Roman de la Rose* all depend upon Wetherbee's erroneous claim that Reason makes "repeated references to the will of Nature, her high court of authority." There is, however, not a single such passage in the entire poem. Instead we find a Reason created superior to the natural realm, capable of judging it from a distance.

I have now sufficiently demonstrated, I believe, the error of two principal points of the Ithacan view of the *Roman*. In the first place, if "man" the species (as opposed to the individual and morally accountable Amant) is incapable of reasonable love, that means nothing else than that mankind lacks free will, and any claim the poem might have to serious philosophical ideas surrenders to biological determinism. But Amant

is conspicuously contrasted to Socrates, an historical mortal
man, precisely to show that "man" is indeed capable of rea-
sonable love. Secondly, we have seen that Reason *repeatedly*
thinks in theological terms and speaks in theological language.
There is also a third error, more narrowly literary in nature.
One signal weakness of Wetherbee's interpretation of the *Ro-
man*, from my point of view, is that it is committed to an
unconvincing reading of the *De planctu Naturae* of Alain de
Lille. It seems to me that Wetherbee fails to distinguish be-
tween the important intellectual transformations that Jean de
Meun brings to the materials of the *De planctu* on the one hand
and the essential continuities between the two works on the
other. This is of course not the place to pursue the debate at
length. Our present concern is Jean de Meun's Reason, and I
shall limit my objections to narrow grounds.

Wetherbee argues that Jean's character Reason is analogous
to, indeed closely modeled on, the character Nature in the *De
planctu Naturae*: "Raison's limitations are those defined by Alain's
Nature in comparing God's power and her own."[8] I find a
serious confusion in these claims. The character in Jean's *Roman*
who is most closely and most coherently modeled on the Natura
of Alain de Lille is obviously and entirely unsurprisingly Na-
ture. One of the texts Wetherbee draws attention to as evidence
of the limitations of Natura's powers as compared with God's
is a passage in which Natura denies knowledge of the "second
birth" of baptismal grace, that is, of the sacramental fruits of
the Incarnation: "Per me homo procreatur ad mortem, per
ipsum recreatur ad uitam. Sed ab hoc secunde natiuitatis mis-
terio mee professionis ministerium relegatur. Nec talis na-
tiuitas tali indiget obstetrice sed potius ego Natura huius
natiuitatis naturam ignoro. Et ad hec intelligenda mei intel-

---

[8] Wetherbee, *Platonism and Poetry*, 258n. In "The Literal and the Alle-
gorical" (271n) the limitations are said to be "stated" rather than "defined,"
but the idea is of course essentially the same. Cf. George D. Economou,
The Goddess Natura in Medieval Literature (Cambridge, MA, 1969), 119-21.

lectus hebet acumen, *mee rationis confunditur lumen.*"[9] Now there is in the *Roman de la Rose* a passage very closely modeled on this one (19115ff.), but it is of course put into the mouth of Nature, not Reason. We note, indeed, in the italicized phrase, that Natura characterizes her own incapacity to understand grace as a limitation not of man's reason but of her own mode of operation (*mea ratio*).[10] Finally, the whole passage comes hard on the heels of a lengthy discussion of the roles of *ratio* and *sensualitas* in the human constitution in which the preeminence of *ratio* is unquestionably established and which ends with the categorical denial that man's natural condition excuses unreasonable behavior with regard to sex: "Nec in hac re hominis natura mee dispensationis potest ordinem accusare."[11] In short, there is in this text no warrant at all to impose the limitations of Alain's Natura on Jean's Raison. The character Reason does not exist in the *De planctu Naturae*, and from her initial appearance in the *Roman de la Rose* she is explicitly elevated above Nature's realm.

I shall have occasion to return to other aspects of Wetherbee's analysis of the *Roman de la Rose* in another chapter. Though his remarks about the poem in *Platonism and Poetry* are brief, they have been taken up by other Ithacan heretics as authoritative. Thus what is merely a nasty rumor about Lady Reason in Wetherbee has become an established truth for Carol Kaske.[12] Her confident misquotation of Wetherbee (who is now supposed to have said that Reason cannot think in theological

[9] Alan of Lille, "De Planctu naturae," ed. M. Häring, *Studi Medievali*, ser. 3, vol. 19 (1978): 829. In italicizing the final phrase, I follow Wetherbee ("The Literal and the Allegorical," 272n) who cites the same passage as though it demonstrated a deficiency in Jean's character Reason.

[10] Man's reason was created by God, not by Nature; see line 19116, and the discussion below pp. 27ff.

[11] "De Planctu naturae," ed. Häring, 827.

[12] Carol V. Kaske, "Getting Around the *Parson's Tale*: An Alternative to Allegory and Irony," in *Chaucer at Albany*, ed. Rossell Hope Robbins (New York, 1975), 147-77.

terms "at all") supports an equally confident misreading de-
signed to reveal the "unchristian" nature of Reason's ideas,
one of which, according to Kaske, is that "Reason disapproves
of clerical celibacy as being against Nature."[13] The text ad-
duced to support this claim is a passage in which Reason
extrapolates on the vices of youth as described in Cicero's *De
senectute*.

Par Jonece s'en va li hons   4409
en toutes dissolucions
et suit les males conpaignies
et les desordenees vies
et mue son propos souvent.
Or se rant an aucun couvent,
qu'il ne set garder la franchise   4415
que Nature avoit an lui mise,
et cuide prendre au ciel la grue
quant il se met illeuc en mue,
et remaint tant qu'il soit profés;
ou, s'il resent trop grief le fes,   4420
si s'en repent et puis s'en ist;
ou sa vie, espoir, i fenist,
qu'il ne s'en ose revenir
pour honte qui l'i fet tenir,
et contre son queur i demeure: 4425
la vit a grant mesese et pleure
la franchise qu'il a perdue
qui ne li peut estre rendue,
se n'est que Dex grace li face,
qui sa mesese li efface   4430
et le tiegne en obedience
par la vertu de pacience.

The subject of this passage is not clerical celibacy in general
but the coerced chastity that Jean de Meun elsewhere in the

---

[13] Kaske, "Getting Around," 152, 153-54.

poem personifies as Constrained Abstinence. As there are distinctions in matters of sexual indulgence—seduction as opposed to rape, for instance—so also are there in matters of constraint. Even so, nothing is said in this passage about either clerical celibacy or constrained abstinence as "being against Nature." Reason says that a young man may "put himself in some convent because he does not know how to control that freedom that Nature has given him." The passage as a whole draws a comparison between two extremes, both of which show an inability of the young man to cope with his own freedom—the dissolution of a "disorderly life" (4412) on the one hand, constrained abstinence on the other. The statement that clerical celibacy and constrained abstinence are against nature is of course unexceptionable in any event, but Reason does not happen to make it. Jean de Meun himself may have disapproved of the ecclesiastical discipline of clerical celibacy; many clerks in his time and later have so disapproved. Reason herself, however, expresses no general opinion on the matter, and no opinion at all that we can call "unchristian." That she does not disapprove of the ideal of religious chastity is manifest from the closing section of the lines cited (4428ff.).

The Ithacan tenet that "Reason cannot think in theological terms at all" is sharply contradicted by these lines, so it is hardly surprising that Kaske chooses to read only "between" them in search of Reason's "self-betraying asides."[14] If "the grace of God" is not a theological term, I do not know what one is. "Obedience" and "the virtue of patience" (4431-32) are likewise, as used by Reason, theological terms; and the word *profés* (4419) is a technical term of the religious life. I suppose we may call this self-betrayal of a sort. Reason betrays her own familiarity with a cherished idea of medieval ascetic theology—to wit, that religious chastity cannot be attained through purely human capacity, but only through the coop-

---

[14] Kaske, "Getting Around," 153.

eration of the human will with God's grace—an idea classically stated in a famous page of Augustine's *Confessions*.[15]

The Ithacan argument staggers on, stumbling up against the sharp corners of Jean's text with increasingly painful effect. We come to the point where Reason tells the Lover,

> Mes conment que la besoigne aille,   4515
> qui veust d'amors joïr sanz faille,
> fruit i doit querre et cil et cele,
> quel qu'ele soit, dame ou pucele . . .

According to Kaske, if only I had considered these four lines, in which Reason "condones premarital sex so long as the 'maiden' manages to become pregnant," I could never have maintained that Reason was associated with Divine Sapience, that her sexual doctrine was Augustinian, or that it was well known to thirteenth-century readers.[16] I take this in poor part, actually, for as it happens, I do remember the lines in question. They come as a kind of thematic recapitulation at the end of an attack on the voluptuary principle that, according to Reason, the Lover has adopted. Even as wrenched from their context by Kaske, however, the lines say absolutely nothing about condoning premarital sex and nothing about a "maiden" getting pregnant. Reason says that people who want to enjoy love correctly, whether they be men or women, ought to seek love's fruit. (She goes on to add that they ought to have a good time while they are at it.) This doctrine, including its parenthetical addendum, is *pure* Augustinianism.[17] There is some theological language in this passage too, incidentally. The word "fruit" has inescapable technical connotations of

---

[15] *Confessions* 6.11.20, citing Wisdom 8:21; for the significance of the scriptural context, see below, pp. 25ff.

[16] Kaske, "Getting Around," 152, 153.

[17] Augustine repeatedly defended the licitness of reasonable sexual delight in his anti-Pelagian writings. See especially *De bono conjugali* 16, the passage used by Thomas Aquinas to authorize his own opinion that "the abundance of pleasure in a well-ordered sex act is not inimical to right reason" (2^a2^{ae}.153.2ad2).

proles in this context, and *sanz faille* refers to *moral* error. I opined that this doctrine would be well known to Jean's readers because it is a commonplace of his contemporary moral theology, the most obvious background against which we can measure the conventionality or originality of the sexual ideas in his poem.[18] I associated Reason with Divine Sapience because Guillaume de Lorris had done so.[19]

There are other points in Carol Kaske's article that invite refutation, but the only other point directly relevant to my present purpose is the imputation of biblical illiteracy to Reason. Supposedly, Reason "never cites the Bible (nor does any speaker on those sexual topics which are the book's main concern; in contrast, the digression against mendicants cites Scripture on every page). . . ."[20] I must reserve for a later chapter a more seriously literary discussion of the relationship between scriptural and classical wisdom in Reason's speech, but one or two points can be quickly made. A contrast between the discussions of sexuality and mendicancy is without force with regard to the density of scriptural citation. There was no other language for the poverty debate than the language of Scripture, for the friars insisted that mendicancy was *the* authentic form of evangelical life.[21] The discussion of sexual morality, on the other hand, had a long prechristian history in the philosophers. The more important point is that Reason *does* cite the Bible. I find numerous passages of scriptural language in her speech, though I shall limit myself to but two—the first because it is actually documented in the explanatory notes of the edition quoted by Kaske, the other because it is closely related to a passage cited by Kaske to refute me. One of the precepts of Reason is the following: "Fei tant que tels envers touz soies /

----

[18] The Augustinian basis of the mainstream of thirteenth-century moral theology in this regard is demonstrated in detail by M. Müller, *Die Lehre des hl. Augustinus von der Paradiesesehe* (Regensburg, 1954).

[19] See the discussion below, pp. 27-28.

[20] Kaske, "Getting Around," 152.

[21] I have discussed this question more fully in my *Introduction to the Franciscan Literature of the Middle Ages* (Chicago, 1977), 83ff.

con touz envers toi les voudroies" (5421-22). As Lecoy notes, this is an obvious rendition of the so-called Golden Rule, "Do unto others as you would that others do unto you" (Matt. 7:12). There cannot be many verses in the New Testament that are better known. Slightly more obscure perhaps, but only slightly, is "Radix enim malorum est cupiditas" (1 Tim. 6:10), the only text on which Chaucer's Pardoner ever preaches. Reason cites it in a very witty way that underscores the continuity of Ciceronian and Christian wisdom. Her discussion of voluptuaries, to which I have earlier referred in my thumbnail survey of the relationships between Reason and Nature, qualifies the pleasure principle of sexual relations by stressing the dangers of pleasure-seeking (4392ff.). Reason's term for pleasure is *delit*, a word that Genius subsequently uses as an index of the wretched "world of necessity" initiated by the castration of Saturn.[22] The explicit source adduced by Reason as an authority on *delit* and its dangers is Cicero's *De senectute* ("Tulles le determine / ou livre qu'il fist *de Viellece*"); but as so often with Reason, the explicit citation brings with it implicit Christian authority. According to Cicero, according to Reason, the man who gives himself over to pleasure makes himself a serf "to the prince of all vices"—a phrase that, incidentally, makes sense only within a Christian theological context—because "C' [delit] est de touz maus la racine" (4399). The Ciceronian word reflected by Jean's *delit* is *voluptas*, a word commonly used in Christian moral theology as a synonym for *cupiditas* in its sexual application. The silent negotiator between Paul and Cicero is Augustine. His wonted use of the word *voluptas* as a technical moral term has been recognized as a borrowing from Cicero's own moral vocabulary.[23] It was Augustine as well who equated *voluptas* with *cupiditas* and *libido*.[24]

---

[22] This nice phrase is Wetherbee's, in a passage that makes the connection between *delit* and fallen nature (*Platonism and Poetry*, 259).

[23] See M. Testard, *Saint Augustin et Cicéron* (Paris, 1958), 1:25ff., and passim.

[24] E.g., "Voluptatem praecedit appetitus quidam, qui sentitur in carne

Kaske's interpretation of the poem exemplifies what is in my view the common error of the Ithacan heretics, and that is to make much of what Reason does not say and either too much or too little of what she does; but it is such an extreme example of misreading that its refutation is insufficient to refute the heresy itself. No interpretation of the *Roman de la Rose* that so consistently misrepresents its literal text is likely to command assent; but the attack on Reason has been much more plausibly and responsibly made.

The most attractive and accordingly from my point of view the most dangerous statement of the Ithacan heresy comes from the pen of Thomas Hill. He chooses for himself a role not unlike that of Reason herself, the pilot who finds the safe mean between the shoals of opposing excess—in this case, modernist naturalism on the one hand and Robertsonian moralism on the other. He is able to agree with some tenets of both schools, maintaining at once that Jean de Meun pillories his Lover and that he is very upbeat about sex. That is, the Lover *is* a fool, but then you have to be one to make babies. The article in which Hill advances his reading of the poem is rich and winsome, and it deals with a number of important matters, including specific points of mythographic interpretation and Augustinian theology, with which I have long been in agreement. With what he says about Lady Reason, however, I cannot agree.

Hill extenuates the Lover's rejection of Reason with a double argument, first by denying Reason's sufficiency as a sexual guide, then by justifying the Lover's means by reference to his

---

quasi cupiditas ejus, sicut fames et sitis, et es quae in genitalibus usitatius libido nominatur, cum hoc sit generale vocabulum omnis cupiditatis" (*De civitate Dei* 14:15); "Libido recte definitur: Appetitus animi quo aeternis bonis quaelibet temporalia praeponuntur" (*De mendacio* 7); "Amor, cum pravus est, vocatur cupiditas aut libido" (*Enarrationes in psalmos* 9.15). These texts and others are conveniently gathered in the article by C. Vaca, "La Sexualidad en San Agustín," in *Augustinus Magister* (Paris, 1954), 2:727-36; see in particular 727-29.

ends: "He does not accept the love which Raison proffers him (which suggests his irrationality), but his dismissal of Raison is in a sense almost justified. That is, when Raison comes to the lover, he loves his rose, and Raison does not directly respond, in any way, to his situation. Raison's remarks about sexuality are brief and cryptic."[25] Again, "The Lover does not follow Raison's advice in most respects . . . but at the end of the poem he does beget a child, and in this respect, at least, the result of his folly accords with the precepts of Raison."[26]

I am convinced by neither of these statements, which seem to me to lack textual warrant; the second in particular suffers from a demonstrable confusion of logic. The implication of the remark that the Lover does not follow Reason's advice in most matters is that he does follow it in one: in begetting a child. But this is not supported by the text. The Lover follows Reason's advice in *no* respect, and the last thing we hear him say of her in the poem sums up his attitude to her throughout: "I did not remember Reason, who wasted so much effort on me."[27] In order to defend the Lover's irrationality by an appeal to his begetting a child, Hill has to imply that one of Reason's "precepts" is that begetting children is a good thing *tout court*. This is a possibly reasonable idea, though capable of irrational manipulation by various characters in the poem, but it is *not* an idea advanced by Reason. Concerning the begetting of children Reason says one thing only: that a man who lies with a woman should earnestly seek the fruit of love, which is of

[25] Thomas D. Hill, "Narcissus, Pygmalion, and the Castration of Saturn: Two Mythographical Themes in the *Roman de la Rose*," *SP* 71 (1974): 420-21. How much justification there is in being "in a sense almost justified" I cannot gauge.

[26] Hill, "Two Mythographical Themes," 417.

[27] "Mes de Reson ne me souvint, / qui tant en moi gasta de peine" (21730-31). Hill's analysis assumes without argument the veracity of the statement that the Lover begot a child. The content of the *Roman* is not history, however, but a nightmarish dream. The claim that everything allegorically described in it actually came to pass is made by a narrator of extremely dubious authority.

course *proles*. Her positive precept concerns the ordering of the will, which is within rational control, not the fertilization of the ovum, which is not. It is logically impossible that any act of folly is in accord with the precepts of Reason, nor can the result of folly exculpate folly itself. As Augustine puts the matter in theological terms, "Good children born of adultery do not justify adultery."[28] What the Lover himself says of his begetting of a child, incidentally, is that it was a *fault*.[29] His fertilization of the ovum is in his own view the single trespass in an otherwise satisfactory sex act.

The argument that improper means are justified by proper ends is not "paradox" but moral error. A man may earn bread for his children by honest toil or highway robbery with similar or identical material results, but the fact of nutrition does not justify larceny, not even "in a sense almost" justify it. Of course, the crime *would* be "morally ambiguous" if that were the only means of the man's feeding his children, for necessity knows no law. This line of argument Hill brings to bear, implicitly, on the *Roman de la Rose*. Human sexuality in the fallen world is irrational; reason has no say in it; fallen man must go it alone, without Reason. The purest statement of the Ithacan heresy might be this: man's fulfillment of the divine will with regard to his sexual nature can be accomplished only by the denial of reason, the image of God within man.

The argument that leads to this unstated conclusion claims to find its basis in "Augustinian sexuality." Let us see. Hill's argument is complex, often elegant, sometimes elusive, and never easily summarized, but the gist of it is that Augustine teaches that, as a result of the fall, reason has been alienated from sexuality. The exemplum of the castration of Saturn signals Jean de Meun's intention to define "man's sexual nature in a post-lapsarian world"; and Reason's bemusement at sexual

[28] ". . . boni adulterorum, nulla defensio est adulteriorum" (*De bono conjugali* 16).

[29] "Vez ci tout quan que g'i *forfis*" (21701).

euphemism exemplifies her failure to comprehend "Augustin-
ian sexuality." The Lover *is* irrational, but he is "in a sense
almost justified" in his irrationality, since reason cannot com-
prehend or address his predicament.

I think that Hill seriously misrepresents Augustine in two
respects: first by failing to stress the centrality in Augustine's
teaching of guilty pleasure (*libido, voluptas*) and second by
underestimating the power of the rational will in controlling
it. Hill cites the well-known passage in *De civitate Dei* 14
where Augustine contrasts the rational and voluntary opera-
tions of the sexual organs in Paradise with their passionate and
disordered stimulation in the fallen world. "Thus, for Au-
gustine one of the most immediate results of the fall is the
alienation of sexuality from reason."[30] This is in a sense true.
The rational will can no longer command a dispassionate erec-
tion. It is not true, however, in the sense that Hill would
persuade us: namely, that human reason is incapable of un-
derstanding or addressing sexuality in a postlapsarian world.
If Augustine actually believed *that*, he could hardly have un-
dertaken numerous books, including the fourteenth book of
the *City of God* itself, in which he rationally analyzes fallen
human sexuality.

That is an error concerning the nature of the "alienation of
sexuality from reason." There is another, I think, concerning
the *extent* of such alienation. On the basis of another well-
known passage (*De civ. Dei* 14.16), Hill concludes that "Even
within marriage human sexuality, according to Augustine, is
affected to some degree by original sin, in that even a wise
man who is attempting to beget children cannot participate
in sexuality and remain wholly rational at the same time."[31]

This is authentic Augustinian doctrine only if the phrase
"participate in sexuality" is a coy indirection for "experience
sexual climax." What Augustine clearly alludes to in the pas-

---

[30] Hill, "Two Mythographical Themes," 420.
[31] Ibid.

sage cited is the moment of orgasm, the most intense experience of sexual *voluptas* ("ita ut momento ipso temporis, quo ad eius pervenitur extremum"). At this moment the rational command of the soul is almost completely abandoned. Neither the orgasmic epilepsy nor its pessimistic moral analysis is original with Augustine. Aristotle, Cicero, and Vergil before him also regarded this frenzied pleasure as a humiliation of human nature; and in Augustine's view it was linked with the sin of primal disobedience,[32] introducing a residual morbid quality into even licit sexual relations. But though this most intense *voluptas* of sexual intercourse is inescapable and compromising to those who engage in intercourse, it does not define all of human sexuality. My benevolent reader will I am sure agree with me when I say that all of life is not one long orgasm. If it were, we could perhaps be justified in ascribing to Augustine a doctrine of radical or irreparable alienation of reason from sexuality—though we might well want the energy to publish our claim. This is not Augustine's teaching, however.

To "participate in sexuality" is not for Augustine an elective course, deferrable in case of headache. Human beings *are* sexual; that is the way God made them. Their choice is not whether they will or will not be sexual, but how they will be sexual. The arena of choice is precisely that of reason and grace. Reasonable responses to sexuality are various. They include marriage, in which *voluptas* is put to honorable use, and continence, by which the sexual instinct is curbed through rational discipline. Continence can be achieved only by the grace of God, but it is a way of handling sexuality, not a way of denying its existence. Augustine himself was still vigorously participating in sexuality when he was seventy years old.[33]

There is also, of course, an unreasonable response to human

[32] See the important materials gathered by Vaca, "La Sexualidad en San Augustín"; and John J. O'Meara, "Virgil and Saint Augustine. The Roman Background to Christian Sexuality," *Augustinus* 13 (1968): 307-26.

[33] See Vaca, "La Sexualidad en San Augustín," 731.

sexuality, typified by the priority of *voluptas* and its excessive
or single-minded pursuit. Though in the fallen state no man
can fully keep in mind the rational ends of sexuality *during
the frenzy of the coital climax*, that does not mean that it is
"natural" or excusable for a man to pursue *voluptas* as the sole
end of love. This, however, is precisely what, according to
Reason, the Lover is doing:

> Mes l'amor qui te tient ou laz   4570
> charnex deliz te represente,
> si que *tu n'as ailleurs entente* (italics mine).

Augustine offers Amant small comfort, but there is another
strand to Hill's argument. It is that Reason is an insufficient
guide for him because she does not know what Augustine
knows: "Raison does give intimations of what rational sexuality
might be, but she does not tell the lover how to attain it . . .
though there is after all an explicitly Christian response to the
lover's situation. Raison does not tell the lover to seek his rose
in honorable wedlock . . . [or] to remain celibate."[34] There
are several responses to this objection.

   Hill's argument is in the first place an argument from
silence. The imputation that Reason has nothing to offer on
subjects not explicitly raised in her discourse is convincing
only if ratified by other evidence. Reason probably knows that
two and two make four, even though she does not say so. She
does not counsel the Lover on how many drinks he can have
before dinner nor on how much he should pay for his shoes,
but that hardly means that there is no reasonable point of view
on such matters. Reason is a universal feature of the human
species, not the particular grace of the sanctified. This means
that there is no special Christian Reason any more than there
is a special Christian digestive system or circulation of the
blood. I shall presently argue that the strategic constraints of
Dame Reason's forensics, like those of her mother Lady Phi-

---

[34] Hill, "Two Mythographical Themes," 421.

losophy, derive from a specific literary tradition in which, for apologetic reasons, Christian revelation was "reduced" to the categories of classical philosophy. This means that Reason speaks as a "philosopher" much of the time, and not as a "theologian"—bearing in mind that what Jean de Meun would mean by "theologian" was an expounder of the Scriptures. The Christian doctrines of the *remedium* and of celibacy, to which Hill alludes, are of course *theological* doctrines to which specific recourse by the *philosophical* Reason need not be expected.

To be sure, Reason's teachings accord with theological truth. Indeed, if we are to have "Augustinian sexuality" in the *Roman*, we must surely have an Augustinian Reason to address it— and Augustinian reason ever operates in cooperation with the truths of revelation.[35] This means for starters that Reason does quite explicitly address the moral presuppositions that undergird Christian teachings concerning sexual intercourse on the one hand and sexual continence on the other. They are, respectively, the connection between sexual love and procreation (4373ff.) and the dangers of pleasure-seeking (4392ff.). Marriage is an arena for sexual intercourse and votive celibacy an arena for sexual abstinence, but marriage and celibacy are forms of life, not states of mind. Being married no more guarantees rationality than does being a plumber or a professor. That the over-ardent lover of his own wife is an adulterer was a current maxim of medieval moral theology, and Augustine points out the poignant physiological irony of sexual impotence, whereby a man may burn with a fierce lust while being incapable of raising an erection.[36]

Hence neither a discussion of marriage nor a commendation of celibacy would address the Lover's "situation" in any event. It is not that he faces uncertain options of his sexuality, but

[35] For a particularly lucid and economical account of this feature of Augustinian thought, see Pierre Thomas Camelot, " 'Quod intelligimus, debemus rationi': Note sur la méthode théologique de saint Augustin," *Historisches Jahrbuch* 77 (1953): 397-402.

[36] *De civitate Dei* 14.16.

that his sexuality is firmly engaged in an obsessive, single-minded, irrational passion: "tu n'as ailleurs entente." The Lover is not an emblem of human sexuality, but of the *libido* that corrupts sexuality. Neither marriage nor celibacy solves the problem of irrational passion; they are both arenas for rational love.

The Lover's problem is not sexuality but irrationality. There is only one cure for irrationality, and that is rationality. Thus Reason does indeed tell the Lover in the clearest possible terms how to attain "rational sexuality." The way in which one "attains" rationality of any sort is by being reasonable or, in the dramatic terms of the *Roman de la Rose*, by believing, following, and loving Reason. "Rational sexuality" for a Christian consists not in an arbitrary mode of life—giving in marriage or not giving in marriage—but in being rational about sex. What Reason says to the Lover is this: Love me, and all other loves will be well.[37] *That* is how one attains rational sexuality. One is reminded of the great line of Augustine, "Love, and do as you please."[38] To attribute the Lover's folly to the putative "limitations" of Reason is to indulge in what the sociologists call "blaming the victim."[39] That the Lover acts contrary to Reason in the *Roman de la Rose* is manifest; that Reason is incapable of coping with "sexuality in a post-lapsarian world" is absurd. A sick man may, out of stubbornness or madness, refuse to take his prescribed medicine; but that is hardly convincing evidence that medicine is incapable of addressing sickness.

[37] See lines 5765ff.

[38] "Dilige et quod uis fac" (*Tractatus in Iohannis epistulam* 7.8).

[39] For a cheerfully jejune example of this process, see Daniel Poirion's cashiering of Reason in his *Le Roman de la Rose* (Paris, 1973), 154: "Son propre échec est la conséquence de son imperfection et de ses équivoques. Il n'est pas en contradiction avec le rôle que lui confie Alain de Lille dans son *De Planctu* et dans son *Anticlaudianus*, textes dont Jean de Meun s'inspire généralement pour construire son personnage. Le pouvoir de la Raison est fait pour être dépassé." Is it unsporting to observe that the character Reason *does not exist* in the *De planctu Naturae* of Alain de Lille?

II. Reason's Divine Lineage

This somewhat distressing review of the argument of the Ithacan heretics, though it has diverted me from the possibility of a more positive contribution to an understanding of the *Roman de la Rose*, has seemed necessary to me for two reasons. The first is that I feel a special obligation in this regard since the heresy was developed as a quite specific rebuttal of my own work. More than a decade ago, when I first began writing about this strange and beautiful poem, I advanced the claim— in my naiveté I thought it an unexceptionable one—that both the language of Guillaume de Lorris and the iconographic assumptions of the illustrated manuscripts linked the character Reason with scriptural Wisdom. What I said specifically was that "to say that Lady Reason shares the iconographical attributes of Lady Philosophy [in the *Consolatio* of Boethius] is also to suggest her kinship with Divine Sapience, the Second Person of the Trinity, a kinship clearly established in the texts of both Guillaume and Jean."[40] This the Ithacans have denied, but my own reexamination of the poem in the light of their arguments has convinced me only that its sapiential theme is more important to its poetic strategies than I had first realized. A second impetus is that the Ithacan view of things has dominated discussions of Lady Reason, at least in English-language criticism, for the past decade; and there are indications that, merely for want of challenge, an ingenious but errant hypothesis might become a canonized "fact" about the *Roman de la Rose*. My own primary appeal must of course be to the text, but I am aided by the work of other scholars as well. Apparently unbeknownst to the Ithacans, what I hinted at concerning "sapiential" Reason has been reiterated in much more detailed fashion by P. Badel, who published an interesting article on "Raison, 'Fille de Dieu,' " in the Frappier festschrift of 1970.[41]

[40] John V. Fleming, *The Roman de la Rose: A Study in Allegory and Iconography* (Princeton, 1969), 114.

[41] P. Badel, "Raison, 'Fille de Dieu' et le Rationalisme de Jean de Meun,"

Badel's article is, among other things, an anthology of those passages of the poem most relevant to the characterization of Reason, both in terms of what the narrator says of her and in terms of what she herself and the poem's other characters say of her. It is particularly helpful in its identification of relevant scriptural materials. With this little guidebook in hand, let us return to the poem in time for Reason's début.

Though there is small critical agreement concerning Jean de Meun's *use* of sophisticated theological materials, the fact of their presence in his poem has long been accepted without cavil. On the other hand, Guillaume de Lorris has not much been accused of a theological perspective—"courtly," "artificial," "psychological" are the adjectives he is wont to attract. It comes as a surprise, therefore, to discover the precisely theological nature of that part of his description of Lady Reason which enlarges what Curtius calls the "Old Woman and Girl" topic and which links her unmistakably with the Philosophia of Boethius. What Guillaume de Lorris has distinctly invented is this:

> A son semblant et a son vis   2969
> part qu'el fu fete ou paravis,
> car Nature ne seüst pas
> ovre fere de tel compas.
> Sachiez, se la letre ne ment,
> que Dex la fist ou firmament
> a sa semblance et a s'image   2975
> et li dona tel avantage
> qu'ele a pooir et seignorie
> de garder home de folie,
> por tant qu'il soit tex qu'il la croie.

Mélanges de langue et de littérature du Moyen Age et de la Renaissance offerts à Jean Frappier (Geneva, 1970) 1:41-52. Some implications of Badel's article are drawn out in an exciting essay by E. Fenzi, "Boezio e Jean de Meun, Filosofia e Ragione nelle rime allegoriche di Dante," *Studi di Filologia e Letteratura (Dedicati a Vincenzo Pernicone)*, 2-3 (1975): 9-69.

The busyness of critical apparatus for these lines perhaps suggests that they are dealing with sophisticated ideas beyond the sure grasp of the normal run of a vernacular amanuensis. The phrase "Dex la fist ou firmament" (2974) raises special problems. I doubt that the words *ou firmament* ever came from the pen of Guillaume de Lorris. And numerous medieval scribes seem to share my doubt, for their "variants" include a number of different adverbs pointing to God's proprietary relationship to Reason: He is said to have created her *demainement, nomeement, meisemement*. The reading adopted by Langlois, *demainement*, strikes me as the most probably authentic. *Demainement* means "personally" or "of His own substance" or something to that effect. The adjective *demaine* relates to a word denoting authority, possession, majesty. It can mean simply "his own," as when Guillaume writes of the hapless Narcissus that he "ama son umbre demain."

Whatever reading we favor in line 2974, it is God who is Reason's maker. The *letre* of the previous line—the textual authority that authenticates the claim—can be nothing but the Bible, and Badel has identified the principal scriptural passages to which Guillaume makes specific allusion. The inescapable phrase *semblance et image*, to which we must shortly return, is particularly insistent, though the richness of Guillaume's theology goes well beyond the first chapter of Genesis. Badel identifies the clear allusion in these lines to the famous medley in Proverbs 8, where the personified Wisdom sings her own praises as the "mistress of discretion, the inventor of lucidity of thought." In this celebrated poem, one of the fundamental texts of medieval Christology, Sapientia speaks of her own preexistence ("God created me when his purpose first unfolded, before the oldest of his works") and of her own cooperation in the creating of the world. That is, before the foundation of the world the Father created His Wisdom; the Wisdom of the Father then called into being the created order: "In the beginning was the word. . . . Through Him all things were made." This sapiential text, taken in its wider context

of the contiguous chapters in the book of Proverbs, inevitably
played a crucial and defining role in early Christological theory.[42]
It specifically informs Paul's sense of Christ, the Wisdom of
God, in the very texts that structure the poetry of Alain de
Lille, Jean de Meun's most conspicuous theological authority.[43]

The affinities between the Sapientia of Proverbs and Guil-
laume's Reason become even more insistent if we examine the
general dramatic situation of the two poems. Reason, "la dame
de la haute engarde," looks down from her elevated chamber,
"sa tor," and sees a foolish young lover. Sapientia looks down
from the window of her house ("De fenestra enim domus
meae per cancellos prospexi" [7:6]) and sees a foolish youth
("vecordem iuvenem") whose folly consists precisely in sexual
indiscretion—his attraction to the blandishments of the "adul-
teress" dramatically delineated in terms of the sensual envi-
ronment of a private arena of love. The heart of Guillaume's
Lover has already been pierced by an arrow. The foolish young
man of Proverbs pursues sexual pleasure like a beast going to
the slaughter, unaware of its fate until an arrow pierces its
liver ("donec transfigat sagitta iecur eius" [7:23]). There are
other details that clearly link the two wise women, as we shall
see when we speak of Jean de Meun. There is a second im-
portant defining text in the Book of Wisdom 6-8.

As for Jean, there is neither descriptive nor dramatic evi-
dence to suggest that he altered the conception of Reason that
he inherited along with the poem of Guillaume de Lorris in
order to reduce her to the purely natural category of the Natura
of the *De planctu Naturae*. Reason reappears in Jean's poem

[42] B. Botte, "La Sagesse et les origines de la christologie," *Revue des sciences
philosophiques et théologiques* 21 (1932): 54-67.

[43] For lucid introductions to this aspect of Paul's thought, see H. Win-
disch, "Die göttliche Weisheit der Juden und die paulinische Christologie,"
in *Neutestamentliche Studien für G. Heinrici* (Leipzig, 1914), 220-34; and
H. Conzelmann, "Paulus und die Weisheit," in his *Theologie als Schriftaus-
legung* (Munich, 1974), 177-90. The classic study is by A. Feuillet, *Le Christ
Sagesse de Dieu* (Paris, 1966).

without obvious alteration of any sort, as though she had
merely run back to her tower for a moment to see to some
brief domestic matter before getting on with the essential
business of sorting out the Lover:

> Tant com ainsinc me dementoie   4191
>
> . . .
>
> lors vi droit a moi revenant   4195
> Reson, la bele, l'avenant,
> qui de sa tour jus descendi.

There are, however, at least two passages in Jean's poem that
clearly reiterate a *supernatural* conception of Reason, and they
both come from the mouth of Nature herself. First, Nature
describes man as the microcosm ("uns petiz mondes noveaus"),
and complains, in a passage that looks back through Alain to
Boethius, of the bitter irony that man, alone of all creation
endowed with reason, alone of all creation unreasonably turns
away from the divine purpose.

> Sain faille, de l'antandemant   19025
> connois je bien que vraiemant
> celui ne li donai je mie.
> La ne s'estant pas ma baillie,
> ne fui pas sage ne poissant
> de fere riens si connoissant.   19030

A hundred lines later (hardly two sentences for the prolix
Nature) she adds: "{Diex} fist l'antandemant de l'ome, / et,
an fesant, le li donna" (19116-17). It is obvious from these
lines, as well as from several other passages in Jean's poem,
that Reason belongs to a realm above that of Nature, that is,
a supernatural realm. Reason in no wise depends, as the Ith-
acans claim, upon the authority of Nature. On the contrary,
Nature herself explicitly states her powerlessness over Reason's
realm. That is not Nature's bailiwick, but God's.

The Latin word *ratio* has many meanings in medieval texts,
so even on the surface of things there is no clear sense of what

Guillaume and Jean certainly "mean" by their shared character.
When we add the further complications of poetic implication
in a demonstrably ironic context, the matter is even less cer-
tain. But whatever we are eventually to make of Lady Reason,
we are surely justified by beginning with a survey of the
lexicon. The most common meaning of "reason" in the Vul-
gate, where it frequently appears as part of the idiomatic phrase
rationem reddere, is account, explanation, justification, or ex-
cuse. At least one critic, G. Paré, apparently wished to limit
Lady Reason to this narrow construction.[44] At the very least,
however, poetical demands seem to call for a generalized psy-
chological or moral capacity, and this seems to be the reading
of the Ithacans. According to Wetherbee, Reason is "God's
daughter and at the same time ignorant of grace, divine in
origin yet limited to strictly rational comprehension."[45] "The
point is, and I believe it is an important one," writes Hill,
"that Raison is what Jean de Meun says she is and nothing
more. She is the faculty of reason, created by God for man,
and man's highest gift, but she is not *sapientia*."[46] The two
implications of this statement—that Jean de Meun somewhere
definitely "says" what Reason is and that reason and *sapientia*
are necessarily quite different things—are nowhere argued out,
though neither is self-evident. I should emend Hill's formu-
lation in the following fashion. For Jean de Meun, Reason is
exactly what Guillaume de Lorris said she was and something
more besides. She is human reason, the image of the sapiential
Christ in man, and the mirror of *sapientia* in the created world.

Let us begin with Alain de Lille, generally recognized as
Jean's most generous literary creditor. Jean looked to Alain
not merely as a "source" for lines, but as a *poeta theologus* who
sought to express complex theological ideas in verse. It is of
some special interest that Robert Javelet, who has written best
of the technical vocabulary surrounding our problems, turns

[44] G. Paré, *Les Idées et les lettres au XIII* siècle* (Paris, 1947), 34-35.
[45] Wetherbee, *Platonism and Poetry*, 259n.
[46] Hill, "Two Mythographical Themes," 421.

precisely to Alain when he wants to illustrate the complexity
of the word *ratio* in twelfth-century theological thought.[47] In
the *Distinctiones* of Alain de Lille we find a long list of meanings
for the word *ratio*, which include, in what might be described
as an ascending hierarchy of dignity, the following. Reason
means argument (*concinnatio*); and it means account or expla-
nation. Passing over various other rhetorical definitions, we
come to its generalized sense as a power of the soul (*potentia
animae*) that comprehends the qualities of things—the Ithacan
ratio perhaps. Moving on, reason is the power of the soul by
which the soul moves to the contemplation of things heavenly
("vis animae qua anima movetur ad contemplationem coeles-
tium"), and it is this meaning that gives force to the distinction
between reason and sensuality. Already with this definition
we are on terrain held by theology. Finally, reason is the Son
of God, the Word. "For just as reason proceeds from the soul
and is separate from it, so also the Son proceeds from the
Father yet is distinct from Him. Thus in Greek he is called
the *logos*, that is *ratio*." Now the *logos* is, of course, the incarnate
manifestation of Divine Sapience, the Wisdom of the Father,
the *sophia* of the Septuagint, and the *sapientia* of the Vulgate.

This Christological *ratio* is far from rare in twelfth-century
writers; it is the word's common meaning in exalted, theo-
logical, and poetical contexts. John of Salisbury's definition of
human reason in his *Entheticus* is this:

> Est hominis ratio summae rationis imago,
> Quae capit interius vera docente Deo . . .
> Subdita sic ratio formam summae rationis
> Sordibus explusis induit, inde micat.
> Tunc mens tota nitet et vero lumine plena,
> Res falsas abigit et bona vera colit.[48]

[47] R. Javelet, *Image et ressemblance au douzième siècle, de saint Anselme à Alain
de Lille* (Strasbourg, 1967), 1:169. My discussion of Alainian *ratio* follows
Javelet's analysis.

[48] "The 'Entheticus' of John of Salisbury: A Critical Text," ed. Ronald
E. Pepin, *Traditio* 31 (1975): 155-56. Cf. Fenzi, "Boezio e Jean de Meun,"
52.

Human reason (that is, what Jean de Meun "says" Reason is, and no more) is, according to John of Salisbury, the Christ teaching within us. God himself is the light that makes visible the image in the mirror (609ff.). Reason teaches philosophy, and philosophy and charity are identical (307ff.). The end of philosophy is the love of God (421ff.). Death has no dominion over those who love wisely (653ff.).

To speak of this Reason as a strictly limited faculty incapable of thinking in theological terms, unable to understand the Fall of Man, or ignorant of divine grace, would be absurd. She is instead the guide to theological understanding, the nurse who offers first aid to fallen man, and the human capacity that responds with reciprocal desire to the importunity of divine grace. She is, to put the matter briefly, the image of God in man, an image that cannot be so obscured, deformed, veiled, or tarnished as to be entirely obliterated. Reason is the absolute and inalienable evidence within human nature of the continuity between creature and Creator. This idea is a commonplace. The theologian David Cairns puts it thus: "In all the Christian writers up to Aquinas we find the image of God conceived of as man's power to reason."[49] The principal focus for the discussion of this great theme in Christian thought is a single verse of Scripture, Genesis 1:26, "Let us make man after our own image and likeness." Its very rich development in twelfth-century spiritual thought, including that of the so-called Chartrians, has been elaborately demonstrated and documented in the remarkable dissertation of Robert Javelet, who does not stop short of the term *raison-sagesse*.[50]

The theological texts gathered by Javelet would by themselves prove nothing about the *Roman de la Rose* (except that in reading it we ought to be prepared for lexical complexity) were it not for the fact that specific passages in the poem make

---

[49] David Cairns, *The Image of God in Man* (London, 1953), 110.

[50] Javelet, *Image et ressemblance*, 1:172.

such clear and explicit reference to the knot of ideas Javelet
has identified. It may be useful to make a brief review of some
of these ideas now. We have already seen that the introductory
description of Reason in Guillaume's poem links her with the
Sapientia of the Old Testament, particularly of Proverbs 7 and
Wisdom 6-8. Those same passages just as clearly link Reason
with traditional Christian teachings concerning the creative
Logos, the sapiential Christ.

> A son semblant et a son vis
> part qu'el fu fete ou paravis   2970
>   . . .
> Sachiez, se la letre ne ment,
> que Dex la fist ou firmament [*or* demainement]
> a sa semblance et a s'image . . .   2975

The reference to Genesis 1:26 ("Faciamus hominem ad ima-
ginem et similitudinem nostram") is inescapable, and because
this text is, as Javelet has richly documented, the literary
control of the theological image of *raison-sagesse*, it seems to
me impossible to deny to the text of the *Roman* the theological
implications that the scriptural text authoritatively commands.
Guillaume is talking not about the creation of man but the
creation of Reason, that is, the emanation of the preexistent
and eternal Logos, the Jesus-Sophia.[51] We do not have here
the precision of theological debate, but the evocativeness of
theological poetry in the manner of Alain de Lille or Dante.
Lady Reason is the link between the God made man and the
God-made man.

We notice that line 2975 ("a sa semblance et a s'image")
is a recapitulative echo of line 2969 ("A son semblant et a son
vis"), where *vis* (face, L. *vultus*) occupies the position of image
(L. *imago*). The "face" of Reason is an important clue to Rea-

---

[51] See B. L. Mack, *Logos und Sophia: Untersuchungen zur Weisheitstheologie
im hellenistischen Judentum* (Göttingen, 1975).

son's identity, as we shall see when we come to examine her
literary lineage, and it is a feature that Jean de Meun con-
sciously picks up at a moment of cardinal dramatic importance
in his poem. In the scene in which Reason tells the Lover that
she is the daughter of God and offers herself to him in muted
but unmistakably sexual terms, she says this:

> Regarde ci quele forme a
> et te mire en mon cler visage (5788–89).[52]

Here we have a striking image, one we have seen before in
the poem, though in a rather different form, the image of a
face that is also a mirror. Look into my face, says Reason to
the Lover in a moment of amorous abandon, and see yourself.
This is an invitation, very much like the one issued centuries
before by Lady Philosophy to her opaque interlocutor, to get
the Lover to recall who he is; but the terms are here much
more inescapably scriptural and theological. Man is made in
the image of God, and he will accordingly see himself in the
face of God, which is our reason.[53] Javelet has written beau-
tifully of the poetry of this thought:

> Il n's'agit donc pas d'une simple réflexion qui renvoie l'esprit
> à Dieu, mais d'une présence de Dieu dont la face est en
> filigrane dans notre raison comme une apparition voilée de
> la Raison ou Sagesse éternelle. *La rationalité*, si elle permet
> la conaissance de Dieu, *n'est pas une ratiocination de faculté,
> mais l'engagement noétique de tout l'être*. C'est-a-dire que tout

----

[52] No one seems to know how to translate these lines. André Mary drops
them altogether. Charles Dahlberg renders them "Look at my form and at
yourself in my clear face," and André Lanly, "Regarde quelle est cette beauté
et mire-toi en mon clair visage." The last named does acknowledge the
difficulty by citing an even less likely rendering from Marteau in his notes.
My own best try is this: "See here what form He has, and see yourself in
my clear visage."

[53] Javelet, *Image et ressemblance*, 1:171, citing Peter Lombard on Ps. 116,
Lumen vultus tui signatum super nos.

l'être en tant qu'esprit, sans recourir aux arguments du dehors, *par son intériorité même*, doit atteindre à ce Dieu qui a un visage, qui est Verbe et qui est personne.[54]

This same passage contains another allusion to the scriptural Wisdom of Proverbs, for it comes as part of a sexual invitation offered by Reason as a surrogate for the lover that Amant seeks. She offers to be his *amie*:

> Ne porquant si ne veull je mie   5765
> que tu demeurges sanz amie.
> Met, s'il te plest, en moi t'entente.
> Sui je pas bele dame et gente?
>   . . .
> Si avras an cest avantage   5783
> amie de si haut lignage
> qu'il n'est nule qui s'i conpere
>   . . .
> Car j'ai de mon pere congié   5792
> de fere ami et d'estre amee . . .

This echoes the tableau of amatory competition of Proverbs 7, where Wisdom would distract the foolish young man from the "alien woman" by offering herself: "Dic sapientiae: Soror mea es, et prudentiam voca amicam tuam, ut custodiat te a muliere extranea et ab aliena, quae verba sua dulcia facit" (Prov. 7:4-5). The sexual theme is an important one in the sapiential traditions of Scripture. Though it will not be found in Boethius,[55] there is an important intermediary text between Solomon and Jean de Meun, and I shall shortly suggest the nature of the linkage. In the present context the very fact of it is not without considerable significance.

[54] Javelet, *Image et ressemblance*, 1:172.

[55] See G. von Rad, *Weisheit in Israel* (Neukirchen, 1970), 217-28. The dramatic possibilities of personified Sapientia are explored in the illuminating study by B. Lang, *Frau Weisheit: Deutung einer biblischen Gestalt* (Düsseldorf, 1975).

There are at least two further explicit statements in Jean's
poem that man is made in the image of God, both of them
from the mouth of Dame Nature. First, Nature causes man
to be born in God's image: "hom, que je fourme et faz nestre /
an la propre fourme son mestre" (18995-96). Nature is the
steward of the human creature, not its author. Again, two
hundred lines later, she speaks of herself as God's bailiff with
regard to man: "Dieu que le [hom] me bailla / quant a s'ymage
le tailla" (19185-86).

Allow me to cite two final passages of his poem to illustrate
that Jean de Meun offers us no escape from Guillaume's "the-
ological" Reason—that is, a Reason constructed of scriptural
language and resonance. In speaking of the nature of man,
Dame Nature signals two special gifts, *naturel franchise*, which
is her own, and *reson*, which is God's:

> . . . reson, que Diex leur done,   18845
> qui les fet, tant est sage et bone,
> semblables a Dieu et aus anges,
> se mort nes an feïst estranges,
> qui par sa mortel differance
> fet des homes la dessevrance

The particular graph that links men and angels through a
horizontal axis of reason and separates them with a vertical
axis of mortality is a popular verbal picture of the monastic
spirituality of the twelfth century.[56]

One significant detail of Reason's self-characterization comes
in the justly famous conversation between Reason and the Lover
concerning words and things, a conversation that we must
explore further in another chapter. For the moment, I will
note only the relevance of the fact that Reason here claims to
be the inventor of human language.

---

[56] See Javelet, *Image et ressemblance*, 1:164ff.; and M. M. Davy, "Le Moine
et l'ange en Occident au douzième siècle," in *L'Ange et l'homme* (Paris, 1978),
115.

. . . ainceis m'opposes   7053
que, tout ait Dex fetes les choses,
au meins ne fist il pas le non,
ci te respoing: espoir que non,
au meins celui qu'eles ont ores
(si les pot il bien nomer lores
quant il prumierement cria
tout le monde et quan qu'il i a)   7060
mes il vost que nons leur trovasse
a mon plesir et les nomasse
proprement et conmunement
por craistre nostre entendement;
et la parole me dona,   7065
ou mout tres precieus don a.

The idea that Reason is the inventress of language, that it is she who "puts names to things," is not a general commonplace, and it has a specific source in Christian thought. The idea is St. Augustine's, in the twelfth chapter of the second book of the *De ordine*, a chapter in which he defines as the three classes of things that are the work of reason teleological relation, language, and pleasure ("Unum est in factis ad aliquem finem relatis, alterum in dicendo, tertium in delectendo"). The shared capacity that leads men to live together in community is the capacity of reason, and reason likewise provides for them a means of rational communication: "Reason recognized the need to put names to things, that is, to establish sounds that might have signification."[57] "Reason" can mean many things, but what it means to Augustine in the discussion that is the specific background for this passage in the *Roman de la Rose* is this: "Reason is the motion of the mind capable of discerning and connecting those things that it knows, by which it comes to an understanding of God and the soul."[58] It would be nonsense

[57] *De ordine* 2.12.35: "vidit esse imponenda rebus vocabula, id est significantes quosdam sonos. . . ."

[58] *De ordine* 2.11.30: "Ratio est mentis motio, ea quae discuntur distin-

to describe the faculty designed to lead men to *know* God and
the soul as incapable of theological thought. Indeed, the proper
role of human reason is precisely to lead men to theological
truth, that is, to knowledge of God and the soul.[59] Thus is it
that Lady Reason's credentials—credentials that are insistently
present in the French text of Jean de Meun's poem—fully
justify her claim to an incomparably *haut lignage*. That lineage
may not be compelling to Jean's Lover, who is a fool, but it
surely must be impressive to us, his readers.

III. REASON'S LITERARY LINEAGE

Though the text of Scripture is the only text explicitly
mentioned by Guillaume de Lorris in his introduction of Rea-
son, it is nonetheless clear that the poet has at least one other
famous book in mind—the *Consolatio Philosophiae* of Boethius.
In the initial scene of that famous work there appears to the
dejected narrator the vision of "a woman of majestic counte-
nance whose flashing eyes seemed wise beyond the ordinary
wisdom of men. Her color was bright, suggesting boundless
vigor, and yet she seemed so old that she could not be thought
of as belonging to our age. Her height seemed to vary: some-
times she seemed of ordinary human stature, then again her
head seemed to touch the top of the heavens." She is, of course,
Lady Philosophy, the most conspicuous type of the literary,
female *puer senex*, or "Old Woman and Girl" as Curtius calls
her.[60] Joachim Gruber, who has written an impressive essay
on the opening scene of the *Consolatio*, has traced her ancestry

---

guendi et connectendi potens, qua duce uti ad Deum intelligendum, vel
ipsam quae aut in nobis aut usquequaque est animam."

[59] Augustine adds: "quid sit ipsa ratio et qualis sit nisi perpauci prorsus
ignorant," a judgment vindicated by the many minds of readers of the
Roman.

[60] E. Curtius, *European Literature and the Latin Middle Ages* (New York,
1953), 101ff. For purposes of economy I shall refer to this allegorical *potentia*
as the Old Girl.

in antique literature, and we know as well that she appears in a variety of guises in important works of medieval Latinity that certainly influenced Jean de Meun and may well have influenced Guillaume.[61]

Guillaume's presentation of his "Old Girl" is admittedly rather oblique, precisely (I would suggest) because he wished to stress her primary allegiance to the Bible rather than to any fiction, however famous or however pious. Thus he describes her in terms of a perfect mean rather than those of oscillating polar ambiguities:

> El ne fu joine ne chanue,   2962
> ne fu trop haute ne trop basse,
> ne fu trop grelle ne trop crasse.

This is fiddling with a formula rather than literary revolution, but it can remind us that Guillaume expects us to look beyond Boethius as well as at him when we meet Lady Reason for the first time. One Boethian detail *is* decisive, her shining eyes: "Li oil qui en son chief estoient / con .ii. estoilles reluisoient" (2965-66). These lines correspond to Boethius' *oculis ardentibus*, a feature that Gruber has shown to be a classical signal of divinity and that the medieval commentator of the *Echecs amoureux* identifies specifically with the goddess of Wisdom, Pallas.[62] These shining eyes, unlike those the Lover has seen in Narcissus' well, are the beacons of knowledge and moral virtue.[63]

Quite as convincing as any details of verbal iconography is the Boethian situation of Guillaume's poem. The Old Girl appears to a man in distress and dejection to attempt to per-

---

[61] J. Gruber, "Die Erscheinung der Philosophia in der Consolatio Philosophiae des Boethius," *Rheinisches Museum für Philologie* 112 (1969): 166-86.

[62] See J. Gruber, *Kommentar zu Boethius de Consolatione Philosophiae* (Berlin, 1978), 59; on the *Echecs* gloss, see Fleming, *The Roman de la Rose*, 114.

[63] This is the interpretation of several commentators. See, e.g., *Scientia et Virtus: Un Commentaire anonyme de la Consolation de Boèce*, ed. Sandor Durzsa (Budapest, 1978), 40.

suade him to abandon worldly concern for moral philosophy. There is nothing quite like this in Alain de Lille, a conspicuous devoté of the Old Girl, and in such twelfth-century texts as we do find it in—notably the *Elegia* of Henry of Septimello— there is the clearest possible reference to Boethius as a specific source. We can hardly believe that Guillaume would ignore Boethius and yet know Henry.

In Jean de Meun's poem the presence of Boethius is even more palpable; the first three thousand lines, in fact, have been recognized as an extended "parody" of the *Consolatio*, with Reason cast as Philosophia and Amant as Boethius. The nature of Jean's interest in Boethius must presently occupy our sustained attention; for the time being, it is perhaps sufficient simply to acknowledge the fact of it.

To be able to claim Lady Philosophy as one's mother is more than most of us can boast; yet it is but the first step in claiming a grander genealogy still. Lady Reason of the *Roman de la Rose* derives her dramatic function from the *Consolatio* of Boethius, but it is not clear that she owes her personal identity to the same work. Philosophia is clearly kin to Reason, but not the same thing as Reason herself—at least not lexically the same. Twelfth-century texts provide us with a very rich sample of Old Girls—Natura and Phronesis are the most famous—but we shall not find among them a Ratio. The Ratio of the *Anticlaudianus* is a fine lady, the charioteer of Phronesis and the tamer of the five wits, but Alain's Old Girls, both in iconographical and in dramatic terms, are Natura and Theologia. In tracing a more complete lineage for the Lady Reason of the *Roman de la Rose* we might legitimately hope to find a literary model that satisfies the dual criteria demanded: we seek a consolatory or didactic dialogue in which the Old Girl— the manifest principle of authority—is named Ratio.

From the later Middle Ages I have found but one work that really satisfies these criteria, but it does so to such perfection that at first blush it seems a highly promising candidate. It is the *De consolatione Rationis* of Peter of Compostella, an obscure

work known only from a single manuscript in the Escorial.
As its title suggests, Peter's work has close and obvious links
with Boethius. It too is a Menippean satire, though of some-
what appalling poetical quality. In it Ratio instructs the nar-
rator (Compostellanus), debates various abstractions of iniquity
(especially Mundus and Caro), and commands the Seven Liberal
Arts. Ratio's initial appearance is particularly "Boethian," both
in the language of her description and in her role as scourge
of the Muses.[64] Peter's book is replete with gobbets of text
shared by Alain de Lille, and J. J. Sheridan has somewhat
imprudently adduced it as an important and unnoticed source
for the treatment of the Seven Liberal Arts in the *Anticlau-
dianus*.[65] Were this identification valid, the possible relevance
of the *De consolatione Rationis* to the *Roman de la Rose* would
seem all the more insistent. Unfortunately, it seems not to be
valid. Peter of Compostella was apparently a fourteenth-cen-
tury friar, and far from being one of Alain's sources, he is
simply another of his debtors, like Geoffrey Chaucer.[66] Though
his book cannot throw a direct light on Jean's *Roman*, it may
nonetheless offer reflected illumination, faint but welcome, as
a parallel essay in the Boethian tradition. We may note two
points about it in the hope that they will later prove relevant.
The first is that although Peter conspicuously follows Boethius
in inspiration and general design, he does not follow his struc-
ture. The *De consolatione Rationis* is a work in two books, not
five. Secondly, in his discussion of the "Boethian" problem of
free will, Peter freely draws on obvious texts from Augustine's
De libero arbitrio as well as texts from the *Consolatio*.

We must, I think, somewhat redirect our search for an
epiphanic Ratio by looking among those books that may have

[64] *Petri Compostellani De Consolatione Rationis libri duo*, ed. P. Blanco Soto
(Münster, 1912), 60.

[65] James J. Sheridan, "The Seven Liberal Arts in Alan of Lille and Peter
of Compostella," *MS* 35 (1973): 27-37.

[66] See M. Gonzalez-Haba, *La Obra de Consolatione Rationis de Petrus Com-
postellanus* (Munich, 1975), 9ff.

inspired Boethius rather than among those he inspired. One of the most surprising facts about the *Consolatio*—and it is, after all, a very surprising book in many different ways—is that there is so little agreement concerning its specific literary antecedents, the question of which, probably inevitably but possibly also unfruitfully, has not often been removed from the polemic concerning whether the *Consolatio* is a "pagan" or a "Christian" work.

I would be happy to finesse this controversy altogether, since it is almost entirely irrelevant to the way in which most Christian writers perceived the *Consolatio* in the later Middle Ages, but my understanding of the *Roman de la Rose* forces me to take a stand in this matter as well. Some commitment is all the more necessary since Pierre Courcelle, to whose great works all students of the medieval reception of late antique texts owe an immeasurable debt, has leant his very considerable authority to the idea that Boethius' book is essentially an essay in pagan neoplatonism. Some of his followers have gone further still, asserting as facts some highly dubious inferences and a few demonstrable fictions concerning the "unchristian" nature of the work.

There is unlikely to be a last word on this subject, but one of the latest, and to my mind the most closely reasoned and the keenest in its sensitivity to the literary nature of the *Consolatio*, comes from the equally authoritative pen of Christine de Vogel.[67] De Vogel's conclusions, briefly summarized, are these: (1) there are *no* passages in the *Consolatio,* including those that have frequently been identified as heterodox from the Christian point of view, that could not have been written by a Christian working within a demonstrable Christian tradition; (2) on the other hand, there *are* passages in the book that only a Christian could have written and that, specifically, no pagan neoplatonist could have; and (3) there is one unquestionable citation of the Bible in the *Consolatio*, and nu-

---

[67] C. J. de Vogel, "Boethiana," *Vivarium* 10 (1972): 1-40.

merous passages that may be conscious echoes. Such conclusions are of course entirely consistent with what we know both about the cultural milieu in which Boethius lived and with the Christian character of his other authentic works; surely de Vogel's articles can lay to rest the most persistently paganizing interpretations of Boethius' life and his best-known book. On the other hand, they by no means seek to make the *Consolatio* a simple work of Christian piety or a work that is religious in any obvious way.

There are important elements of the *Consolatio*, including its intellectual and rhetorical conclusion, that only a Christian could have written; and there are no ideas in it that are totally unthinkable within the context of fifth-century Christianity. At the same time, there are evidences throughout the work of a somewhat eccentric syncretism. All of them are extenuated, and some perhaps entirely explained, by the fictional presupposition of the work—it is very consciously a consolation of *philosophy*, after all—but we cannot escape the fact that some of them challenge formal theological analysis. De Vogel finds this markedly true with regard to the doctrine of chance expressed in I m5, which she is disposed to consider "as just a pagan element . . . a 'wild' element, so to speak," in Boethius' thought.[68] This means that doctrinal rigorists—Bovo of Corvey in the tenth century, or Pierre Courcelle in the twentieth—will not be disappointed if they search the work for doctrinal "error." Such is their right and perhaps, from their perspective, their duty. We should not, however, confuse such scholastic demonstration with either the historically proper identification

[68] C. J. de Vogel, "The Problem of Philosophy and Christian Faith in Boethius' Consolatio," in *Romanitas et Christianitas: Studia Iano Henrico Waszink . . . oblata* (Amsterdam, 1973), 364. De Vogel's discussion ignores the distinction between Boethius the author and Boethius the literary character. The "pagan" opinions cited are those of the latter expressed at a very early point of the fiction—that is, at a time before he has enjoyed the enlightening teachings of Philosophia. They are *not* the beliefs of the author, Anicius Manlius Torquatus Severinus Boethius.

of Boethius' conscious intention or with an indictment of those
medieval humanists like John of Salisbury who were happy to
read the *Consolatio* in a more poetic and optimistic way. I have
already suggested what "heresy" means as a term of *literary*
discourse—it means other people's reading texts in ways with
which we disagree. When Courcelle accuses William of Conches
of approaching "heresy," that means little else than that Wil-
liam of Conches read the *Consolatio* rather differently from
Pierre Courcelle.[69]

Reopening our minds to the fact of Boethius' Christian
culture, however promiscuous or syncretistic the *Consolatio* may
show it to be, leads us also to reopen some old issues swept
aside by Courcelle—that is, to consider among Boethius' pos-
sible sources of inspiration some of the classics of his own Latin
Christian tradition. For a Latin Christian of the sixth century,
there is one obvious luminary in that tradition who demands
to be heard: Aurelius Augustinus. In 1930 Raoul Carton pub-
lished a lengthy essay on "Le Christianisme et l'augustinisme
de Boèce."[70] Carton examined a number of the themes and
ideas in Boethius' *Theological Tractates*, identifying some as
deriving directly from Augustine and others as sharing a com-
mon Christian response to certain neoplatonic conceptions.
Making good use of the excellent work of Klingner in philology
and Bruder in philosophy, he tried to demonstrate the broad
consistency of Boethius' theological thought and method with
those of Augustine. A decade later the American classicist
E. T. Silk, already well known for important work on Boe-
thius, wrote an impressive article in which he argued, mainly
on the basis of literary parallels, that the *Consolatio* owed at
least some of its literary inspiration to Augustine's early dia-
logues.[71]

[69] P. Courcelle, *La Consolation de Philosophie dans la tradition littéraire* (Paris,
1967), 313.

[70] R. Carton, "Le Christianisme et l'augustinisme de Boèce," *Revue de
philosophie* 30 (1930): 573-659.

[71] E. T. Silk, "Boethius's Consolatio Philosophiae as a Sequel to Augus-

Carton's article has certain obvious limitations. It was written for a special journal number commemorating the fifteenth centenary of Augustine's death, and pressures of meeting a deadline kept him from writing as fully about the *Consolatio* as he had written about the tractates.[72] A further undeniable unevenness of argument and a somewhat vague technique of textual analysis characterize the essay and perhaps have made it vulnerable to unceremonious dismissal. That, in any event, is how I would have to characterize Courcelle's treatment of it. Silk's essay has usually been described as though it were merely an appendix to Carton, and thus thrown out in the same bathwater. In fact, Silk's approach is significantly different from Carton's, for it is based essentially in the perceptions of literary criticism rather than in those of historical theology. Unlike most attempts to find precise "sources" for the *Consolatio*, it takes as its very foundation the fact of Boethius' profound literary originality: "Nearly every discovery of Boethius' supposed or real debt to earlier writers has brought with it fresh evidence of Boethius's power to mould and transmute what he borrowed."[73] In their responsiveness to the transformations of literary ideas as they move from one great mind to another, Silk's intuitions are in my view altogether more subtle, suggestive, and illuminating than Courcelle's much more ambitious but conventional demonstrations of "literary tradition."

---

tine's Dialogues and Soliloquia," *Harvard Theological Review* 32 (1939): 19-39. While my manuscript has been negotiating its deliberate progress through the press, several relevant studies of Boethius have reached me—too late for my consideration but too important for the question of "Boethian Augustinianism" not to mention. See in particular the collections of essays in the *Atti* of the Congresso Internazionale di Studi Boeziani of 1980 (Rome, 1981) and in *Boethius, His Life, Thought and Influence* ed. Margaret Gibson (Oxford, 1981); and the books by Henry Chadwick, *Boethius: the Consolations of Music, Logic, Theology, and Philosophy* (Oxford, 1981), and Edmund Reiss, *Boethius* (New York, 1982).

[72] Carton, "Le Christianisme . . . de Boèce," 628n.

[73] Silk, "Boethius's Consolatio," 20.

Two points in Silk's essay strike me as particularly convincing, though as he well knew, they make no pretense of positive demonstration. The first is the parallel between the presentation of idle poetry as an impediment to the truth in the *Contra academicos* with Philosophy's banishment of the Muses in the *Consolatio*. The second is the formal similarity of the dialogue structure in the *Soliloquia* and in the *Consolatio*. This latter point is particularly significant. The construction of the *Consolatio* is sufficiently similar to that of the *Soliloquia* and sufficiently dissimilar to anything else we know in the vast body of late antique dialogues, pagan and Christian alike, as to argue the near certainty of a specific relationship between them.[74]

The discussion of Boethius' possible use of Augustine has suffered somewhat from a dialectical fallacy akin to that which characterizes the debate between Reason and the Lover. To say that Amant should eschew loving *par amours* does not mean, as he would have it, that he is being counseled to hate. To suggest that Boethius was a reader of Augustine—and does anyone actually imagine that the author of a Latin treatise on the Trinity in the early sixth century could *not* be a reader of Augustine?—is not the same as to say that Boethius was an "Augustinian" or a "disciple of Augustine," or that he had no ideas *other* than those of Augustine. Nonetheless, the principal positive argument against the "Augustinian thesis" (the other being the *argumentum ex silentio*) is that there are things in the *Consolatio* not in harmony with Augustinian theology. The work of Klingner and de Vogel, and now the new commentary by Gruber, demonstrate the remarkable eclecticism of Boethius' sources of inspiration. There is no byway of neoplatonic thought of which we can certainly accuse him of ignorance, yet there is no school or text—and this includes Porphyry—

---

[74] See further B. R. Voss, *Der Dialog in der frühchristlichen Literatur* (Munich, 1970), 351; and P. L. Schmidt, "Zur Typologie und Literarisierung des frühchristlichen lateinischen Dialogs," in *Christianisme et formes littéraires de l'antiquité tardive en occident* (Geneva, 1977), 124ff.

that claimed his exclusive or even his decisive allegiance. I would say the same thing of Boethius that I would say of Origen, Augustine, or for that matter, Paul of Tarsus: he was a Christian whose philosophical instincts and vocabulary owed much to neoplatonic commonplace.

The specific point of structural similarity between the *Soliloquia* and the *Consolatio* that is of particular significance to the dialogue between Reason and the Lover in the *Roman de la Rose* is this: both of them are soliloquies in dialogue form, dialogues of the mind with itself, or to put the matter more precisely, dialogues between Augustinus and Ratio on the one hand and between Boethius and Philosophia on the other. E. K. Rand, speaking as of something obvious, noted this relationship many years ago when he characterized the *Soliloquia* as "really not a soliloquy, but a dialogue between Augustine and his Reason, a device that reappears, in a more elaborate and picturesque form, in the *Consolation of Philosophy* of Boethius."[75] One scholar has called Ratio the "elder sister" of Philosophia.[76] I prefer to think of her in more dynastic terms as her mother, but however we characterize the relationship, the Ratio of the *Soliloquia* is the direct lineal ancestress of Lady Reason in the *Roman de la Rose*. Raison favors her mother in looks, but she was named for her grandmother. I find nothing astonishing in the fact that there should be a positive relationship between the two most famous Reasons in European literature. On the other hand, it *is* a little surprising that no one has, to my knowledge, ever suggested it.

My own view is that Boethius fairly reeks of Augustine. The distinctive impress of literary competition marks nearly every page of the *Consolatio*, though it is not of the sort that manifests itself in servile imitation or extensive parallel passages. Augustine's achievement in the Cassiciacum dialogues

---

[75] E. K. Rand, *Founders of the Middle Ages* (Cambridge, 1928), p. 257.

[76] H. Scheible, *Die Gedichte in der Consolatio Philosophia des Boethius* (Heidelberg, 1972), 43.

surely inspired Boethius, but it probably also challenged him to reexplore the resources of Latin neoplatonism to see whether, after all, the wisdom of the Christians could not there be found in garb that pleased the eye of the mind if not the longing heart. Augustine the convert had said that many paths led to Truth, only to be contradicted by Augustine the bishop. In the *Consolatio Philosophiae* there is no such palinode, and in its fiction of the sufficiency of naked Philosophia we see perhaps the optimism of Augustine's intellectual infancy expressed with an authority and a literary confidence of which his own intellectual maturity could not allow.

The old idea of Silk is in my view entirely correct if somewhat misleadingly stated. The *Consolatio* is not so much a sequel to Augustine's *Soliloquia* as it is their prolegomenon. We are wont to talk of "building on" the work of our predecessors; but Boethius has found a way of building "under" Augustine. His subterranean industry, though secret, is not sinister. His work is one of undergirding, not of undermining. Our understanding of the relationship between the *Consolatio* and the *Soliloquia* in particular can best be advanced by removing our gaze from the Old Girls to refocus on their authorial narrators. Augustine and Boethius are no less manipulated fictions than are Ratio and Philosophia, and we can understand what and how the latter teach only when we realize who their pupils are. Augustinus, when we first meet him, is engaged in Ciceronian meditation on how to achieve good and flee evil. Boethius, when we first meet him, is "deeply depressed" as de Vogel puts it. The first rhetorically ambitious statement of Augustinus is an exquisite "neoplatonic" prayer of surpassing beauty, which asks for divine grace to lift the mind to God. The *Consolatio* begins with a self-indulgent lament that memorializes Boethius' earth-bound sorrows. Boethius is a sick man who needs two books of first aid before Philosophia can as much as begin to effect a cure. Augustinus is a mental athlete ready immediately to enter into strenuous dialectical calisthenics with his trainer.

The distance between the narrative *personae* of the two books—
a distance at once psychological, moral, and intellectual—is
a crucial fact about them. The great enterprise of the Cassi-
ciacum dialogues taken as a whole is the defense of rationality
against academic skepticism, an insistence that human beings
can indeed know truth by reasonable demonstration and mental
exertion. At the same time, Augustine believes that faith itself
is reasonable and that the role of reason is to know those things
that faith believes. It is entirely logical, therefore, that Au-
gustinus should begin an inquiry into the rational knowledge
of God with a long prayer to God that proclaims His attributes
and asks His help in the undertaking of knowing the truth of
His existence. By the middle of his seminar with Philosophia,
Boethius too will approach the capacity for such a prayer, but
in the despair of the opening "scene" of the *Consolatio* such an
aspiration would be unthinkable. Boethius the *persona* must
come first to that confidence in God's just recompense of the
willed actions of free men which is the starting point of the
persona Augustinus. There is a sense in which the ending of
the *Consolatio* is the beginning of the *Soliloquia*.

The final paragraph of the *Consolatio Philosophiae* is one that,
as Christine de Vogel has taught us, could be written only by
a Christian. A confident statement of man's free will justifies
the efficacy of prayers of petition and impels the quest of the
first line of the *Soliloquia*—to seek virtue and to flee vice: "Our
hopes and prayers are not directed to God in vain, for if they
are just they cannot fail. Therefore, stand firm against vice
and cultivate virtue. Lift up your soul to worthy hopes, and
offer humble prayers to heaven." The sentence that introduces
this final paragraph is this: "Quae cum ita sint, manet inte-
merata mortalibus arbitrii libertas nec iniquae leges solutis
omni necessitate uoluntatibus praemis poenasque propo-
nunt."[77] I am not prepared to credit that the author of that
sentence wrote it without a conscious memory of the statement

[77] *Consolatio* 5.644, ed. Bieler (Turnholt, 1957), 105.

of free will in the great opening prayer of the *Soliloquia*: "Deus, cujus legibus in aevo stantibus . . . cujus legibus arbitrium animae liberum est, bonisque praemia et malis poenae, fixis per omnia necessitatibus distributae sunt."[78]

Even so, there is no need to insist on positive relationships between the *Soliloquia* and the *Consolatio* to demonstrate the deep relationship between Ratio and Philosophia as literary characters, Old Girls. There is another sort of kinship founded in intellectual concept, one wherein indeed the women can be said to share an identity. Sapientia, or Wisdom, is, so to speak, the common denominator shared by Reason and Philosophy. Just as there is a "Reason-Wisdom" as identified and documented by Javelet among the spiritual writers of the twelfth century, so also is there a "Philosophy-Wisdom." Ficino's commentary on Plato begins with a proemium, a dedication to Lorenzo dei Medici, in which the fabulous birth of Philosophia from the head of Sophia herself is couched in the unmistakable language of the eighth chapter of Proverbs. Sophia emanates from the head of Jupiter; she in turn projects a daughter, Philosophia, who delights to make her habitation among the children of men.[79] M. T. d'Alverny, the teacher of sapiential iconography, warns us that we shall mistake ourselves to search for pagan mysteries of the Renaissance in such a formulation. It grows instead, she says from one of "the *traditional tendencies of Christian thought.*"[80] That tendency of Christian thought considerably antedated Boethius, but it was doubtless greatly nourished by the almost unexaggeratable success of his book. The magisterial Philosophia of the *Consolatio* provided medieval literature with an enduring allegorical type, to be sure, but she did much more. The plenary

[78] *Soliloquia* 1.4.2; ed. Müller, 140-41.

[79] *Marsilii Ficini Florentini in commentaria Platonis prooemium in Opera Omnia* (Basel, 1576), 1,128-1,130.

[80] M.-T. d'Alverny, "Quelques Aspects du symbolisme de la 'Sapientia' chez les humanistes," in *Umanesimo e esoterismo* [*Archivio di Filosofia*, 1960] 321.

meaning of the very world *philosophia*, which is a commonplace of twelfth-century literary culture, seems directly related to the ubiquitous reading of the *Consolatio*. A recent study by M. M. Davy has sketched out for us the rich intellectual and poetic genealogy of the word among many of the same great spiritual writers studied in a different context by Javelet. What we find should not surprise us. The *normal* meaning of "philosophy" among Jean de Meun's teachers was "Christian Wisdom"—as body of teaching, as divine emanation, and as way of life.[81]

The literary history of personified Philosophia suggests the degree to which such possibilities had already been prepared by the Latin moralists, Cicero and Seneca in particular, who most deeply influenced the Fathers of the Church. Seneca, though not the first to declare Philosophy the mother of the liberal arts, says so with a dignified authority.[82] It is this conception of Philosophy, and the many others to which it is akin, that we find in Augustine's statement that *Reason* is the inventress of the arts.[83] As early as Justin we find a conscious design to present Christian truth *as* philosophy, *verissima philosophia*, the competitor and supererogator of antique Wisdom.[84] The identification of personified Philosophia with Christ, the eternal Wisdom of the Father, is conspicuous.[85] Rochais has published a western monastic text that uses the remarkable phrase "ipsa philosophia Christus."[86]

Philosophia-Sapientia, the mistress of moral life, is the pre-

---

[81] See M. M. Davy, *Initiation médiévale: La Philosophie au douzième siècle* (Paris, 1980), 96ff.

[82] Seneca *Nat. Quest.* 2.53.3, as quoted by P. Courcelle, "Le Personnage de Philosophie dans la littérature latine," *Journal des Savants* (1970), 209-52.

[83] *De ordine* 2.12.35.

[84] See P. Courcelle, "Verissima Philosophia," in *Epektasis: Mélanges patristiques offerts au Cardinal Jean Daniélou* (Paris, 1972), 653-59.

[85] See Davy, *Initiation médiévale*, 109.

[86] H. Rochais, "*Ipsa Philosophia Christus*," MS, 13 (1951): 244-47.

ceptor of ascesis. Here we shall find an unbroken continuity
linking the Christian holy man with the ancient wise man.
The way of Philosophy is *par excellence* the way of the monk,
who chains the flesh that the spirit may soar. Philosophy was
the programmatic priority of mind over matter, and in that
sense, "philosophy" and "religion" were the same. The re-
markable extent to which this is true is evidenced on every
page of Augustine's *De vera religione*, a work that Petrarch in
his day would claim was entirely inspired by one noble state-
ment of the ascetic aspiration in the *Tusculan Disputations* of
Cicero. The "message" of the *Soliloquia* and the *Consolatio* is
inescapably "religious" in Christian terms, not because it ex-
pounds systematic theology but because it advances an un-
mistakably Christian view of human nature. That nature is
sacramental, consisting both of a body with its appetites and
a soul with its "motions." In the relationship between the two
will be found the materials of the Christian dramatic dialogue.

The search for Lady Reason's grandmother has led us into
difficult terrain. For the purposes of this essay on the *Roman
de la Rose*, questions of the Christian orthodoxy of the *Consolatio*
are not so much luxuries as unwanted but unavoidable burdens.
What actually is of concern here is not the unrecoverable and
controverted contents of the mind of Boethius in the sixth
century, but the nature of the reception of his book in the
vernacular period. I do think that the Christian Boethius wrote
a Christian *Consolatio*, and I do believe that he was explicitly
aware of and responsive to the Cassiciacum dialogues of Au-
gustine when he did so. Yet I presume to press these views
on my readers only because I think that they were also the
views of Jean de Meun in the thirteenth century and that they
can offer help in understanding the nature of his poem.

First, as regards Boethius himself. We must remember that
the widespread questioning of his orthodoxy is the result of
modern intellectual sophistication unknown in the Middle
Ages. The astonishing, perennial popularity of the *Consolatio*,
its early and repeated translation into all European languages,

its especial associations with truly distinguished men of letters like Bono Giamboni, Jean de Meun, and Geoffrey Chaucer, its prominent place in what might be called the Christian academic curriculum beginning at the latest with King Alfred—all of this argues that the work was accepted as a treasured item in the cultural deposit of medieval Christianity, one of a handful of books that those who knew books at all would know and cherish. Even those very isolated and eccentric voices in which Courcelle could detect cavil are raised in the course of formal commentaries on the work—one of the more flattering forms of attack. De Vogel has some wise words on this subject:

> No doubt Jean de Meun and Chaucer, King Alfred and Queen Elisabeth, Notker Labeo and Maximos Planudes read and enjoyed Boethius' *Consolatio* as a work of piety written in the language of philosophy. They liked that kind of syncretism and made it theirs. None of them was a rationalist philosopher hostile to Christianity, nor were they narrow-minded Christians, afraid of Greek philosophical thought, even when in certain details they would find a difference between Platonist philosophy and Christian faith.[87]

At least three scholars—Cherniss, Fenzi, and Ott—have reviewed the schematic fashion in which Jean de Meun has linked his dialogue between Reason and the Lover with the model of the *Consolatio*.[88] Though as we have seen, Jean does

[87] De Vogel, "The Problem of Philosophy and Christian Faith in Boethius' Consolatio," 359-60.

[88] Fenzi, "Boezio e Jean de Meun"; Michael D. Cherniss, "Jean de Meun's Reson and Boethius," *Romance Notes* 6 (1975): 678-85; and K. A. Ott, "Jean de Meun und Boethius. Über Aufbau und Quellen des Rosenromans," in *Philosophische Studien: Gedenkschrift für Richard Kienast*, ed. U. Schwab and E. Stutz (Heidelberg, 1979), 131-65. Of these essays, which are entirely independent of one another, the most perspicacious (in my view) is that of Fenzi, the most comprehensive in its source study, that of Ott. Cherniss' argument (again, from my point of view) is like a printer's form—full of carefully selected materials arranged upside down and backwards.

not here or elsewhere contradict the overtones of biblical sa-
pience so prominent in the description of Reason given by
Guillaume de Lorris, he manipulates the actual dialogue in
ways that draw attention to Boethius. Thus the pattern of
"consolation" or at least of pedagogy in the two works is
identical, or nearly so, as is much of the doctrine concerning
Fortune and her works, lengthy passages of which are taken
directly from the *Consolatio*. In one important passage Reason
actually gives preemptive praise to whoever would translate
the work into French. It is possible, as Cherniss speculates,
that Jean may have already framed his projected *Boèce* by the
time he penned those words, and that indeed all of "Reason
and the Lover" may have been drafted at a time when a formal
translation was much on his mind. In my earlier work on Jean
de Meun I tried to suggest the importance of his brief pro-
emium to his translation as a possible index of his interpre-
tation of the work, and Cherniss has repeated the suggestion.[89]
We now know that this proemium has a close but not entirely
clear relationship with the prologue to a Latin commentary
ascribed to one William of Aragon.[90] We thus find in it,
perhaps, our sole surviving evidence of the formal academic
career of Jean de Meun. The *Roman*, though not exactly a
school poem, is characterized nonetheless by a lively academic
wit.

The religious parody involved in Amant's submission to
Amours and his reception of the Ten Commandments of Love
is inescapable, and it appears that Guillaume de Lorris intended
that the playful ambiguity of the term *dieu d'Amours* should
enrich his text from the moment that the god first appeared
in his pages, a silent hunter stalking the Lover. With Jean de

[89] Cf. Fleming, *The Roman de la Rose*, pp. 110-11; and Cherniss, "Jean
de Meun's Reson and Boethius," pp. 680-81.

[90] See R. Crespo, "Il Prologo alla traduzione della 'Consolatio Philoso-
phiae' di Jean de Meun e il commento di Guglielmo d'Aragona," in *Romanitas
et Christianitas: Studia Iano Henrico Waszink . . . oblata* (Amsterdam, 1973),
55-70.

Meun, the double-entendre involved in service to a *seigneur* is developed more insistently and with more theological bite. The reappearance of Reason in his poem is prefaced by a verse paragraph (4121-44) in which the Lover moves from a clear and accurate statement of his situation to a formal abjuration of his own brief moment of good sense. He must not, he concludes, betray his *seigneur* (4128), and in one of Jean's more outrageous (and unnoticed) lines, he collates true and false divinity in ludicrous illogicality:

> Ja, se Dieu plest, dou dieu d'Amors
> ne de lui plaintes ne clamors,
> ne d'Esperance ne d'Oiseuse . . .[91]   4139

Reason's term for Amours, *bon seigneur*, is of course more heavily ironic yet ("As tu or bon seigneur servi?"), and in its interrogative context it introduces the significant thrust of her argument. She first suggests, then insistently states, that the Lover does not know the god whom he serves:

> mes sanz faille tu ne savoies
> a quel seigneur affere avoies.   4213

Out of this assertion grows the first of the lively, stichomythic arguments that are a conspicuous dramatic feature of the dialogue between Reason and the Lover in Jean's poem.

> Quenois le tu point? — Oïl, dame.   4223
> — Non fez. — Si faz. — De quoi, par t'ame?
> — De tant qu'il me dist: 'Tu dois estre
> mout liez dont tu as si bon mestre
> et seigneur de si haut renon.'
> — Quenois le tu de plus? — Je non,
> fors tant qu'il me bailla ses regles
> et s'an foï plus tost c'uns egles,   4230
> et je remés an la balance.
> — Certes, c'est povre connoissance.

[91] Even here Guillaume has prepared the way; see lines 1897-1901.

I have nowhere seen this passage much discussed, but it raises
what is in a sense the heart of the matter at dispute between
Reason and the Lover, and that is what men know and how
they know it. Simple contradiction ("Yes"—"No"—"Yes, I
do!") is dialectically sterile; so Reason moves on to inquire
into the grounds of the Lover's alleged knowledge of his *sei-
gneur*. How does he know this "lord"—"De quoi, par t'ame?"
(4224). This is a very curious line, and we must return to it
momentarily. The Lover's response is a classical assertion from
unexamined authority. He trusts the god of Love because the
god of Love says that he is jolly lucky to have such a *bon mestre*.
Reason opines that there is not much knowledge in *that*, and
their debate, though hardly begun, is over. But let us return
to line 4224. With the phrase *par t'ame* Reason, obviously, is
not uttering an oath. She does not say, "By my soul, tell me
how you know him!" Rather, she inquires thus: "By what
means? By means of your soul?"

The *Soliloquia* of Augustine begin with a long and beautiful
prayer—neoplatonic in its imagery but decisively Christian in
its hope of a graceful divine response—but the real dialectical
beginning of the book is Reason's question to Augustine con-
cerning what it is he wants to know:

R.   Quid ergo scire vis?
A.   Haec ipsa omnia quae oravi.
R.   Breviter ea collige.
A.   Deum et animam scire cupio.[92]

Augustine wants to know *God and the soul*, the fundamental
objects of theological knowledge. And he wants to know these
matters, as he says in another place, just as surely as he knows
that seven plus three make ten; and it is such knowledge that
Reason confidently sets out to help him find. The argument
of the *Soliloquia*, of the *De immortalitate animae* (which we know
is a rough draft of what was once intended to be a third book

---

[92] *Soliloquia* 1.7.1; ed. Müller, 143.

of the *Soliloquia*), and to a certain extent of the *De quantitate animae* is in essence a demonstration of God "by means of the soul" and vice versa. That is, the existence and qualities of the soul are first demonstrated, by entirely rational means, and then used to lead to equally rational knowledge of God. I think that the very strangely phrased question "De quoi, par t'ame?" refers to this argument and to its correspondingly initial position within the dialogue between Reason and Augustine in the *Soliloquia*. To it the Lover gives no explicit response, but what he *does* say is an obvious parody of the epistemological chain in Augustine. The Lover, that is, bases his faith in his "god" not upon the rational examination of his own soul but directly upon the unmediated authority of the god himself. That is, his "knowledge" is based on unexamined faith. This intellectual ascent might actually be described as Augustinian were it not for the want of one crucial stage. For Augustine too the path to sure knowledge moves from faith (*fides*) to authority (*auctoritas*), but it can do so only by coming first to an absolutely crucial intermediary stage, reason (*ratio*). André Mandouze, who has most lucidly described Augustine's epistemology, puts it this way: "Chargée d'éprouver l'objet de la foi, la *raison* est l'instrument et non le concurrent de l'autorité."[93] Jean de Meun's Reason is not in the least degree disposed to confirm the authority of his Lover's faith in the *dieu d'Amours*. She considers that faith "madness," not knowledge, and she says so repeatedly in the distinctive voice and intonation that no one who knew her grandmother is likely to mistake.

There are further suggestions of positive textual relationships between the *Soliloquia* and the *Roman de la Rose*. I have already argued that the scene in which Reason makes a pass at the Lover (5765ff.) reflects what Gerhard von Rad has called the "spiritual eroticism" of Jewish Wisdom literature, and

[93] A. Mandouze, *Saint Augustin: l'aventure de la raison et de la grâce* (Paris, 1968), 283.

specifically that manifested in the seventh chapter of Proverbs. I think, however, that Jean was aware also of two important Augustinian texts that had, in differing ways, dramatized the same theme. The most famous of them—though the latter from the point of view of the chronology of composition—comes as the prelude to the climactic moment of conversion in the eighth book of the *Confessions*. In his final moments in the garden at Milan, just before he walked some little distance apart from Alypius to sit with his Bible on his lap beneath the fig tree, Augustine experienced a tense internal struggle: "This argument within my heart was nothing else than myself fighting against myself." The dispute is there dramatized as a "personification allegory" in which Continentia speaks to Augustine, attempting to win him to her and away from his "old friends," the worldly cares and affections, especially sexual pleasure, which he still fears he cannot live without. Continentia's presence is made known by her chaste dignity, "casta dignitas continentiae, serena et non dissolute hilaris, honeste blandiens, ut uenirem neque dubitarem, et extendens ad me suscipiendum et amplectendum pias manus plenas gregibus bonorum exemplorum."[94] This last phrase refers to the votaries of Continentia, who surround her even as the votaries of Amours surround *him* in the Garden of Deduit.

The implied contrast of chaste and unchaste allurement, of sensual and intelligible embrace, is that of the harlot or the "foreign woman" of Proverbs on the one hand and Sapientia on the other. Biblical authority certainly lies behind the passage, but Augustine probably knew other examples both in Christian and in pagan literature as well.[95] By the time Au-

---

[94] *Confessions* 8.11.26.

[95] See the Christian texts adduced by Richard Horsley, "Spiritual Marriage with Sophia," *Vigiliae Christianae* 33 (1979): 30-54; and the rich materials in P. Courcelle, "Le Visage de philosophie," *REA* 70 (1968): 110-20; for the importance of Cicero as an intermediary, see M. C. Waites, "Some Features of the Allegorical Debate in Greek Literature," *Harvard Studies in Classical Philology* 23 (1912): 13-14.

gustine wrote it out in the *Confessions*, he had long since tried
another version of it in the *Soliloquia*.[96] There Reason proposes
to inquire of Augustine "what kind of lover of Wisdom" he
is. The language is explicitly sexual. Augustine wants to see
Wisdom without a veil, to embrace her in her nudity: "She
allows this favor to but a few select lovers. And indeed if you
burned with love for some beautiful woman, would it not be
right for her to deny herself to you if she discovered that you
loved another besides herself?" The sexual competition between
Reason and the Rose, like that between Continentia and Au-
gustine's "old friends," draws a distinction between a superior
and an inferior love. I believe that informed readers would
have been instinctively open to the possibilities of such reso-
nances. It is of some interest that one of the most important
poets of fourteenth-century England alludes to the *Roman de
la Rose* in a spirit similar to that in the passages cited from
the *Soliloquia*.[97]

The discovery of positive "influence" of Augustine's *Soli-
loquia* on the conception of Reason in the *Roman de la Rose* is
perhaps chiefly interesting for its novelty. From the point of
view of poetic understanding, the mere fact that the two most
famous Reasons in European literature have a familial rela-
tionship is banal; we could, after all, hardly expect less. At
the same time, it is not without considerable potential utility
for our understanding of the nature of Jean's poem, for it
provides us with an important and entirely untried means of
approaching his "intertextual" proclivities. There can have
been few poets in the history of literature with more insistent
reasons for meditating on the relationships, anxious or com-
placent, between the literary artifact of "tradition" and the
poetic act of present composition. He was in the first place a
translator, and a "literary" one at that—that is, one specifically

[96] *Soliloquia*, ed. Müller, 161-62.
[97] See *Cleanness* [*Purity*], lines 1054ff.

conscious of the literary decisions that a translator must make.[98]
Next, his own great poetic creation, the *Roman de la Rose*, was
actually built on the abandoned site of Guillaume de Lorris
out of the carefully chosen debris of a liberal education. Finally,
he was an ironist whose chosen métier was the manipulation
of literary contexts and the deadpan citation or miscitation of
revealing textual authority.

The poem that he inherited offered the *donné* of a Lady
Reason already heavily mortgaged to the Bible and to Boethius.
We have already seen that Jean de Meun honored those two
liens on his inherited property, and that he went further still
by honoring, with the form of his own dramatic dialogue, the
debt that he knew Boethius owed to Augustine. But I suggest
that his interest in Augustine was not that of the literary
archaeologist: it was that of the poet. The *Soliloquia* would
have interested him—as the Augustinian dialogue on friend-
ship by Aelred of Rievaulx would also interest him—for a
number of distinctively "humanistic" features of its literary
form. For Jean de Meun, master of the liberal arts, the *Soli-*
loquia—in a manner yet more radical than that used by Boethius
in the *Consolatio*—addressed theological problems from the
point of view of the arts of the trivium.

Two features of the Cassiciacum dialogues considered as a
group are of particular interest for their wider implications for
literary posterity, and both have been identified in the brilliant
and classic study of H. I. Marrou, which has taught us to read
the early Augustine with new eyes.[99] They are the dialogues'
propaedeutic strategies and their formal Ciceronianism. If we
are surprised that the Christian Boethius should choose to write
as he did in the *Consolatio*, we should be absolutely astounded
at the Augustine of Cassiciacum. It is as though Augustine

---

[98] Jean makes a distinction between word-for-word translation and the
freer attempt to capture an author's sense; see "Boethius' *De Consolatione* by
Jean de Meun," ed. V. L. Dédeck-Héry, *MS* 14 (1952): 168.

[99] H. I. Marrou, *Saint Augustin et la fin de la culture antique*, 4th ed. (Paris,
1958), 299-327.

had abandoned the profession of rhetoric as a pagan only in order to take it up again on an amateur basis as a Christian. The "historical" dialogues—that is, those that certainly record the gist of Augustine's actual disputations with his friends— reveal the old pedagogue reveling in all the tricks of the trade, never happier than when setting the cat among the pigeons in order to withdraw to silent observation from the sidelines, apparently eager to sustain the argument at all costs, and particularly at the cost of avoiding the stated issue at hand.

The Cassiciacum dialogues are, from the point of view of most sensible schools of literary criticism, among the most trying books ever written, a distinction they share with Jean's *Roman*, especially with its long "chapters" given over to individual characters. Almost every literary vice of which Jean de Meun has been accused is conspicuous in the Cassiciacum dialogues: prolixity, apparent aimlessness of argument, elephantine digressions that overwhelm the central "plot," absence of conclusion or clear point of authorial view, encyclopedic proclivity, an abundance of scientific lore of dubious relevance.

Marrou rescues us from confusion by showing—though he had not McLuhan's phrase—that for Augustine "the medium is the message." His intellectual strategy is clear enough once we grasp it, and in one famous paragraph of the *De quantitate animae* he makes it explicit.[100] We can know by reason the theological truths we believe through faith, but this is a matter of considerable difficulty, requiring exertion and perseverance. *Knock*, and it shall be opened unto you. The liberal arts do not hold wisdom, but they are useful for the pursuit of wisdom. That human reason which would reach out to know, reasonably and certainly, the truths of faith, must be trained like an athlete, exercised, honed, trimmed, tested. As Marrou has taught us to see, all the literary "vagaries" of Augustine's literary dialogues—all the "dialectic," the logic, the verbal

[100] See the discussion in Marrou, *Saint Augustin*, 307-308.

distinctions, the sophistries, the mathematics and geometry, in short all the materials which constantly seem to divert the interlocutors (and the reader) from the "point"—are the means of preparing the human reason to grasp that truth reserved for the fit and supple mind alone. Thus the convert of Cassiciacum returned to the "dialectic" that he knew to be, as an end in itself, a vanity, but only that he might make, in Marrou's phrase, a "reductio artium ad philosophiam."

One final perception of Marrou's concerning the Cassiciacum dialogues, including conspicuously the *Soliloquia*, has a special relevance for our consideration of Jean de Meun, and that has to do with their own immediate literary models. Marrou calls them "dialogues of the Ciceronian mode," and he identifies those specifically Ciceronian features that make them quite distinct within Augustine's vast oeuvre.[101] Augustine never again wrote quite as he wrote at Cassiciacum, for there he wrote, at least in literary guise, as a "philosopher." It was natural that he turned to the greatest Latin doctor of philosophy, Cicero. The specific models that he had before his eyes at Cassiciacum are confirmed by Testard's tables of citations and parallels: the *Hortensius*, the *Tusculans*, the *Academica*, those dialogues characterized by wide-ranging debate, by sharp and sometimes witty exchange, by the impetus to sustain the dialectic and to press ever further and harder in the exercise of the mind's capacities. The insistent presence of Cicero in the *Soliloquia* begins with its first line, a pastiche from the *De oratore* and the *De divinatione*, and Cicero looms as a benevolent genius behind the whole work.[102]

---

[101] Marrou, *Saint Augustin*, p. 308.

[102] "Wer die Soliloquien zu lesen beginnt, erkennt gleich im ersten Satz eine Wendung, die Augustin Cicero nachgestaltet hat: *volventi mihi multa ac varia mecum diu ac per multos dies sedulo quaerenti memetipsum ac bonum meum quidve mali evitandum esset* . . . Dieser Eingang ist offensichtlich geschaffen nach den berühmten ciceronischen Eingängen von *De oratore: cogitanti mihi saepenumero et memoria vetera repetenti* und *De divinatione: quaerenti mihi multumque et diu cogitanti, quanam re possem* . . ." (*Soliloquia*, ed. Müller, 59-60).

Cicero is not without his specific contribution to our genealogy of Lady Reason. If we seek to know what Augustinian "reason" might be, we can hardly do better than to inquire of Ratio herself. In *Soliloquia* 1.6 she draws a distinction between *looking* and *seeing*. The spiritual looking is the capacity of reason; the fact of spiritual seeing is the work of divine illumination. Ratio speaks: "Aspectus animae, ratio est; sed quia non sequitur ut omnis qui aspicit videat, aspectus rectus atque perfectus, id est quem visio sequitur, virtus vocatur; est enim virtus vel recta vel perfecta ratio." Both the concept and the language are neoplatonic, and the inventor of their Latin expression is Cicero, who says in the *Tusculans* (4.15.34) "ipsa virtus brevissime recta ratio dici potest" and the *De legibus* (1.45) "est enim virtus perfecta ratio."[103] Here, in the optimistic possibilities of "right reason," we find the ancient posterity of one of the perennial themes of western thought, but we find also one of those places where Augustine and Boethius most clearly diverge. An Ithacan view of reason is not unjust with regard to the *Consolatio*, where the word *ratio*, whether or not accompanied by the demeaning adjective *humana*, usually speaks of those limitations and constraints of the lower range of the word's lexical dignity. For Boethius the guide of life is Philosophia, the love of Wisdom, and nowhere in his book is Reason the same or even nearly the same as Wisdom. As we have seen, it is quite otherwise in the *Roman de la Rose*, where a personified, epiphanic Reason has usurped the place of Boethius' Philosophia. But to speak of usurpation is misleading. Reason's queenly beauty is hers by right of birth. In the *Roman de la Rose* she has justly reclaimed the title of her ancient lineage.

[103] See the notes in Müller, 228; and the *Soliloqui*, ed. A. Marzullo (Milan, 1972), 231.

2.

LOOKING FOR LOVE IN CARTHAGE

Lady Reason's dazzling credentials assure us that we can believe her, indeed that we must believe her. There are no inadequacies of her poetic conception and no limitations to her moral vision that can cloud the title of her authority. Hers is the single voice within the *Roman de la Rose* that consistently articulates the moral and intellectual standards against which Amant's erotic drama is to be understood and finally judged. Not to believe Reason is, in a word, unreasonable; and to reject her as Amant does, with repeated rhetorical and dramatic flourishes that bespeak a willful desire to be rid of her entirely, is flagrant madness. Such is, I would argue, the inescapable intellectual fact of the literary lineage that we have just traced.

What might be called the poetic fact of Jean de Meun's text, on the other hand, may seem to lead in a somewhat different direction; and those critics who have been of the Lover's party can justly argue that if Jean de Meun has really intended Lady Reason to illuminate the moral landscape of his rose garden, he seems strangely to have gone to pains as well to hide her lamp under a bushel. Readers have found her teachings "cryptic," "equivocal," and "paradoxical"; and her whole pedagogical mode evasive, subjunctive, or diffident. In particular, the Ithacans have repeatedly objected that her doctrine lacks any specific Christian character that might signal unequivocally the transcendent authority that I have claimed on her behalf. We circle back to the allegations of Reason's "limitations." By way of chiding me for describing her teachings as "the store of traditional Christian wisdom," Michael Cherniss says that "it is clear from a careful reading of the colloquy between Reson and Amant that she, too, is a secular figure and an inadequate instructor on the subject of *amor*. Her wisdom is not exclusively or uniquely Christian; rather, it is the sort of rational wisdom available to the great pagan writers who lacked Christian revelation. . . . She is limited and inadequate precisely because she cannot discuss love from a Christian perspective."[1]

I have already permitted myself an opinion as to how "careful" a reading it actually is that leads to such conclusions, but I must acknowledge that the issue here raised, the relationship between classical and Christian wisdom in the dialogue between Reason and the Lover, is indeed the heart of the matter. If we remove the adjective "careful" from the first sentence cited above—or better yet, replace it with another, such as "uncareful," "unwary," or "unsuspecting"—its judgment will surely reflect our own experience as common readers. That is the kind of character Lady Reason seems to be, and that *is* the kind of stoic wisdom she seems to expose—up to the point, that is, when we do in fact become *careful* readers. I myself can find no escape from the uncomfortable fact that Jean de Meun repeatedly and entirely consciously invites us to mistake his poem by making rather less of Lady Reason than we should. But the reader's underestimation of Reason is, ironically, born of Reason's overestimation of the reader.

Lest I myself be thought cryptic or equivocal, I should

---

[1] Cherniss, "Irony and Authority," 230. See also Donald W. Rowe, *O Love O Charite! Contraries Harmonized in Chaucer's Troilus* (Carbondale, IL, 1976), 64-65: "But then even Reason, whom Jean characterizes as the likeness of God in man, cannot understand the mysteries of divine love. Jean associates Reason with pagan wisdom; her heroes are such men as Socrates and Plato. . . . Thus both nature and reason remain highly hazardous guides to truth."

perhaps say explicitly that I believe that the problem here identified reflects a conflict between the expectations of the poet and those of the reader. If Lady Reason has disappointed us as a guide, it is for the same reasons, or cognate ones, that Lady Philosophy has disappointed some of Boethius' readers. She seems insufficiently "Christian"; she is a teacher but not a preacher. Her literary garments are rich and silky, not the burlap habit of the friars. There are, to be sure, numerous medieval poems in which the voice of Christian authority speaks in a harsh voice, unmelodious in its intonation and unsubtle in its formulations. To say that Jean's *Roman* is not one of them is perhaps already to say a good deal, but it is far from saying that the *Roman* (or its privileged voice, Lady Reason) is "secular" or "unchristian," to borrow two adjectives that recur in the criticism.

We have identified a pattern in the *Roman de la Rose* that links it directly with Augustine's dialogues "in the Ciceronian mode," and if we judge it according to the intellectual conventions of its own tradition, and not according to those of a real or imagined simplistic Christian didacticism, it becomes harder to read and easier to understand. The paradoxical fact is that the critics have belittled Lady Reason because they have expected too much from her. They want her to do all of the work, cross all the *t*'s, tie up all the loose ends. Her failure to do so is misdiagnosed as incapacity and moral debility. But as Marrou has taught us, the dialogue in the Ciceronian mode demands strenuous readers. It is the reader, trained by the dialectic of dialogue but nonetheless the accountable steward of his own brainpower, who is expected to respond in kind to the importunity of the text, to sustain the dialectic, to discover the truth arduously sought. The important point is that the truth must be *discovered*; it is not delivered parceled to the door. The reader of Augustinian dialogue can be no spoon-fed catechumen. One of our clearest early indications of Amant's lamentable condition must surely be his appalling inadequacy as a "reader" of his own poem. He botches Ovid, expresses a philistine ignorance of allegory, does not know so much as what language Lady Reason speaks. For the reader in the *Roman de la Rose*, such details bear a double warning. It is not enough to avoid the more flamboyant idiocies of the dreamer-narrator. The greater challenge is to respond with verve and spirit to the stimulating indirections of Lady Reason's "Ciceronian" dialectic. What I mean by "indirections" can perhaps be demonstrated best by reference to a single example—the example of Lady Reason on the subject of friendship.

The long dialogue between Reason and the Lover is as it were the proemium to Jean's poem, but it contains also his denouement, when, with fifteen thousand lines yet to go, the two characters part company forever. Their rift, whether viewed as comic or tragic or both at once, as I believe Jean would have us view it, is the inevitable outcome of their protracted and often spirited quarrel about love—the thing itself, and the words used of the thing. The episode is lengthy—three thousand lines—yet dense with a complexity of argument and image that no critic has so far addressed. It might be said of the *Roman* as a whole that it is a poem so foreign to us that we understand its easiest ideas only with great labor. Its real difficulties we may never even identify.

All of the subjects touched upon in that lengthy dialogue are of crucial importance for the broader strategies of the whole poem, but one subject in particular, friendship, has a privileged status, pointing as it does to the major character Amis, to the meaning of the Lover's compact with the god of Love, and to the more bizarre alliances of Reason and Danger, Amours and Faussemblant, the Vekke and the Lover, and so forth. Within the more limited economy of the episode itself, it is the subject of friendship that most clearly displays the distance between Reason and the Lover and thus adumbrates their definitive parting of the ways.

The *Roman de la Rose* is a poem of contexts; every part of it explains, qualifies, illuminates another part. It is therefore useful to note the general context of the argument about friend-

ship, which in fact comes in the midst of Reason's taxonomy
of *love*. Reason defines a number of different *kinds* of love,
always at some length and often with copious literary exem-
plification. Among love's genres are sexual passion (a mental
illness), natural concupiscence (an innate proclivity), and so
forth. One of the loves here defined is friendship, "mutual
good will among men, without any discord, in accordance
with the benevolence of God." This love called friendship is,
according to Reason, virtuous; and she contrasts it sharply
with that love which has captured the Lover, love *par amours*.
The Lover's response to this lecture is highly irrational—ir-
rationality is, after all, what is signified by the dramatic tableau
of a man arguing against Reason—but also richly comic. The
beginning and the end of the argument, omitting several hundred
lines of exemplification, are as follows:

Amistiez est nomee l'une,	4655
c'est bone volanté conmune	
des genz antr'els, sanz descordance,	
selonc la Dieu benivolance,	
et soit entr'els conmunité	
de touz leur biens en charité,	4660
si que par nule entencion	
n'i puisse avoir excepcion.	
. . .	
[Amant:] Ci ne finastes hui de dire	5345
que je doi mon seignor despire	
por ne soi quele amor sauvage.	
Qui cercheroit jusqu'an Quartage	
. . .	
n'avroit il pas aconseü	5356
. . .	
Neïs Tulles, qui mist grant cure	5375
en cerchier secrez d'escripture,	
n'i pot tant son engin debatre	
qu'onc plus de .iii. pere ou de .iiii.,	

de touz les siecles trespassez
puis que cist mond fu conpassez,   5380
de si fines amors trouvast.

That is, Reason defines friendship as a species of love that she
recommends instead of the love of Amours (the Lover's *seignor*
[5346]); and the Lover says, in effect, "the kind of love you
are counseling—namely, friendship—cannot be found on earth.
I would not find it even if I were to go as far as Carthage.
Not even Cicero could find more than three or four examples
of true friendship in the whole history of the world."

These passages of Jean's text are very curious, and they raise
a number of problems that the poem's editors and commen-
tators have never recognized, hence never addressed. Yet the
kinds of problem here raised—linguistic precision, Jean's at-
titude toward his sources, the nature of the classical learning
of the *Roman*, the whole question of the poem's "intertex-
tuality"—are among those that offer most promise for the
understanding of a work concerning which there is little com-
mon critical agreement beyond the shared perception of its
crucial presence in the history of the poetry of late medieval
Europe. The specific questions that the texts ask include two
I shall pursue in this chapter: Why is friendship an *amor
sauvage*? And why would the Lover not find it even were he
to go to Carthage? The search for answers to those questions
will involve the discovery that for Jean de Meun a "text" is
sometimes a pretext and sometimes a supertext.

What I mean by the term "supertext," a neologism I advance
with some embarrassment, will presently emerge, though in
the most general terms I allude to the operation within a poem
of a secondary literary presence of a specially, and often uniquely,
powerful authority. A supertext is not a text, for it appears
only by inference or implication; it is not a subtext because it
does not infiltrate from below but commands from above. The
concept is necessarily related to that of "intertextuality," and
it has a particular vitality with regard to medieval literary

culture, which in many ways fostered real or feigned subservience of original genius to literary authority and encouraged complex patterns of literary dependence, appropriation, imitation, and what in our own day would be downright plagiarism.

Such problems are acutest of all, perhaps, precisely with those major figures of the vernacular period for whom the literary calling inevitably yoked translation and original composition. There were many such artists, but for representative purposes two conspicuous poet-translators immediately present themselves: Jean de Meun and Geoffrey Chaucer. These two men, whose literary careers viewed in their totality are so strikingly similar, are in one sense *always* translating an anterior text.[2] Jean's French *Boèce* is one way he "handles" the *Consolatio*; the central metaphor of the *Roman de la Rose* is another. Chaucer's actual translation of the *Roman* we do not have, yet we see him "translating" Jean de Meun on virtually every page he wrote. We search for canons by which we can hope to adjudicate complex literary relationships that include, in one and the same instance, deference if not servility on the one hand and an assertive competitiveness on the other.

II. *VETERA ET NOVA*: Cicero and Some Christians

In the text from the *Roman de la Rose* that is the subject of our inquiry there is one explicit appeal to the authority of an *auctor* outside of the poem: Cicero. As it happens, no classical author could be better suited to exemplify the dilemma of the Christian writer interested in the "classics," a dilemma that, in the early Christian period, created some of our surest models

[2] Two particularly stimulating articles relevant to the general phenomenon that I have in mind are Douglas Kelly, *"Translatio Studii*: Translation, Adaptation, and Allegory in Medieval French Literature," *PQ* 57 (1978): 287-310; and Nancy Freeman Regalado, " 'Des Contraires Choses': La Fonction poétique de la citation et des *exempla* dans le 'Roman de la Rose' de Jean de Meun," *Littérature 41 (1981): 62-81.*

of the medieval supertext. Cicero presented the problem of "Christian humanism" in its acutest form, for he combined in his life and reputation unassailable literary authority and an unimpeachable moral character. He was not merely a great writer, the greatest prose stylist of all time, but a great man; and his severe platonic morality so often approached the categories of Pauline righteousness that whole paragraphs and indeed essays could be appropriated in their integrity to the schoolbooks of Christian children for a thousand years. Yet it is precisely Cicero who presents the paradigm case for our discussions of the ambiguous attitude of the Church Fathers to the classics, an attitude traditionally illustrated in scholarly discussion by reference to Jerome and Augustine.

Two famous set pieces, the first in Jerome's letter to Eustochium, the other in the third book of the *Confessions*, offer apparently stark alternative Christian possibilities. Jerome, convicted by Christ himself of being a "Ciceronian," is scourged for that crime till his sobs of pain mingle with cries for pity.[3] On the other hand, Augustine is half converted to true religion by his reading of the *Hortensius*, a book that "contained an exortation to the love of wisdom. Indeed, Lord, that book changed my way of thinking and turned my prayers toward you."[4] The two anecdotes are actually not so far apart as they seem, and the one can help explain the other. Augustine says of Cicero's readers that they generally admired the chaff rather than the fruit. If that is culpable in a pagan, how much worse in a Christian? Yet such is Jerome's real crime—an educated embarrassment at the stylistic crudities of the Scriptures and a guilty preference for the polished cadences of Tully.

For the purposes of finding the fruit of Lady Reason's theory of friendship, it is Augustine's attitude that is of the greater

[3] *Epistola xxii (Ad Eustochium)*, 30; St. Jérome, *Lettres*, ed. J. Labourt (Paris, 1949), 144-45.

[4] *Confessionum libri xiii*, 3.4.7; ed. M. Skutella (Stuttgart, 1969), 41. This is the text used throughout. English translations are my own, closely following those of Pusey and Watts, and the French translation of Labriolle.

interest; yet though his be the model of a "positive" Christian response to pagan culture, it is a response by no means free from ambiguity. It would be hard to give Cicero a greater compliment than to say that he initiated Augustine's search for Wisdom, a search that as we know would end only with Christ, the eternal Wisdom of the Father; but even in proffering it, Augustine exhibits certain grudging and patronizing reservations: "Et usitato iam discendi ordine perueneram in librum cuiusdam Ciceronis, cuius linguam fere omnes mirantur, pectus non ita."[5] Maurice Testard has argued that in using the categories of "heart" and "tongue," Augustine defers to Cicero's own opposition of "wisdom" and "eloquence," an hierarchy often suggested in medieval texts by "gold" and "silver" and one easily enough included among the clichéd metaphors of scriptural exegesis—spirit and letter, fruit and chaff, grain and husk.[6]

Yet it is precisely the continuity with scriptural Wisdom that Augustine seeks to destroy with the odd word *pectus*. Christine Mohrmann must certainly be right in suggesting that Augustine has chosen it instead of *cor* precisely because *cor* is a privileged scriptural word with privileged scriptural associations.[7] Augustine wants to make the point that though Cicero has *philosophia*, it is not the revealed *philosophia* of Christ. And however we understand the extraordinary phrase *cuiusdam Ciceronis*, it is difficult to avoid its supercilious and patronizing overtones. We cannot believe that the source of Augustine's archness is literary vanity; he does not patronize Cicero because he thinks himself a better Latinist. On the other hand, he clearly thinks he is possessed of a higher wisdom; and that, perhaps, makes him a better *writer*.

This famous passage in the *Confessions* gives a clear example of how it was that Christian writers of the Middle Ages could

[5] Ibid., 40-41

[6] Testard, *Saint Augustin et Cicéron*, 1:18ff. For "silver and gold," see H.-J. Spitz, *Die Metaphorik des geistigen Schriftsinns* (Munich, 1972), 191ff.

[7] *Vigiliae Christianae*, 30 (1959): 239.

at once revere the great masters of classical antiquity and, with a logic as sincere as their respect, recognize their own inevitable superiority. Christian "Ciceronianism" is, in fact, a fairly common phenomenon in late antique literature. One particularly impressive example, the *De officiis* of St. Ambrose, has been repeatedly examined by students of the classical tradition in early Christianity but nonetheless neglected with respect to its implications for *Augustinian* literary tradition.[8] There is the clearest, most explicit, generative relationship between the *De officiis* of Cicero and that of Ambrose.[9] The subject of the latter work and its principal philosophical assumptions, its tripartite structure, its very title—all this and more Ambrose has taken from Tully, explicitly and, so far as one can tell, without apology or self-conscious tension. I do not mean, of course, that Ambrose's attitude toward his pagan source is uncomplicated by a certain assumption of superiority and, at times, an implicit censoriousness. Yet throughout the book Cicero is regarded with manifest respect and deference as a grave moral authority, and the authority *par excellence* on Ambrose's chosen topic, duty. The debts of philosophical substance and literary form are acknowledged cheerfully and without "anxiety," certainly without the breast-beating, literal or metaphorical, of Jerome.

The considerable controversy surrounding the nature of Ambrose's *De officiis* has in fact been excited by the author's optimistic approbation of the main lines of Cicero's thought, so that Ambrose has been identified by some as a thoroughgoing stoic and credited by others with a conscious and syncretistic fusion of Ciceronian and scriptural philosophy.[10] But Ambrose is a "Ciceronian" only insofar as Cicero approaches being a

[8] But see Testard, *Saint Augustin et Cicéron*, 1:119-20.

[9] *De officiis libri tres*, ed. G. Banterle [*Sancti Ambrosi Episcopi Opera* 13] (Milan/Rome, 1977), 369ff., lists the parallel readings.

[10] See the excellent review of scholarship in Goulven Madec, *S. Ambrose et la philosophie* (Paris, 1978), 161ff. The most helpful single study is still R. Thamin, *Saint Ambrose et la morale chrétienne au iv⁴ siècle* (Paris, 1895).

Christian, and the distance between Cicero and Christ is some-
times a short step and sometimes a great chasm. There can be
no doubt that Cicero is the giant on whose broad shoulders
Ambrose rests in his *De officiis*, but it would be rash to call
Ambrose, the master of Augustine, a dwarf. A giant on the
back of a giant sees not merely a little further; he sees an
altogether new horizon. Cicero, however grave a moral au-
thority, lived before the illumination of Christ and beyond the
illumination of the Scriptures. Ambrose pays homage to the
classical moralist on every page of his book, but he likewise
corrects him, confidently, and at times sharply, from the priv-
ileged perspective of Christian revelation.

I shall limit myself to a single example, though any number
could be adduced. Cicero begins his third book by evoking
the busy leisure of Scipio Africanus, of whom it was first said
that "he was never less at rest than when he was at rest."[11]
His point is that Scipio turned his leisure to useful and social
purpose, in reflection and internal dialogue. Ambrose in his
turn ratifies the importance of *otium* and *solitudo* to the ethical
man, but his attitude toward Cicero's exemplary use of Scipio
is one of peeved condescension. *His* third book begins not with
Scipio, but with David and Solomon, models of contemplation,
and what he has to say of Scipio is that "he was *not* the first
to understand that he was not alone when he was alone, nor
less at leisure than when he was at leisure."[12] The first was
Moses. Ambrose's *exemplum* is implicitly truer than Cicero's
because it is taken from sacred history, not from the history
of the earthly city. By implication, the moral quality that it
exemplifies—though sharing a Latin vocabulary with Cicero—
is likewise of a higher order than that described by Cicero.
This has nothing to do either with the comparative literary
abilities of the two writers or even with their comparative

[11] *De officiis*, ed. P. Fedeli (Turin, 1965), 153: "nunquam se minus otiosum
esse, quam cum otiosus."
[12] *De officiis* 3.1.1-2; ed. Banterle, 274.

moral characters. It results from the simple fact that one writer is illuminated by the grace of Christ, and the other not. In the final paragraph of his *De officiis* Ambrose summarizes his claim for the work's moral utility, which, quite independent of the possible stylistic inadequacy of the essay, is firmly established in its copiousness of scriptural *exempla*.[13]

In certain manifestations this attitude could be little more than a kind of literary self-righteousness, an uncomplicated rejection of "lies" in favor of "truth." In what might be called the Dominican attitude toward poetry in the later Middle Ages, there is a coarseness that does not stop short of philistinism, and even great poets, the Chaucer of the "Retractions" or the Jean de Meun of the "Testament," were not untouched by it. But it has another vein too, one poetically much richer, and there is a major tradition of medieval Christian poetry in which biblical self-confidence led to fruitful literary competitions rather than literary suppression or censorship.

The *Psychomachia* shows one strategy for taking on Vergil, the *Divine Comedy* another. Here is poetry as serious and elevated as we shall find in the Middle Ages; yet in differing ways the response of Prudentius and Dante to the *Aeneid* is witty, even playful. One particular poetic tradition, in which materials from pagan mythology and Christian history are brought together in what might be called competitive collation, is especially relevant in the present context. The Bible epic of "Eupolemius" gives a good example of the technique from the high Middle Ages. "Eupolemius" structures much of his poem about parallels—Joseph and Hippolytus, the golden calf and Europa's bull, the Tower of Babel and the revolt of the giants, Noah and Deucalion, Jacob and Diomedes.[14]

The classic of this genre is an older work, dating from the

---

[13] *De officiis* 3.22.130; ed. Banterle, 358; cf. Madec, *S. Ambrose et la philosophie*, 163n.

[14] Eupolemius, *Das Bibelgedicht*, ed. K. Manitius (Weimar, 1973), 19; for further examples, see M. Manitius, "Mittelalterliche Umdeutung antiker Sagenstoffe," *Zeits. f. vergl. Lit.* 15 (1904): 151-58.

first Christian millennium, the so-called *Eclogue* of Theodulus. It enjoyed a long life as a medieval schoolbook, and as one of the *Octo Auctores Morales*, it helped keep intact in the Renaissance the remarkably enduring marriage of elegant Latin and ascetic doctrine.[15] The eclogue is a debate between the shepherd Pseustis (Falsehood) and the shepherdess Alithia (Truth). Pseustis proposes examples of elegant classical mythology only to be topped every time by Alithia's examples from Bible history. The final adjudication is reserved for Phronesis, well-known as a grave censor from the poems of Alain de Lille and Henry of Septimello, among others, and of course her judgment is for Alithia. The eclogue thus presents an elegant model of how a Christian poet might at once delight in classical texts and avoid the errors of seeing final truth in them. The *Dialogus super auctores* makes the point quite explicitly that Theodulus' intention is not to dissuade his audience from *reading* pagan poetry, but to point out its deficiencies as a model for moral imitation.[16]

III. Friendship, Classical and Christian

The *De officiis* was not the only moral essay of Cicero's to which great Christian writers paid the high compliment of "Christianization," for there is a yet more magnificent example in the *De spiritali amicitia* of St. Aelred of Rievaulx. Aelred's book is one of the greatest masterpieces of twelfth-century Cistercian literature, and that perforce means one of the great-

[15] *Theoduli eclogam*, ed. J. Osternacher, *Jahresbericht des bischoflichen Privat-Gymnasiums am Kollegium Petrinum in Urfahr* 5 (1902). The more recent edition by Huygens, with the complete commentary of Bernard of Utrecht, has been unavailable to me. On the *Octo Auctores*, see R. Bultot, "La *Chartula* et l'enseignement du mépris du monde dans les écoles et les universités médiévales," *Studi medievali*, ser. 3, vol. 7 (1967), pp. 787-834.

[16] "Intentio eius est sacrae paginae veritatem commendare et fabularum commenta dissuadere, non quidem ut non legantur, sed ne lectae credantur vel in actum transferantur" (*Accessus ad auctores*, ed. R.B.C. Huygens [Leiden, 1970], 94).

est books in medieval European literature. In it Aelred does
for friendship what Ambrose did for duty; he examines a Cic-
eronian category from the advantage of Christian revelation,
exploring, in effect, what difference Christ makes for friend-
ship. Aelred was entirely conscious of the Ambrosian pattern
he followed, and he repeatedly cites Ambrose's *De officiis*.

The *De spiritali amicitia* thus provides a splendid example
of twelfth-century "Christian humanism"; but its relevance for
the *Roman de la Rose* is more pointed still. Jean de Meun
translated the book from Latin into French, and in the famous
dedicatory epistle to his *Boèce* he proudly lists its title (*Espi-
rituelle amistié*) along with other translations and the *Roman de
la Rose* in the catalogue of his oeuvre.[17] This is in some ways
a remarkable fact, but more remarkable still is the fact that
scholars have not stampeded to explore a major work devoted
to a subject developed at length in the *Roman de la Rose* and
known to have been translated by the *Roman*'s author. This
neglect is to some extent explained by the fact that no copy
of the French translation is known so that the text has not
been able to force itself upon the attention of students of French
literature; but I think also that the prevailingly fashionable
descriptions of Jean de Meun as an "immoralist," a "bourgeois
realist," a "phallicist," and a social and political revolutionary
have made it seem unlikely that his poetry could be much
illuminated by monkish books on monkish friendship.

Such assumptions were fruitfully challenged some years ago
by Lionel Friedman, who set out to examine Reason's definition
of friendship (4655ff.) in the light of a comparative exami-
nation of relevant portions of the *De amicitia* and the *De spiritali
amicitia*.[18] In analyzing this passage, he concluded that "it is
impossible to consider Raison's definition a 'translation' of
Cicero's and difficult to believe it a paraphrase." He makes a

[17] "Boethius' *De Consolatione* by Jean de Meun," ed. Dédeck-Héry, 168.
[18] Lionel J. Friedman, "Jean de Meun and Ethelred of Rievaulx," *L'Esprit
créateur* 2 (1962): 135-41.

good attempt to sort things out, but his own discussion is muddled by the fact that he cites, as Cicero's definition of friendship, that of Aelred, thus rather begging the case.[19] The mistake is understandable, for the two definitions are nearly identical—yet crucially different. We shall do well to have them before our eyes.

Cicero's definition of friendship in the *Laelius* (6.20) is this: "Est enim amicitia nihil aliud, nisi omnium diuinarum humanarumque rerum cum beniuolentia et caritate consensio."[20] It is this definition, in a slightly different form, that Aelred and his friend Ivo adopt, tentatively, as a kind of "working position" for their dialogue in the *De spiritali amicitia* (1.11-12).

> AELREDUS. Nonne satis tibi est hinc quod ait Tullius: *Amicitia est rerum humanarum et diuinarum cum beneuolentia et caritate consensio?*
>
> IVO. Si tibi sufficit ista diffinitio, mihi iudico satisfactum esse.[21]
>
> [*Aelred.* Is not what Tully says sufficient for you: "Friendship is agreement concerning things human and divine, with benevolence and charity"?]

It does suffice, but only for a moment, for when Aelred next cites it, it has enjoyed a crucial increment. In the first place, he insinuates the definition into the midst of a scriptural quotation (Acts 4:32), which identifies friendship with the apostolic communism of the church at Jerusalem. Of the early Christians he then says (1.29), "Quomodo non inter eos *rerum diuinarum et humanarum cum caritate et beneuolentia* fuit summa

---

[19] Friedman, "Jean de Meun and Ethelred of Rievaulx," 136.

[20] Cicéron, *L'Amitié*, ed. L. Laurand (Paris, 1965), 6.20; p. 13.

[21] *De spiritali amicitia*, ed. A. Hoste, in *Aelredi Rievallensis Opera Omnia* [Corpus Christianorum Continuatio Mediaevalis, 1] (Turnholt, 1972), 291. All citations are from this edition.

consensio, quibus erat *cor unum et anima una?*"[22] It is the *summa*, awarded by Friedman to Cicero, which is in fact the insight of Aelred; and it is the kind of superlative that can indicate the presence of a supertext. Basil Pennington observes that "Aelred is here repeating the definition of Cicero, adding however the significant adjective 'complete.' "[23] The two definitions are not very different, merely definitively different.

A close textual analysis will make it obvious that Reason's definition does not come from the *Laelius* but from the *De spiritali amicitia*. This is to say that on the question of friendship her wisdom *is* exclusively and uniquely Christian and that it pointedly supersedes what Cherniss calls "the sort of rational wisdom available to the great pagan writers who lacked Christian revelation." Her mind is Ciceronian only insofar as Aelred is Ciceronian—and that is so far and no further. Aelred's definition of friendship is a kind of *reductio Ciceronis ad sacram paginam*, for in it Cicero has been captured and purified by the Acts of the Apostles. Lines 4659 through 4660 ("et soit entr'els conmunité / de touz leur biens en charité") have no basis at all in Cicero; but they are a clear echo of Acts 4:32: "Neither did any one say that aught of the things which he possessed was his own; but all things were common unto them."

Aelred's *De spiritali amicitia* was a famous book in its day, and we have long known that it was one of a select group of "humanist" texts translated by Jean de Meun. Under these circumstances we may be moved to inquire why successive editors and critics of the *Roman* have attributed Reason's concept of friendship to Cicero when it is in fact drawn from Aelred of Rievaulx.[24] There are several possible answers to this

[22] *De spiritali amicitia*, 294.

[23] Aelred of Rievaulx, *Spiritual Friendship*, trans. M. E. Laker (Washington, 1974), 57n. The notes for this translation, from which my own renderings differ somewhat, are by Fr. Basil Pennington.

[24] Naive readers of this passage include, among others, editors E. Langlois and F. Lecoy, the translator A. Lanly, and most recently, the critics M.-R. Jung, "Jean de Meun et l'allégorie," *Cahiers de l'Association internationale des*

question, but one of them must surely be that readers of the
poem have been misled by one of the strategies by which Jean
de Meun hoped most wittily to signal his ironic intentions.
We are misled because both Reason and Amant himself men-
tion Cicero by name.

Shortly after defining friendship, Reason adduces a passage
from Cicero's *De amicitia* in her exemplification of the theme:
so says Tully *in one of his books*. This vagueness ("dist Tulles
en un suen distié" [4718]) is a lovely Augustinian touch,
almost as good as *cuiusdam Ciceronis*. The implication is that
Reason is not intimately familiar with Cicero's work: her *pri-
mary* source is Aelred. But this is mere *jeu d'esprit*. The truly
false *cicerone* is the Lover himself, who, although he affects not
to know what friendship is beyond the name for some category
of uncouth love, is nevertheless certain that it is impossible
to find, an opinion that he rests squarely in the authority of
Cicero:

> Neïs Tulles, qui mist grant cure   5375
> en cerchier secrez d'escripture,
> n'i pot tant son engin debatre
> qu'onc plus de .iii. pere ou de .iiii.,
> de touz les siecles trespassez
> puis que cist mond fu conpassez,   5380
> de si fines amors trouvast.
> Si croi que mains en esprouvast
> de cels qui a son tens vivoient,
> qui si ami de boiche estoient;
> n'encor n'ai ge nul leu leü   5385
> qu'il onc en ait nul tel eü.
> Et sui ge plus sage que Tulles?
> Bien seroie fols et entulles,
> se tex amors voloie querre,
> puis qu'il n'en a mes nule en terre.   5390

études françaises 28 (1976): 34-35; and John M. Fyler, *Chaucer and Ovid* (New
Haven, 1979), 178-79.

Now that indeed *is* Tully who, near the beginning of his essay, reports with a sigh that one can scarcely find in all of history "three or four pairs of friends."[25]

The Lover's crippling pessimism concerning the possibility of friendship is perhaps appropriate for a pagan; those who live without Christ can hardly know what friendship is, since Christ is its beginning and its end.[26] As an argument in the age of grace, however, it is feeble indeed. Aelred cited this same Ciceronian text long before the Lover ever laid eyes on his rose garden, and he rejected it as risible.

> Ivo. As Tullius says, "In so many past ages, tradition extols scarcely three or four pairs of friends." But if in our day, that is, in this age of Christianity, friends are so few, it seems to me that I am exerting myself uselessly in striving after this virtue which I, terrified by its admirable sublimity, now almost despair of ever acquiring.
>
> Aelred. It is no wonder, then, that pursuers of true virtue were rare among the pagans since they did not know the Lord, the Dispenser of virtue, of whom it is written: "The Lord of hosts, he is the King of glory." Of those who had faith in him I will give you indeed not three or four but a thousand pairs of friends, who (though the pagans take the example of Pylades and Orestes as a great marvel) were ready to die for one another.[27]

A catalogue of the ironies in Amant's response to Reason would be a long one with his talk of searching out the secrets of texts and the circumstances under which he would be a stupid fool. But the central and great irony—here and elsewhere in the *Roman de la Rose*—is the folly of his appeal to moral teachings of antique pagans successfully and definitively

---

[25] *L'Amitié*, 4.15; ed. Laurand, 11.

[26] "Constat enim Tullium uerae amicitiae ignorasse uirtutem; cum eius principium finemque, Christum uidelicet, penitus ignorauerit" (*De spiritali amicitia* 1.8; ed. Hoste, 290).

[27] *De spiritali amicitia* 1.25, 27-28; trans. Laker, 56-57.

refuted by the living experience of Christians: "Et sui je plus sage que Tulles?" No, alas—though he *should* be. Not three or four pair but a thousand pairs! To wallow in Ciceronian pessimism while ignoring Aelred—whose book manifestly controls this narrative moment of the poem—to align himself with the torpid interlocutor of Aelred's dialogue but, unlike him, never gain enlightenment, is a species of pagan folly toward which neither Jean de Meun nor the audience for whom he translated the *Espirituelle amistié* and wrote the *Roman de la Rose* could conceivably have taken an indulgent attitude. Nor, incidentally, could Cicero himself. Amant's desire has nothing at all to do with a *consensio* in benevolence and charity but with a *copulatio* in hypocrisy and concupiscence. *That* is the sort of friendship Cicero thought was *sauvage*.[28]

One German critic has deplored the tendency of certain scholars, whom he elsewhere identifies as "the American school," to substitute patristic authorities for Jean de Meun's obviously identifiable sources.[29] I can answer only that what is obvious in the *Roman de la Rose* seldom takes the reader very far. The *obvious* source of Reason's doctrine of friendship is Cicero's *De amicitia*. The covert source is Aelred's Augustinian reworking of Cicero, the *De spiritali amicitia*. It is the latter which informs the passage with its special significance, a significance we can hardly doubt that Reason and her poetic creator Jean de Meun, fully intend. It is Jean de Meun, and not "the American school," who has compromised his own "obvious" source with unobvious but powerful patristic doctrine.

[28] *L'Amitié*, 21.79-81; ed. Laurand, 42-43.

[29] Ott, "Jean de Meun und Boethius," 208: "Und ebenso zeigt sich . . . bei D. W. Robertson und seinen Schülern die Neigung, das gesamte Schrifttum der christlichen Theologie von den Kirchenvätern bis ins 12. Jahrhundert als die allgemeine 'Quelle' des Rosenromans anzusehen, anstatt sich an die nachweisbaren bestimmten Quellen Jean de Meuns zu halten." Speaking only for myself, modesty forbids that I accept the compliment. I have not yet lived long enough to peruse "das gesamte Schrifttum der christlichen Theologie von den Kirchenvätern bis ins 12. Jahrhundert," and indeed there are days when I fear that I may be forever mired among the semi-Pelagians.

IV. Carthaginian Love

The analysis of our passage from the *Roman de la Rose* has identified one controlling text and one amusing pretext, the *De spiritali amicitia* and the *Laelius*, but neither of them tells us why the Lover will not find *amor sauvage* in Carthage or why it would occur to him not to look for it there in the first place. To understand that, we must identify yet another book hidden in the lines, like a spirit, present everywhere and visible nowhere, the supertext that actually commands Jean's use of Cicero and Aelred alike. Jean de Meun's supertext is the *Confessions* of St. Augustine.

The suggestion of an Augustinian "source" for an important part of the *Roman*, though it is the poem's inexorable implication, must face the opposition of tradition. Ernest Langlois, who wrote an important book called *Les Origines et sources du Roman de la Rose*, limited Augustine's influence on the poem to a few phrases from one of his lesser books, the *De opere monachorum*.[30] Even these phrases came to Jean's attention indirectly through the polemics of William of Saint-Amour.

I myself have never shared the view that Augustine exercised only a marginal influence on Jean's poem. Quite apart from the evidence adduced in the last chapter concerning the *Soliloquia*, it seems to me that the burden of sexual doctrine in the *Roman de la Rose* reflects commonplace Augustinian statements, and especially those found in the fourteenth book of the *City of God*.[31] The present suggestion is a new one, though there is, *a priori*, hardly anything extraordinary in the possibility that Jean de Meun, a poet who mined for his own vernacular purposes classics from the Latin repertory of medieval letters like the *Consolatio Philosophiae* of Boethius or the *De planctu Natura* of Alain de Lille, could also have mined the

---

[30] E. Langlois, *Les Origines et sources du Roman de la Rose* (Paris, 1891), 133.

[31] See Fleming, *The Roman de la Rose*, 134, and the discussion above, pp. 19ff.

Confessions, a work that, as Pierre Courcelle has shown, proved almost inexhaustibly fecund to later medieval writers. But since what goes without saying too often goes unsaid, I might make the explicit point that there is an overarching generic kinship between the *Confessions* and the *Roman de la Rose*, which all the differences between the two works, however marked, cannot compromise. This kinship is reflected both in theme and in structure.

The great theme of both works is, of course, love. Guillaume de Lorris, in the proemium to the romance, claims that he will expose nothing less than the whole art of Love

> ce est li Romanz de la Rose,   37
> ou l'art d'Amors est tote enclose.

There is throughout the *Roman* an urgency about love that, however carefully circumscribed, is always intense and often does not stop short of the comic. Whether in the practices of mental eroticism taught by the god of Love in Guillaume's part of the poem or in the altogether more robust sexuality of Jean's denouement, we see the Lover in the grip of a power that will not be denied, over which he has no control, and toward which the only appropriate posture is that of submission. This phenomenon has been universally remarked but diversely explained by the poem's critics, often in terms of such concepts as "courtly love" and "naturalism."

For our limited purpose of examining the dialogue between Reason and the Lover it is not necessary to enter into an extended discussion of the large and problematical issues that such concepts bring with them. Nonetheless, I do want to point out that the poetic situation of the *Roman* is consistent with fundamental Augustinian teaching. Love is, for Augustine, inexorable, the absolutely basic fact of what has come to be called his "anthropology." He can imagine a human life without love no more than he can imagine human life without food. Man was born for love, will have it, must have it. Man's viciousness, but also his promise of glory, are tied to a desperate and abandoned quest for love. Love is, indeed, man's destiny. "Thou hast made us for thyself," he writes in the justly famous opening paragraph of the *Confessions*, "and our heart is restless until it finds its rest in Thee." Moral analysis in Augustine does not depend upon the *fact* of love, which is assumed, but on the *object* of love, a determination of reasonable volition. And this, I have argued (and by no means I alone), is likewise the moral presupposition of the authors of the *Roman de la Rose*.

As there is basic congruence of theme between the two works, so also are there important parallels of form and structure. The *Roman de la Rose* is an extended erotic autobiography in which the first-person voice of the narrator is sounded with considerable artistic skill and artistic tact. The fictional—or if that be too controversial a word, the self-consciously artistic—use of the first-person voice in the *Confessions* is now widely recognized.[32] I am convinced, indeed, that it is the *Confessions* that provided the Middle Ages with its aptest model of vivid, exemplary fiction as we find it in such diverse works as the *Divine Comedy*, the *Canterbury Tales*, or the *Libro de buen amor*. This comes tolerably close to saying that in some sense St. Augustine's *Confessions* enabled most of what is best in medieval "moral fiction." As far as the *Roman de la Rose* is concerned, there are other, more specific parallels, as for example, the structural metaphor of pilgrimage.

This is, I hope, bearable speculation, but it is speculation nonetheless. Of the positive relationships between Augustine's *Confessions* and Aelred of Rievaulx, on the other hand, we have abundant and conclusive proof. "His reading was in edifying books whose words are wont to bring tears," writes Aelred's biographer, "and in particular he generally had in his hands the *Confessions* of Augustine, for it was these which had been

---

[32] See Eugene Vance, "Augustine's *Confessions* and the Grammar of Selfhood," *Genre* 6 (1973): 1-28; and Charles Dahlberg, "First Person and Personification in the *Roman de la Rose*," *Mediaevalia* 3 (1977): 37-58.

his guide when he was converted from the world."[33] What was generally in his hands was always in his heart, and his heart poured forth its fullness into the pages of the *De spiritali amicitia*.

The agenda of this chapter cannot allow a thorough or even adequate survey of the extent of Aelred's debt to the *Confessions*, but I must at least acknowledge it. The first sentence of the prologue to *De spiritali amicitia* explicitly states the Augustinian theme of Aelred's work ("When I was just a lad at school . . . nothing seemed to me more sweet, nothing more agreeable, nothing more practical, than to be loved and to love"), and the debt increases with every succeeding paragraph. The debt is of three sorts. There are in the first place innumerable direct citations and verbal echoes of the *Confessions*, so much a part of Aelred's mind that they are an inevitable part of his writing: "The easy and almost unconscious reliance on the Scriptures and the reminiscences of the *Confessions* of St. Augustine and the devotional writings of John of Fécamp derive from deep personal meditation nourished by the *lectio*."[34] Next, Aelred is thoroughly and explicitly Augustinian in his doctrine of love, as he is indeed in all his works and most conspicuously in the stunning *De speculo caritatis*, his most extended treatment of the subject. Aelred regards friendship as a species of love, and we recall that the discussion of friendship in the *Roman de la Rose* follows Reason's similar definition: "Amors sunt de pluseurs manieres. . . . Amistiez est nomee l'une" (4650, 4655). In itself such a taxonomy would be a mere medieval commonplace, but Aelred goes much further, for he unmistakably identifies his own conception of friendship with Augustine's search for love in the *Confessions*. At the appearance of Gratian, one of the personae in Aelred's dialogue, Walter thus identifies him: "Here comes our friend Gratian. . . . I might rightly

---

[33] *The Life of Aelred of Rievaulx by Walter Daniel*, ed. F. M. Powicke (London, 1950), p. 50.

[34] Ibid., lxvii.

call him friendship's child for he spends all his energy in seeking to be loved and to love."[35]

The third point, and the one most immediately relevant to the central argument of this chapter, is this: Aelred adopts a quite self-consciously Augustinian attitude toward Cicero. That Cicero is the "source" of Aelred's treatise there is, from its very first page, no doubt whatsoever. There is not in the two books called *De amicitia* the same structural imitation that exists between the two books called *De officiis*, but when we move from form to content, Cicero's mind and matter are decisive. In the prologue to *De spiritali amicitia*, Aelred paints a brief history of his adolescence on top of the clear design of the master: "I was drawn now here, now there, and not knowing the law of true friendship, I was often deceived by its mere semblance. At length there came to my hands the treatise which Tullius wrote on friendship, and it immediately appealed to me as being useful because of the depth of his teaching and the gracefulness of its style."[36] The terms *gravitas sententiarum* and *suavitas eloquentiae* are the obvious reflexes of Augustine's *pectus* and *lingua*. The young Aelred, like the young Augustine, was attracted to Cicero both by his eloquent style and his weighty matter.

Two or three sentences more trace the history of his conversion from the world—a journey for which his guide was Augustine's *Confessions*, as we have already heard in the testimony of his friend Walter Daniel—and his entry into the cloister. It was a pilgrimage of a few short years, recounted in perhaps two hundred words; yet how far it took him from the "world"—and from Cicero! "From that time on Sacred Scripture became more attractive and the little learning which I had acquired in the world grew insipid in comparison. The ideas I had gathered from Cicero's treatise on friendship kept recurring to my mind, and I was astonished that they no longer

[35] *Spiritual Friendship*, 73.
[36] Ibid., 45-46.

had for me their wonted savor. For now nothing which had
not been sweetened by the honey of the most sweet name of
Jesus, nothing which had not been seasoned with salt of Sacred
Scripture, drew my affection so entirely to itself. Pondering
over these thoughts again and again, I began to ask myself
whether they could perhaps have some support from Scrip-
ture."[37]

This is a perfect paradigm of Augustinian Ciceronianism
and, more generally, of "Christian humanism"—the impulse
to redeem the wisdom and eloquence of ancient writers who
had themselves lived without the knowledge of the source of
all Redemption. Aelred knows exactly whose track he follows,
and he sees in the intellectual career of Augustine a useful
parallel to his own enterprise of "Christianizing" the moral
philosophy of a pagan. Augustine's guide at the beginning of
his search for Truth had been none other than the ancient
Tully, whose *Hortensius*, much admired by the college profes-
sors for its rhetorical flourishes, in fact contained an invitation
to Wisdom. A beginning is not an end; and the search that
began with Cicero could end only with the God of Abraham,
and Isaac, and Jacob, and the God made man, Jesus Christ.
All this Aelred saw in the *Confessions*, so that when he came
to write of friendship, he began with Christ that he might
understand Cicero.

Jean de Meun knew the *De spiritali amicitia* intimately, as
perhaps only a skilled translator can, and although we have
no external evidence that demonstrates the chronological re-
lationship between the *Roman* and the *Espirituelle amistié*, Jean's
very sophisticated use of Aelred's text in his poem strongly
argues the priority of the latter. We may even wish to think
that with Aelred, as with Boethius, we see the evidence of
Jean's interest in two different kinds of *translatio*. Jean's reliance
on Aelred can only in part be explained by his eclectic search
for learned and authoritative "matter," for he found in Aelred

[37] Ibid., 46-47.

not merely elegant wisdom on a given topic but a shared vision of the literary enterprise. Jean wished to write about friendship, and the *De spiritali amicitia* indeed offered wonderful teaching about it; but for Jean de Meun the artist, it taught a far greater lesson as well, for it provided a model, one might say *the* model, of what a work of "Christian humanism" might be. In its pages the ancient wisdom of the pagan Cicero lives on intact in all its clarity and power, yet wonderfully increased, the teaching graced by that revelation denied to the teacher. This does not mean, of course, that the difference between the *De amicitia* and the *De spiritali amicitia* is trivial. Christian friendship is to Ciceronian friendship as Christ is to Cicero. If this comparison seems too bizarre we may wish to think of one that, while actually stranger, we have learned to accept— that of Beatrice and Vergil. The Christian concept of friendship does not destroy Cicero's concept; it fulfills, perfects it. Aelred began the *De spiritali amicitia* with the following sentence: "Here we are, you and I, and I hope a third, Christ, is in our midst." The presence of Christ transforms friendship, just as his presence has transformed history.

Aelred formulates this idea with striking originality, but the idea itself is far from new. It finds its classical Latin expression in Augustine and, in particular, in Augustine's famous account of his relationship with an unnamed boyhood friend in Thagaste.[38] That friendship, one of the most moving and affective of Augustine's life, ended for him in inconsolable desolation at his friend's untimely death. Reliving the experience a quarter of a century later, Augustine would speak of the sweet (*dulcis*) bond between them, born of a Ciceronian *consensio* of shared interest, yet deny that it was "true friendship": "Sed nondum erat sic amicus, quamquam ne tunc quidem sic, uti est vera amicitia, quia non est vera, nisi cum eam tu agglutinas inter haerentes sibi caritate diffusa in *cordibus nostris per spiritum sanctum, qui datus est nobis.*"[39]

[38] *Confessions* 4.4ff.; ed. Skutella, 58ff.

[39] *Confessions* 4.4ff.; ed. Skutella, 58. I have italicized the citation of Romans 5:5.

We can now return to Jean's poor Lover, for we are in a
position to assess his despair at ever finding friendship. Amant
himself has misled us to Cicero, but though editors and critics
dally there, Jean has set our path straight again and taken us
to Aelred. Aelred, for his part, takes us back to Augustine.
This is a complicated route, perhaps even a tortuous one; but
the *Roman de la Rose* is a complex and difficult poem.

> Ci ne finastes hui de dire   5345
> que je doi mon seignor despire
> por ne soi quele amor sauvage.
> Qui cercheroit jusqu'an Quartage   5348
>   . . .
> n'avroit il pas aconseü.   5356

The task is an impossible one. *Amitiez*, this "ne soi quele amor
sauvage," could not be found even in Carthage. Now if the
Lover were a rational man and not a fool, and if he were
conscious of those arts of poetic indirection that he explicitly
contemns, he too might have followed *amicitia*'s traces back
to the *Confessions* of St. Augustine. There, at the beginning of
the third book, he would have found a youth very much like
himself, in love with love, in the throes of a search of an object
of his love, a confused lover who mistook a hollow courtliness
for virtue, and lubricity for friendship. The scene of that des-
perate search? Carthage, of course. "To Carthage I came, where
there sang all around me in my ears a cauldron of unholy
loves."[40]

Augustine identifies the fundamental carnality of his search
for love in Carthage with a bold play on words, a rhyme in
fact, though one shallowly concealed by the oblique case of
one of its members: "Veni *Carthaginem*, et circumstrepebat me
undique *sartago* flagitiosorum amorum." I admire Pusey's old
rendition of this last phrase, "a cauldron of unholy loves"; but
the more accurate rendition of *sartago* is "frying-pan." *Cartago/*

---

[40] *Confessions* 3.1; ed. Skutella, 36.

sartago: Carthage, a frying pan of lusts: *Carthage/sauvage*. Carthage was to be the setting of Augustine's desperate infatuation with love itself, his confused immersion in the flesh; so of course Carthage is the city in which Jean de Meun's willful and confused Lover says he would never find the love that Reason calls good. Jean demands that we read his poem very carefully. Here, in a single topographic noun, is the only "textual" evidence of his supertext.

My concern in this chapter is not the art of Augustine but the nature of intertextuality in a passage in the *Roman de la Rose* of Jean de Meun. I think, however, that we shall not see the wittiness of the latter if we do not first appreciate something of the profundity of the former. The phrase "veni Carthaginem," which opens the third book of the *Confessions* and thus the episode of Augustine's search for love in Carthage, recurs at the end of 4.7, the terminal punctuation of his account of his wild grief for his dead friend. The grief itself he calls a kind of madness (*dementia*), and its extravagant symptoms, the inability to find refreshment for his spirit, are the familiar topics of many a description of unlucky medieval lovers: "Not in the delightful groves, not where mirth and music was, nor in the odoriferous gardens, nor in curious banquetings, nor in the pleasures of the bed and chambering; nor, finally, in reading over either verse or prose, took I any contentment."[41] So Augustine leaves Thagaste, knowing even as he does so that he cannot flee from his own heart by fleeing from his home town: "atque a Thagastensi oppido veni Carthaginem."

The Carthage of the *Confessions* provides Jean de Meun with an elegant ornament of geographical iconography; but the deeper Augustinianism of Reason's *amistié* is most clearly exposed in the *Soliloquia* themselves. There (in 1.7) Augustine discovers that reason alone makes human beings the possible objects of friendship and (in 1.20 and 22) that the actual end

---

[41] *Confessions* 4.7; ed. Skutella, 62.

of friendship is *sapientia*.[42] Lady Reason is entirely justified in telling Amant that God has given her leave to be his *amie*.

Augustine gave to Carthaginian love a definitive literary expression and a definitive moral meaning, but that love itself he did not invent. Jean de Meun, whom we must surely by now credit with a deeply sensitive appreciation of poetic contexts, has of course seen that what spiritual friendship does to the greatest writer of pagan prose, Carthaginian love does to the greatest writer of pagan poetry. Several scholars, but in particular John O'Meara, have sought to identify definite patterns of artistic self-consciousness in the construction of the *Confessions*.[43] O'Meara has shown that Augustine is engaged in a clandestine literary competition with no less a rival than the great Vergil himself, and he has sketched the careful, sustained, indeed the almost schematic parallels by which Augustine has collated the experience of his own epic journey from darkness to grace with the epic journey of the *Aeneid*. These two journeys met most happily in the Latin word *errores*, the wanderings of the young Aeneas and the delusions of the young Augustine, the word that the author of the *Confessions* would use to denote both.

But the wanderers themselves also met in a particular geographical location, the city of Carthage. There Aeneas had dallied in Dido's arms while destiny languished. Augustine, who as a lad had lived beneath the shadow of those ramparts from which the distracted Dido searched the empty harbor for her lover, was in his own time to have his own amatory experiences there. We know from several passages in the *Confessions*, among them some of the most moving in the book, the powerful impact that Vergil's Carthaginian episodes had upon

[42] See the very full analysis of these passages in Agostino de Ippona, *L'Amicizia cristiana*, ed. L. F. Pizzolato (Turin, 1973), 5, 8-12.

[43] Two essays by O'Meara are particularly important: "Augustine the Artist and the *Aeneid*," *Mélanges offerts à Mademoiselle Christine Mohrmann* (Utrecht/Antwerp, 1963), 252-61; and "Virgil and Augustine: The Roman Background to Christian Sexuality," *Augustinus* 13 (1968): 307-326.

the young Augustine, and how, when he came to write of his own triumph over the slavery of sexual passion, he alluded naturally, almost inevitably, to Aeneas's flight from Carthage.

"Carthage" is, then, a witty stroke, but perhaps not so witty as the word *sauvage*, which stands to the French *Cartage* as *sartago* stood to *Cartago*. *Sauvage*, which defies translation, is the French reflex of the Latin *salvaticus*, and it can mean, in recorded medieval French examples, wild, rustic, bestial, and primitive. All of these meanings inform Jean's use of the word. Dahlberg, in his excellent English version, chooses "bestial love," and that is of course correct. The French translator, André Lanly, glosses the word as "un amour des premiers ages du monde"; that is also correct.[44]

The Lover no doubt intends the pejorative force of Dahlberg's "bestial." The *amor sauvage* recommended by Reason, like her frank French terms for the sexual organs, is just too *outré* and uncouth for words in its inconvenience for the Lover's program of seduction. But any reader of Aelred (or Aelred's teacher Augustine) *will agree with Lanly's gloss as well*; *amor sauvage* belongs to the province of social archaeology. *Amor sauvage* is Christian friendship, and Aelred's clear teaching (1.51ff.) is that honest friendship is the faint vestige in the postlapsarian world of that natural charity which characterized human nature in "the first ages of the world" before the Fall.[45]

In saying that he knows nothing of *amor sauvage*, the Lover is saying no more and no less than that he knows nothing of *caritas*. We insult Jean and his poem if we maintain that he seriously commends to us as a model of "belief to be transferred into action" this Lover who knows nothing of charity and willfully rejects the promptings of Reason, which would teach him its rudiments. There is a fine irony in the fact that what the Lover calls bestial love is what Aelred calls friendship, and that what the god of Love teaches the Lover is what Aelred

---

[44] *Le Roman de la Rose*, trans. A. Lanly (Paris, 1973), 2:174.

[45] Friedman, "Jean de Meun and Ethelred of Rievaulx," 141.

calls a "bestial impulse": "Longing undirected by reason is a bestial impulse, inclined to all illicit things, indeed unable to distinguish between licit and illicit."[46]

The great men of the Christian Middle Ages, the governors, churchmen, lawyers, and poets who made the most admirable contributions of medieval cultural and intellectual life, knew that they had much to learn from the great writers of pagan antiquity, and for the most part they turned to their ancient masters with a respectful eagerness. First of all, they sought tutelage in the skills of literacy—in the Latin language and in the modes of writing well and speaking well in it—but they also gladly sat at the feet of ancient authorities on law, warfare, medicine, history, agriculture, architecture, and a hundred arts and sciences useful to the nourishment of their spiritual and material lives.

On one subject, however, they would have thought it madness to seek authoritative instruction from pagans, and that was on the subject at the very heart of their stated social aspirations, the subject of Christian love. The pagans had nothing to teach about it, for they knew not what it was. As Ivo says to Aelred in the *De spiritali amicitia*, quite without disingenuousness, "I do not see what the pagan [Cicero] meant by the words 'charity' and 'benevolence.' "[47] Christians, of

[46] *De spiritali amicitia* 2:57; ed. Hoste, 313; *Spiritual Friendship*, 83.

[47] *De spiritali amicitia* 1:14; ed. Hoste, 291; *Spiritual Friendship*, 54. Reason's classification of friendship as a category of charity is an Augustinian gesture (see Marie Aquinas McNamara, *Friendship in Saint Augustine* [Fribourg, 1958], 191). As such, Christian friendship has no real counterpart in ancient wisdom. Far from being an aspect of the "rational wisdom available to the great pagan writers who lacked Christian revelation," brotherly love was the absolutely unique feature of Christianity, and it transformed a world that Socrates and Cicero had scarcely touched. A. J. Festugière ("Aspects de la religion populaire grecque," *RThPh*, ser. 3, vol. 11 [1961], pp. 30-31) has put it thus: "Cette charité fraternelle . . . c'est cela le fait nouveau, la nouveauté totale du christianisme. . . . S'il n'y avait eu cela, le monde serait encore païen. Et le jour où il n'y aura plus cela, le monde redeviendra païen."

course, did know what pagan love was, both from old books
and from their own lives. The sexual norms and conventions
appropriate for pagans, as readers found them in the pages of
Vergil and Ovid, clearly spoke to the felt experience of me-
dieval people, but the voice was that of moral admonition,
not of historical envy: "Lo here, of payens corsed olde rites."

One final point about *amor sauvage* can bring us back to the
supertext responsible at once for the complexity of these lines
from the *Roman de la Rose* and for their satisfactory explication.
Amor sauvage would mean "bestial love" to the Lover, and to
Augustine "primitive love," "a love from the first ages of the
world." Surely they would find common ground in yet another
implication of the term—rustic, simple, uncourtly love. That
the Lover considers it dreadfully unsophisticated, coming fresh
as he does from the fancy finishing school of his master Cupid,
is clear both from the consistent tone of the context of our
lines and from the marvelously apt term, *fines amours*, he uses
for the legendary friendships of the ancients. There is good
reason to think that neither Augustine nor Aelred would cavil
at this imputation of rusticity.

The kind of elegance and urbanity that characterize the
operation of the god Amours, the Lover's liege lord in the
Roman de la Rose, is flatly inconsistent with moral virtue.
Augustine makes this point in the same passage at the begin-
ning of the third book of *Confessions*: "To love then, and to be
beloved, was sweet to me; but much more, when I obtained
to enjoy the person whom I loved. I defiled, therefore, the
spring of friendship with the filth of concupiscence, and I
beclouded its brightness with the hell of lustfulness; and thus,
foul and unseemly, I would fain, through exceeding vanity,
be fine and courtly."[48] The phrase here rendered "fine and
courtly" is "elegans et urbanus," and it provides, perhaps, a
classical source for our Procrustean concept of "courtly love"
frequently invoked to explain the amatory mysteries of me-

---

[48] *Confessions* 3.1; ed. Skutella, 37.

dieval poems, the *Roman de la Rose* conspicuous among them. I suggest that another concept might be more useful still: Carthaginian love. I prefer it for what I regard as its augmented specificity, its closer kinship of word and thing. Yet, as we must now go on to explore, there is no agreement between Reason and the Lover on the question of words or things either.

3.
WORDS AND THINGS

Most readers who have looked closely at the dialogue between Reason and the Lover have pointed to the special significance of their intermittent exchange about the nature of language. The episode has a somewhat elliptical structure, and its implications reach deep into the poem, far beyond the delimited subject of my present study, but it might be briefly sketched as follows.

In the course of proving to the Lover the superiority of Love to Justice, Reason alludes to the myth of the castration of Saturn, the violent and aberrant act that brought to an end the Age of Gold; and in her reference to the myth she uses the word *coilles* (5507) to denote Saturn's testicles. About a hundred and fifty lines later (5680 f.) the Lover indicates that he has been shocked by some of her language. Reason intuits the specific lexical cause of his distress, promising to explain to him why she has spoken in such a manner whenever he may request her to do so; and he tells her that he certainly will call for such an explanation, since smutty talk has been forbidden him by the god of Love. More than a thousand lines, most of them given over to a discussion of Fortune, elapse before the Lover brings up the accusation again (6898f.). Reason defends her use of the word *coilles* and adds another "dirty" one to shock the Lover—viz., *viz* (penis) (6936). There follows a discussion of the relationship between words and things. Reason claims that the words had an allegorical sense in the context of the fable of the end of the Golden Age but that when she talked about them a second time, she used the words in their literal sense. Amant claims to understand their literal meaning but denies any knowledge of the "metaphors of poets." He holds her use of the words entirely vindicated, but nonetheless dismisses her—this time permanently—from the poem.

Most critical discussion of the passage has concentrated on the subject of the myth of the Golden Age itself, a topic of crucial importance to the understanding of the poem, and one that is taken up, explicitly or implicitly, by Amis, La Vieille, and Genius in passages of cardinal importance. I should suggest, however, that such discussion is somewhat premature pending our fuller appreciation of the linguistic context in which the subject is first raised, a context that, I should argue, in some ways controls the meaning of the myth of the Golden Age for the poem as a whole. Given the somewhat curious way in which the argument progresses, it is perhaps more helpful to approach its discussion of language in topical as opposed to sequential fashion, making our beginning somewhere near Jean de Meun's end, in a passage that addresses the general utility of language (7056ff.).

In a brief glance at this passage in my first chapter I pointed out that Reason's claim to be the inventress of human language as we now know it is unmistakably Augustinian. This perception should alert us to the possibility of a coherent and unified theory of language operating within the passage as a whole. The only authority cited on the surface, to be sure, is Plato; but by now we must be alert for Reason's curious habit of citing the "philosophers" in their Christian redactions. What of Reason on language?

> Et ce que ci t'ai recité   7067
> peuz trover en auctorité,
> car Platon lisoit en s'escole
> que donee nous fu parole   7070
> por fere noz volairs entendre,
> por enseignier et por aprendre.
> Ceste sentence ci rimee
> troveras escrite en *Thimee*
> de Platon, qui ne fu pas nices.   7075

The allegedly Platonic theory of the origins of language in
lines 7070-72 is thus translated by Dahlberg: "speech was
given us to make us want to understand, for teaching and for
learning." I think, however, that it rather means "speech was
given us in order to make our desires known, in order to teach,
and in order to learn." The word *sentence* (7073) is ambiguous,
since it can denote either a specific apothegm or simply the
general "sense" of what has been said. Langlois found a passage
in Chalcidius that he took to be the specific source of the
passage, and this has been reproduced by Lecoy's notes: "Eadem
vocis quoque et auditus ratio est, ad eosdem usus atque ad
plenam vitae hominum instructionem datorum, siquidem
propterea sermonis est ordinata communicatio ut praesto forent
mutuae voluntatis indicia."[1] There are two points of rather
general correspondence between the idea expressed in the *Ti-
maeus* and that expressed by Reason. The latter says that lan-
guage was invented "in order to teach and in order to learn,"
and Plato likewise speaks of "instruction." Secondly, there is
a general correspondence between the French "fere noz volairs
entendre" and the Latin "forent mutuae voluntatis indicia."

These are merely general echoes, however, and they have
already been mediated by Augustine, the genius who has left
us the most important essays in linguistic theory to survive
from the antique world. In a famous passage in the first book
of his *Confessions*, Augustine traces the development of infantile
speech as he can recall it from his own earliest memories and
as he observes it in babies around him. The most elementary
way in which he could express himself was by enjoying his
milk or by weeping; next came the power to smile and laugh.
Next, he became somewhat aware of his immediate location,
and it was at this point that he began to try to make his desires
known to others—but in vain, since as yet he had no words.
What he says specifically is this: "Et ecce paulatim sentiebam,

[1] *Timaeus a Calcidio translatus comentarioque instructus*, ed. J. H. Waszink
(London, 1962), 44.

ubi essem, et voluntates meas volebam ostendere eis, per quos implerentur, et non poteram, quia illae intus erant, foris autem illi nec ullo suo sensu valebant introire in animan meam."[2] Here Lady Reason's phrase "por fere noz volairs entendre" finds a closer parallel than in Chalcidius: "et *voluntates meas* volebam *ostendere* eis." We here have a clear hint of the Augustinian "control" of Lady Reason's linguistic theories, but it is only that. The phrase "por enseignier et por aprendre"—the purpose of speech is to teach and to learn—puts matters quite beyond question.

Augustine's most systematic treatise on linguistic theory is the *De magistro*, a dialogue between Augustinus and Adeodatus, written in 389, shortly after his baptism. In it Augustine advances his theory of linguistic "signs," which is such an important element of his mature thought, and which is the foundation of his classic hermeneutic in the *De doctrina christiana*. The *De magistro* can, without reservation, be described as the last word on language in the circles in which Lady Reason grew up; and the first word of the *De magistro* is this:

AUGUSTINUS. Quid tibi videmur efficere velle cum
   loquimur?
ADEODATUS. Quantum quidem mihi nunc occurrit, aut
   docere, aut discere.[3]

For Reason the purpose of language is roughly that adduced by Plato, but it is exactly that adduced by Adeodatus on the first page of the first chapter of the most authoritative essay on the nature of language known to the Middle Ages: "por enseignier et por aprendre." Such a discovery is hardly astounding, but it is very useful, for a reading of this part of Jean's poem from the perspective of the *De magistro* offers considerable poetic illumination. That is to say, every linguistic idea raised in this discussion is posited in explicitly

---

[2] *Confessions* 1.6.8.
[3] *De magistro* 1.1; ed. F. J. Thonnard (Paris, 1941), p. 14.

Augustinian terms, and almost everything that the Lover has
to say about the subject is in Augustinian terms highly risible.

To justify at least the latter part of that claim, I should
adduce Amant's own recollection of the "clean speech com-
mandment" given him by Amors:

> Donc le ramentevré je voir,   5680
> dis je con remanbranz et vistes,
> par tel mot con vos le deistes.
> Si m'a mes mestres deffendu,
> car je l'ai mout bien entendu,
> que ja mot n'isse de ma boiche   5685
> qui de ribaudie s'aproiche.
> Mes des que je n'en sui fesierres,
> j'en puis bien estre recitierres;
> si nomeré le mot tout outre.   5689

According to one of the Ithacans, the discussion of language
between Reason and the Lover reveals the former's inability to
understand sexuality in the postlapsarian world; but if we
assume that Jean de Meun is actually responsible for his text,
it is surely the Lover, not Reason, whose limitations are here
exposed. Amant babbles a good deal of foolishness during the
course of this long poem, but there can be few of his opinions
more fatuous than this one. The god of Love has instructed
him in language, and I think it is an intentional nod to the
De magistro that Amant—who has previously called him *sei-
gneur*—now calls him *mestres* (L. *magister*). In any event, the
specific magisterial pronouncement concerning words and things
was uttered by Amors in Guillaume's poem, and it is this:

> Aprés gardes que tu ne dies
> ces orz moz ne ces ribaudies:
> ja por nomer vilainne chose
> ne doit ta bouche estre desclouse.   2100
> Je ne tien pas a cortois home
> qui orde chose et laide nome.

Now this is a quite remarkable statement in its own right, for there is a clear confusion in it, in Augustinian terms, between words and things. Amors seems to be condemning the use of coarse *words* (*orz moz, ribaudies*), but he is actually proscribing the nomination of coarse *things*. It is forbidden to name a low thing "(por nomer vilainne chose")" or a low and ugly thing ("orde chose et laide"). This seems to be a clear linguistic doctrine. The impropriety of dirty *words* stems from the dirty *things* they signify. The word is the captive of the thing. This is a good principle to remember.

What does Amant make of this commandment? His immediate response to the word *coilles* is that it is *ribaudie*. If that is true, it can only mean that a man's balls are low, base, or ugly things and that, as *things*, they are unmentionable; but that the Lover does not in fact think they are unworthy things is strongly suggested by the high evaluation he puts on his own penis in line 21,362—a figure in excess of 50,000,000 pounds, a considerable sum even in an inflationary economy. The implication is that the villainy of dirty talk resides in dirty *words*, and that as long as he avoids uttering dirty *words*, he has obeyed the clean speech commandment.

This is only the beginning of the absurdity, however. Amant next offers his ingenious gloss on Cupid's linguistic decretal. The prohibition against uttering dirty words applies only to new words—that is, I presume, to words that one makes up oneself. As long as you are not the maker (*fesierres*) of a dirty word, but only its reporter, you have committed no sin against Cupid. There seem to me to be certain intellectual insufficiencies in this theory that have so far escaped the literary critics. It implies, in the first place, an absolute moral or aesthetic status to words, quite independent of the things they signify or of any other context of social convention. Since Reason has called these things *coilles*, the Lover can call them *coilles* too, without villainy. Whether he could also call them "nuggs" or "zyglots" is less certain. That would depend upon whether his invented words are dirty words, and his linguistic theory gives us no means of adjudicating that question. There is an even greater inconvenience in Amant's theory, for it seems to make the whole category of *ribaudie* a logical impossibility. We have already seen that the one who gives names to things is Reason. She is the inventress of language, not the Lover. If the Lover cannot invent the names for things, he can use only names that have been invented by others. But there is no *ribaudie* in using words invented by others. Hence it is impossible to utter *ribaudie*—hardly *quod erat demonstrandum*.

The tongue of the wise adorneth knowledge; but the mouth of fools bubbleth out folly. The Lover's remarks about language in the passage cited are, in a word, foolishness, but they serve a more brilliant poetic purpose than the demonstration of a fact long since made obvious by the poem. They offer a fine example, in the first place, of the careful way Jean de Meun has worked with the materials inherited from Guillaume de Lorris. He uses Guillaume's poem as grafting staddle, not as a display column, and he draws the essential linguistic problem of words and things out of Guillaume's clean speech commandment. In the second place, he carefully orchestrates the speech around central themes in his silent supertext, the *De magistro* of St. Augustine.

The degree to which this is true becomes apparent only when Amant returns to the subject of language as he promised to do, more than a thousand lines later. A portion of the ensuing discussion I have already cited. It is one of the most sophisticated parts of Jean's dialogue and, as it were, Reason's last stand in the poem. She makes one final plea to the Lover that he abandon Amors. Amant replies that he cannot, that he must follow his teacher (*mestre* again, 6872), that he is tired of hearing about Socrates, that he must stay with his teacher even if it lands him in hell, and that Reason talks dirty.

An interesting analysis of this passage by Daniel Poirion finds, among other things, that the confusion between word and thing, *vox* and *res*, reveals "the vestiges of a magical *men-*

talité."[4] The larger linguistic conflict of the poem reflects a radical assault by Jean de Meun on the "social realities" of Guillaume's world of "courtly love." Even if one could allow the facile social history of "courtliness" as applied to Poirion's argument, however, it would remain unconvincing in my view because it fails to recognize the intellectual tradition of the discussion of words and things in Jean's poem. The *Roman de la Rose* owes nothing to Michel Foucault and much to Augustine, who authoritatively established for the Middle Ages the formulation that *all* teaching has as its subject either signs or things, and who also drew the distinction, among the former, between natural signs and conventional signs—the distinction that defines systems of human language.[5]

Natural signs, for example smoke, are *things* that have a necessary, organic, and inevitable relationship to other things they signify—in the case of smoke, fire. The words of ordinary human speech on the other hand are conventional signs, and they signify their things within a context of social custom and general usage that is neither inevitable or unalterable. Fire is always signified by the natural sign *smoke*, but it can be signified by many conventional signs—*fire, Feuer, feu, fuego,* or *phub* for that matter—as long as the sign commands conventional agreement.

There are numerous clear allusions to these ideas in Jean's poem. In the first place, the Lover carries into his discussion

[4] D. Poirion, "Les Mots et les choses selon Jean de Meun," *L'Information littéraire* 26 (1974): 8. The most illuminating treatment of Jean's "linguistics" is G. Ineichen, "Le Discours linguistique de Jean de Meun," *Romanistiche Zeitschrift für Literaturgeschichte* 2 (1978): 245-53. Some further discussion will be found in Maureen Quilligan, *The Language of Allegory: Defining the Genre* (Ithaca, 1979) and the same author's "Allegory, Allegoresis, and the Deallegorization of Language: The *Roman de la rose,* the *De planctu naturae,* and the *Parlement of Foules,*" in *Allegory, Myth, and Symbol,* ed. Morton W. Bloomfield (Cambridge, MA., 1981), 163-186.

[5] Augustine's classic delineation of his theory is in the *De doctrina christiana,* but he treats the subject repeatedly. See the full bibliography in L. Alici, *Il Linguaggio come segno e come testimonianza: Una Reliettura di Agostino* (Rome, 1976).

the essential confusion of words (signs) and things that characterized the clean speech commandment as it came from the lips of Amours. He first suggests that it is the *coilles* themselves that are unworthy ("qui ne sunt pas bien renomees" [6900]), but then fudges the matter with qualification. *Coilles*, he says, "ne sunt pas bien renomees / en bouche a cortaise pucele"— which seems to suggest that as a word *coilles* is an inappropriate conventional sign for a woman of Reason's social station. The emphasis is certainly on the word rather than the thing in what follows:

> Vos, qui tant estes sage et bele,   6902
> ne sai con nomer les osastes,
> au mains quant le mot ne glosastes
> par quelque cortaises parole,
> si con preude fame en parole.   6906

The Lover suggests specifically that Reason "gloss" the word *coilles* the way nurses do when bathing babies. Indeed, one controlling idea of the passage as a whole is that of glossing. At first (6902ff.) Amant wants to gloss and Reason refuses. Then (7128ff.) Reason wants to gloss and Amant refuses. Perhaps "glosyng is a glorious thing, certayn," as Chaucer's friar puts it, precisely because we shall not find an apter example than the verb *gloser* to illustrate the ambiguous possibilities of verbal signs. It is a word with no single trunk of meaning, branching from its very root into a fork of precise contradiction. To gloss is to *conceal* the meaning of words. To gloss is to *reveal* the meaning of words. In general, we may say that Amant, one of whose allies is after all named Bien-Celer, is interested in disguising truth, and that Reason is interested in exposing truth.

For the moment, it is the Lover who commands our attention. As Poirion and Hill have well understood, what the Lover means by "gloss" is "to disguise with a euphemism."[6] Sexual

---

[6] On the other hand, the Lover's meaning of *gloser* does not seem to be recognized by Winthrop Wetherbee in his article, "The Literal and the Allegorical."

organs can be mentioned, as long as they are mentioned by
some other name than their own. The Lover predicts that he
will, before the poem is over, gloss his own shameful members,
and he fulfills his word with elaborate euphemisms of pilgrim's
gear: his scrotum becomes a scrip, his penis a staff, and so
forth. His theory here implies, as it does elsewhere as well,
that evil resides not in things but in words; yet Reason defends
both thing and word—the thing because it was made by God
in paradise, the word because it is the "proper name" of a
thing. In the case of *coilles*, incidentally, this latter claim would
seem to be fully justified in the light of the etymological history
of Latin *culleus* in the Romance languages.[7]

Poirion maintains that euphemism is a part of the social
reality of the courtly world and that Reason's linguistic crudity
or at least pragmatism is an attack on the values of that world.[8]
This is convincing only if the "courtly world" is the abstract
kingdom of Chartrian theology, for the literary object of Rea-
son's implied reprimand here is not Guillaume de Lorris but
Alain de Lille.[9] Reason's rejection of euphemism is indeed one
of the clearer examples of the way in which Jean's Reason does

[7] Ironically, the Lover's "gloss" would make *culleus* literal once again. For
a usage of the word that so shocks Amant in a work of fourteenth-century
religious didacticism, see J. Le Fèvre, *Le Respit de la Mort*, ed. G. Hasenhohr-
Esons (Paris, 1969), 35.

[8] Poirion, "Les Mots et les choses selon Jean de Meun," 9ff.

[9] The Lover's reproach to Reason (6898ff.) that the word *coilles* is improper
"en bouche a cortaise pucele" is a clear reflection of Natura's refusal to name
the sexual organs as being improper "in ore virginali" (*De planctu Naturae*,
ed. Häring, 839, lines 193-94). We note also that the image of the penis
as a writing instrument, which several critics have regarded as deeply sig-
nificant and highly original, likewise comes from Natura (Häring, 845-46),
as do many, though not all, of the genital euphemisms used by various
characters in the *Roman*. In general, it seems likely that Jean's linking of
irrational sexuality with linguistic imprecision echoes Alain's equation of
sexual perversion with grammatical blunder. Jean has certainly chosen a
higher poetical path, for in the *Roman*, as Wetherbee has nicely illustrated,
the remote and labored figures of Alainian allegory take on a convincing
literal substance.

not share the limitations of Alain's Natura. Hill's analysis is at once more convincingly grounded in the text of the poem and more perverse in its Ithacan conclusion, which is, curiously, that the linguistic debate between Reason and the Lover brings out *Reason*'s putative "limitations." Hill writes thus: "Raison by herself cannot resolve the dilemma which the lover faces, any more than she can understand why men should use euphemisms to describe their sexual organs. Rationally, of course, there is no reason why men should not refer to *coilles* directly; but as Augustine points out, the shame which men feel about sexuality—even a man enjoying natural and honorable sexual relations with his wife seeks privacy—is a sign of the disordered irrational aspect of post-lapsarian sexuality."[10] Hill cites *De civitate Dei* 14.18 and adds in a note, "In connection with Raison's use of the term 'coilles,' note Augustine's comments on how the very concept of obscenity derives from the fall (*De civitate Dei*, xiv, 23)."

Though I am not finally sure of the terms of Hill's argument here, I believe that I am in substantial disagreement with it. In *De civitate Dei* 14.18, Augustine quite explicity ascribes the natural and universal shame attendant upon sexual relations to *sin*—the shameful feeling grows *ex poena*. In Augustine's moral vocabulary this *poena* is always the guilty pleasure of concupiscence (*voluptas, libido*). Augustine is very careful in his use of the word "sign," and if we are to speak of shame as a sign, it is more precise to say that it is a sign of sin than of "the disordered irrational aspect of post-lapsarian sexuality"; but this may be regarded as mere verbal quibble. A more serious difficulty arises from Hill's apparent assumption that this shame is itself irrational, an assumption I find in his statement that Reason "cannot understand why men would use euphemisms to speak of their sexual organs." The shame of irrationality is one thing, the irrationality of shame quite another. The shame men feel with regard to *libido* is entirely

[10] Hill, "Two Mythographical Themes," 421-22.

understandable and rational, and in the *Roman de la Rose* Honte
is appropriately allied with Reason. In fact, Hill's argument
runs just backwards. The effect of the discussion about lan-
guage is to demonstrate that Reason does understand, and that
the Lover does *not* understand, the relationship between words
and things, between obscenity and sin.

Hill cites *De civitate Dei* 14.23 to demonstate that "the very
concept of obscenity derives from the fall"—without men-
tioning, however, that I myself had already adduced this same
passage as the "almost certain" specific source of Jean's inspi-
ration.[11] The passage does not advance Hill's argument, but
it does advance Reason's. Reason nowhere directly addresses
the question of why the Lover does or does not, should or
should not, feel shame with regard to his shameful members
and their nomination. She does not need to, since the "inter-
textual" authority of Augustine's argument does it for her.
The rhetorical assumption of *De civitate Dei* 14.23 is that
Augustine must defend himself before a reader offended by his
discussion of sexual organs. Let that reader feel shame, writes
Augustine, because of his own sin, *not because of nature*. Let
him condemn his own works of filthiness, not the words that
must perforce be used to discuss them: "Quisquis ergo ad has
litteras inpudicus accedit, culpam refugiat, non naturam; facta
denotet suae turpitudinis, non verba nostrae necessitatis."[12] In
the *Roman de la Rose* a guilty auditor thinks that shame resides
in the words used by an innocent teacher. We must remember
that Reason has described *libido* (carnal delight) as the Lover's
sole motivation. Of course he will find shame in the operation
of his shameful members, because that shame reflects the *poena*
of the *libido*. To say that "Reason cannot understand why men
would use euphemisms to speak of their sexual organs," how-
ever, is to read the poem upside down. Only Reason *can*
understand that. The Lover wants to place the shame of his

<hr>

[11] Ibid., 422; cf. Fleming, *The Roman de la Rose*, 134.
[12] *De civitate Dei* 14.23; ed. cit., 3.444-46.

sexual quest in *words*. Reason knows that words are conventional signs—and that as far as sexual organs are concerned, shame lies neither in the things themselves (which are honorable and serviceable) nor in the words that denote them (which are apt and useful) but in the *libido* that rules them (which is disordered and sinful).

One general strategy of the satirist is to flatter the reader at the expense of the satiric butt, and this is an evident technique of the "dialectical" dialogues of the Ciceronian mode. We laugh at the torpid Evodius, or Augustinus, or Boethius, or Amant precisely at those moments when we see that they are being rather stupid; for the laughter that discovers their stupidity may at the same time celebrate our own cleverness as readers. We see the truth that evades the lethargic interlocutor. While Adeodatus of the *De magistro* is more than a mere straight-man of dialectical dialogue, he is nonetheless the occasional voice of opacity within the work. It is he who must be taught the proper relationship between words and things. That Jean de Meun is schematically playing off the Lover against Augustine's Adeodatus is the suggestion that arises from a comparison of the two texts.

Augustine gives two specific examples of words that, according to his theories, demonstrate some of the possible relationships between words and things.[13] The first is *caenum* (filth, offal, mud). The thing *caenum* is loathly and disgusting; but the word *caenum* is a fine word, as can be evidenced in the fact that by simply changing a single letter it can become *caelum* (heaven).[14] The point here demonstrated is that in this instance, and in contradiction of Amant, it is the thing, not the word, that is filthy. Augustine's second example is the word *vitium* (vice). To know the word *vitium* is better than to

[13] *De magistro* 9.25, 28.

[14] On the classical background of this word-play, see the edition and Dutch translation of the *De magistro* by G.E.A.M. Wijdeveld (Amsterdam, 1938), 163; and the German translation and commentary by Erwin Schadel (Bamberg, 1975), 168.

know the thing *vitium*, but neither word nor thing is to be preferred to the *doctrina* relating to *vitium*. Now let us compare the two specific examples of filthy words adduced by Amant. They are the words for the male organs, *coilles/coillon* (testicles) and *viz* (penis). In an earlier exchange Amant suggested his incomprehension of Reason by telling her to speak to him "not in Latin, but in French" (5810), and this may suggest the utility of some comparative Romance philology.

AUGUSTINE		JEAN DE MEUN	
caenum/		*coilles/*	< L. *colleus/*
caelum	> Fr. *ciel*	*coillon*	*culleus*
vitium	> Fr. *vice*	*viz*	< L. *vis*

There could hardly be a more clever vindication of the Augustinian theory of the pure conventionality of language than in the gratuitous, purely superficial, accidental—but nonetheless consciously exploitable—similarity between the sounds of the Latin and the French pairings. The word *caenum* has no direct reflex in Old French, but it is, happily, the very root of Latin obscenity, and thus resonates to the Lover's theme of dirty talk. There may be the further connection in Jean's mind that in Augustine's vocabulary *caenum* often has the special meaning of "the filth of lust," since the Lover, who has accused Reason of obscenity, is of course motivated exclusively by lust.[15]

There is another layer of wit in Jean's genital linguistics. The Augustinian theory of the conventionality of linguistic *signs does not deny that certain sounds have a naturally af*fective dimension: merely to hear them is to know whether they be nasty or nice. For example, the very name "Artaxerxes" conveys harshness and cruelty, while the name "Euralys" arouses expectations of civility and generosity. These examples, along with others, come from the chapter of the *De dialectica* on "the

[15] This interpretation is also common in the exegesis of one of the few passages in the Bible (Jer. 38:22) where the word appears—in the form of *coenum*.

force of words."[16] Augustine's word for "force" is the Latin *vis*, the same word that denotes the male organ, Jean de Meun's *viz*. In discussing the *vis verbi* Augustine adduces a passage from Sallust that is strikingly relevant to this playful moment in the *Roman de la Rose*: "When, however, a word moves a hearer both on its own account and on account of what it signifies, then both the statement itself and that which is stated by means of it are attended together. Why is the chastity of the ears not offended when one hears 'He had squandered his patrimony by hand, by belly, and by penis (*pene*)?' It would be offended if the private part of the body were called by a low or vulgar name, though the thing with a different name is the same. If the shamefulness of the thing signified were not covered over by the propriety of the signifying word, then the base character of both would affect both sense and mind. Similarly, although a harlot *is* no different, she nevertheless looks different because of the clothes she wears when she stands before a judge than she looks when she lies in her dissolute bedchamber."[17] Against this background, the Lover's attempt to deny Reason's verbal *vis* is comical; and his own euphemisms have the obvious intention of trying to tart up his harlotry.

What of the second sense of the word "glossing," Reason's sense? For her the word "gloss" means to make clear what is obscure or hidden in a text. At least this is the clear textual implication. She fully understands the Lover's superficial use of the word (7051ff.) and reproves him for it. She finds it not courteous but jejune that women should call the male organs such things as *borses, harnais, riens, piche,* or *pines* (7113). The

---

[16] Augustine, *De dialectica*, ed. J. Pinborg, trans. B. Darrell Jackson (Dordrecht, 1975), 101ff. The importance of this text for modern critical theory has been recognized by Todorov, *Théories du symbole* (Paris, 1977), 37. I regard the *De dialectica* as a genuine work of Augustine's, but its relevance to medieval linguistic theory is, of course, in no way clouded by the doubts concerning its authenticity first raised by the Benedictine editors.

[17] *De dialectica*, 101, 103; the citation of Sallust is from the *Bellum Catilinae* 14.2.

word "prick" is particularly inapt for suggesting the actual
nature of the sexual act. Reason here serves not as a censor of
smut, but as the adjudicator of the "doctrine" surrounding
verbal signs. The most penetrating studies of Augustinian
linguistics have, in fact, demonstrated that for Augustine the
relationship between *ratio* and *auctoritas* is analogous to that
between the thing signified and the sign.[18] The word itself is
necessarily a part of the sensible world, but the thing signified
may be something higher, an intelligible concept. The "au-
thority" of the word must be confirmed by the rational faculty,
which in the *De magistro* is identified with the indwelling
Christ. As far as the *Roman de la Rose* is concerned, the *auctoritas*
of the god of Love is entirely spurious, so Reason declines to
confirm it. Reason's linguistic authority manifests itself es-
pecially in confirming the *doctrina* of things. The doctrine of
Saturn's *coilles* is the allegorical understanding of the "second
sense" of signs that should not be taken "literally" (*autre sen,
a la letre*, 7127-28).

The presence of commonplace terms of exegesis—terms used
of biblical and poetic allegory alike—can offer important guid-
ance for understanding of the general significance of the lin-
guistic sport of our dialogue. I have written at some length
of the Lover's comic literalism in this passage, and I have
nothing useful to add on that subject.[19] At the same time, it
may be helpful to examine Jean's materials, briefly, within a
wider context. The connection between a theory of language
and a theory of interpretation or hermeneutics is a natural but
not an inevitable one; yet we are likely to regard it as inevitable
precisely because of Augustine.[20] That is, Augustine's impact

[18] See Holte, *Beatitude et sagesse*, 329-31; Alici, *Il Linguaggio come segno*,
35n.

[19] The idea has been further elaborated, however, in the article by M. R.
Jung cited above, "Jean de Meun et l'allégorie."

[20] See L. Alici, "Per una ermeneutica 'in interiore homine,' " in *Storio-
grafia ed ermeneutica* [Atti del xix convegno di assistenti universitari di filosofia]
(Padua, 1975), 227-36.

on medieval linguistic theory was definitive, and his discussion
of language brought with it its own context, which was a
theory of interpretation. In the *De magistro* there is, to be sure,
a definite hermeneutical interest, but it is developed only
obliquely, in the second part of the work, in the discussion
of the magisterium of the indwelling Christ. In the much more
famous treatment of his intellectual maturity, the *De doctrina
christiana*, the "sign theory" of language is radically and ex-
pressly linked with a theory of scriptural interpretation. Nu-
merous scholars, but especially D. W. Robertson, have drawn
attention to the general importance of the *De doctrina christiana*
in defining the discussion of literary aesthetics for the Middle
Ages, and there is no need to cover that ground here.[21] We
may, however, make a pointed observation about the Augus-
tinian theory of the relationship between language and history.

Most students of antique culture now believe that there is
considerably more continuity between the techniques of "pa-
tristic exegesis" and pre-Christian literary traditions than was
once allowed, but the discovery of relevant Greco-Roman models
has also served the purpose of throwing into stark relief what
was the essentially original aspect of early Christian allegory.
It is this: scriptural allegory was, for the Church Fathers, rooted
in works rather than words. It was an *allegoria facti* or *allegoria
in factis*, an allegory that took as its "signs" the history of
salvation as it was recorded in the Old Testament.[22] In the
Roman de la Rose the discussion of language between Reason
and the Lover introduces the allegorical "history" of the cas-
tration of Saturn, a history that is a major idea in the poem.
Concerning Reason's understanding of the Fall of Man, Weth-

[21] See especially the introduction to Robertson's translation of *On Christian
Doctrine* (New York, 1958). Stanley E. Fish, *Self-Consuming Artifacts* (Berke-
ley and Los Angeles, 1972), 21-42, gives a sophisticated demonstration of
some critical implications of Augustine's linguistic theories.

[22] See J. Pépin, *Les Deux Approches du christianisme* (Paris, 1962), 38-50,
cited by G. Ripanti, "L'Allegoria o l' 'intellectus figuratus' nel De doctrina
christiana di Agostino," *REAug* 18 (1972): 226.

erbee has written this: "Raison is incapable of conceiving the problem in theological terms, and the historical account she gives of man's lapse from participation in the all-embracing *joutice* of his original condition rests in unresolved contradiction to her confidence that *joutice, largice,* and Raison herself can still claim his affection."[23] I admit that I do not understand the second independent clause in this sentence, but I want to argue that the contrast between the "theological" account Reason is allegedly incapable of and the "historical account she actually gives is a fallacious one. Reason speaks as an exegete for whom the facts of theology are to be drawn from the facts of history. There are in the dialogue between Reason and the Lover repeated appeals, implicit or explicit, to "ancient writings." We see them in Reason's exemplary authorities and in the playful praise of the prospective translator of Boethius. The Lover speaks of Cicero as one "qui mist grant cure / en cerchier secrez d'escripture" (5375-76), and the *escripture* probably there connotes what Augustine had earlier called "certain books of the platonists," that is, the Greek philosophical texts that Cicero made it his duty to Latinize. In reproving a particularly egregious idiocy of Amant's, Reason tells him:

> tu n'as pas bien por moi mater   5724
> cerchié les livres anciens;
> tu n'iés pas bons logicien.

The Lover's argument is without reason and without authority alike.

Of ancient writings that offered theological truth beneath the figment of poetic history, the myth of the Golden Age is a conspicuous and a common example. Reason's implication that it is one of the "obscure fables" requiring academic exegesis from the *integumanz aus poetes* (7133, 7138) is something

---

[23] Wetherbee, "The Literal and the Allegorical," 271-72. The same statement in slightly altered wording is repeated in *Platonism and Poetry*, 258-59.

of an overstatement, given its currency in medieval poetic texts and its long tradition of patristic understanding. The fable of the end of the Golden Age was taken by the Latin Middle Ages as an antique "parallel" to the scriptural account of the Fall of Man. The one was *narratio fabulosa*, the other historical truth, but both, as events that had "another sense" beyond the letter of their texts, spoke of the theological condition of fallen man. Many critics have followed Robertson in identifying this trope within the poem, and Thomas Hill in particular has made an important contribution to our understanding of its specific mythographic background, a contribution independent of the critical argument in which it is implicated.

It *is not necessary*, however, to appeal to a vague "mythographic tradition," for the Christian understanding of the Golden Age was above all the gift of two influential writers, Lactantius and Boethius—and of the two it is the former who is both more explicitly theological and more explicitly mythographic. In my earlier study of the *Roman*, I did draw attention to the particular relevance of Lactantius' use of the Golden Age "topic," but in my ignorance I failed to grasp what I now believe is its real significance for the poem.[24] I am now convinced that Lactantius provides more than an early example of literary "tradition." He provided Jean de Meun with a quite specific *model of unimpeachable Ciceronian Christian rhetoric.*

Although modern patristic study has not, on the whole, credited Lactantius with a profundity of theological thought or granted to him a continuing cultural importance, he was very widely studied in the Middle Ages and the Renaissance, and there are numerous features of his literary personality that might have recommended him to medieval poets, especially to poets with the "humanistic" interests that we associate with Jean de Meun.[25] Although like Jean himself he came in time

---

[24] Fleming, *The Roman de la Rose*, 145.

[25] For a general survey of the career, see J. Stevenson, "The Life and Literary Activity of Lactantius," *Studia Patristica*, ed. K. Aland and F. L. Cross (Berlin, 1957), 1:661-77.

to serve the highest people of the realm—in his old age he became the tutor of Crispus, eldest son of the emperor Constantine—he began his literary life, as Augustine would begin his after him, as a pagan professor of rhetoric. Upon his conversion to Christianity, which took place under the reign of Diocletian, he lost his job and his patronage; and the imperial persecution of Christians, so much a fact of his times, is likewise a major theme of his literary work, especially the *De mortibus persecutorum*. His greatest book, the *Institutiones*, is what defines his more lasting literary contribution. In it he sets out a systematic work of apologetics, consciously and explicitly designed to be at once more comprehensive and more effective than the books of his African predecessors, especially Tertullian and Cyprian.

The audience that Lactantius envisioned for the *Institutiones* might be described as the pagan intelligentsia, the clients of rhetoric and its cultural champions. Though not philosophers, such men dabbled in "philosophy" at least to the extent of knowing Cicero, whose career had been devoted to their service, in a sense, by making available to them in a vocabulary that was already at least half their own the main currents of Greek thought and letters. Such men certainly knew the historians and the poets of the City. They were reasonable, fashionable, urbane. Their instinctive view of Christianity was that it was irrational, unfashionable, and unsophisticated. Lactantius knew that he must speak to them in a special way. He must speak in the philosophical vocabulary of Cicero, not in what Peter Brown has nicely called "the exotic jargon of the psalms." He must appeal to the rational authority of the poets and the historians, not the supernatural revelation of a book crude in its style and incredible in its content. He must argue the theological case for Christianity on the basis of immutable moral truth demonstrable from their shared cultural experience and the evidence of their own greatest writers. His is not the voice of the Nicene Fathers, spelling out the dogmas to be held by faith, but it is nonetheless an authentic "patristic"

voice, just as the voice of the *De vera religione* is an authentic
Augustinian voice. There was no single face of early Christian
culture.

If it is to be held a remarkable qualification of the Christian
intention of Boethius or Jean de Meun that Lady Philosophy
and Lady Reason do not cite Scripture—or rather, as we have
seen, that they do so with sufficient discretion as to please
those readers who do not want to have their noses rubbed in
Scripture—what are we to make of Lactantius, who in the
midst of a comprehensive apology for Christianity against its
pagan detractors, actually criticizes his great predecessor St.
Cyprian for quoting the Scripture to them?[26] Though he com-
pares his own undertaking with that of Tertullian and Cyprian,
he at the same time distances himself from them. Unlike
Tertullian, who merely addressed in a defensive manner the
agenda raised by his adversaries, Lactantius will present a
coherent body of Christian *Institutiones*. Unlike Cyprian, who
based his argument in Scripture, Lactantius will present an
argument founded in generally approved philosophers and his-
torians. What he says of Cyprian specifically—concerning his
presentation to the pagan Demetrian—is this:

> Qua materia non est usus ut debuit: non enim scripturae
> testimoniis, quam ille utique uanam, fictam, commenticiam
> putabat, sed argumentis et ratione fuerat refellendus. Nam
> cum ageret contra hominen ueritatis ignarum, dialtis pau-
> lisper diuinis lectionibus formare hunc a principio tamquam
> rudem debuit eique paulatim lucis principia monstrare, ne
> toto lumine obiecto caligaret. Nam sicut infans solidi ac
> fortis cibi capere uim non potest ob stomachi teneri-
> tudinem, sed liquore lactis ac mollitudine alitur, donec fir-
> matis uiribus uesci fortioribus possit, ita et huic oportebat,
> quia nondum poterat capere diuina, prius humana testi-

[26] *Institutions Divines, Livre* V (5.4.3ff.), ed. Pierre Monat (Paris, 1973),
1:149ff.

monia offerri id est philosophorum et historicorum, ut suis potissimum refutaretur auctoribus.[27]

One particularly nice feature of this passage denying the utility of scriptural argumentation is that it is built out of an obvious scriptural metaphor, that of the "milk and solid food" of Hebrews 5:12-14 (cf. I Cor. 3:1-2). This is the sort of thing Jean de Meun loved: quote the Bible, but call it Cicero.

The two historical theologians share other attitudes as well. One feature of the theme of the Golden Age common to Lactantius and Jean de Meun is particularly distinctive against the background of the larger poetic history of the topic's treatment in medieval texts. It might be described as a certain chronological confusion or ambiguity. For Lactantius, at least for the Lactantius of one poetic voice, the Golden Age was an actual historical epoch, a definite state in the religious and anthropological history of mankind, an age of monotheism before the advent of polytheistic idolatry. But the Golden Age is also *our* age, in which Christianity has restored *justitia*, its governing characteristic, at least for its righteous adherents. Furthermore, and somewhat vaguely, the Golden Age is an important metaphor of Lactantius' chiliasm: it is a *future* restoration of justice. Louis Swift has written nicely of the unresolved syncretisms of Lactantius' use of the myth, in which we can detect the different perspectives of the cultivated amateur of pagan poetry, the irenic apologist, the pre-Nicene believer.[28]

It is of some significance that there is a similar surface polysemousness in Jean de Meun's Golden Age. Reason alludes to the myth as but a remote memory of human bliss, an age closed forever by the violence of Jupiter and the banishment of Justice. Much of the wit of Jean's treatment of Amis and La Vieille, on the other hand, depends upon our seeing that

[27] *Institutions Divines* 5.4.4-6.
[28] Louis J. Swift, "Lactantius and the Golden Age," *AJP* 89 (1968): 144-56.

their social and sexual "programs" demand that we suspend our belief in what Reason has taught us about the Golden Age. Both, in differing ways, insist—with risible results— that we act as though the Golden Age *were* our age. Finally, for Genius, the discussion of the fall of primal justice is conspicuously if incoherently linked with the eschatological vision of copulators' heaven.[29] Thus in the *Roman* as in the *Institutiones*, the Golden Age exists beneath various *species* as time past, time present, time to come.

There is further and more compelling suggestion that Jean is animated by the conscious memory of Lactantius, and that is his use of Vergil. The fullest and most "classical" account of the dethronment of Saturn by Jupiter is that given by Genius (20002ff.), where the source adduced is Vergil, but adduced in that peculiarly involuted way that suggests Jean's fascination with the relationships of literary history:

> Et, si con dit an *Georgiques*   20085
> cil qui nous escrit *Bucoliques,*
> —car es livres greizeis trouva
> conment Jupiter se prouva—

This is supplemented, however, by a number of details (20151ff.) from the first book of the *Metamorphoses* of Ovid, who is also cited in Jean's text: "Ausinc le dit Ovides."

These same texts, cited in the same order, are those used by Lactantius in the chapter that actually takes up his announced topic of justice: "Nunc reddenda est de iustitia proposita disputatio."[30] These are, in a sense, *the* classic texts on the Golden Age, so that their common citation by Lactantius and Jean de Meun could be fortuitous. More significant, however, is the way in which both the *Institutiones* (5.5.10) and the *Roman de la Rose* (20089ff.) use the Vergilian lines for obviously eccentric purposes. Swift has written of Lactantius

---

[29] See in particular lines 19971ff.

[30] *Institutions Divines* 5.5.1; ed. Monat, 1:150.

that "Vergil's lines from the Georgics . . . are wrested from context and made to serve the apologist's purpose."[31] Certainly it would be difficult to imagine a more bizarre purpose than that which they serve for Genius. Though he himself is within the *Roman* the principle of natural concupiscence or delight, and though he promises the heavenly rewards of a new Golden Age to those who follow his lead in the procreative act, he strangely characterizes the *end* of the Golden Age as the beginning of the reign of pleasure.

The cardinal word is *delit*. The usurper Jupiter is a hedonist, and hedonism is the order of his reign (20071f.). "Jupiter the likerous" Chaucer calls him, suggesting the specific proclivity of the fallen race that Jean points to with the word *delit*. We have already seen that *delit* is, in the moral vocabulary of the *Roman de la Rose*, a precise, privileged term. It is the *voluptas* of Cicero's *De senectute*, the *cupiditas* of the Bible, the *concupiscentia* and *libido* of Augustine. It is for Lady Reason—and for St. Paul—the "root of all evils." Now in this specific regard, the text of the *Institutiones* is crucial, for Lactantius identifies *cupiditas* as the defining characteristic of the age initiated by Jupiter's violence. Furthermore, he does so with the same inescapable Pauline echo we have earlier heard from the mouth of Lady Reason: "Fortasse aliquid eiusmodi Iupiter fecerit ad expungnandam tollendamque iustitiam et idcirco efferasse serpentes ac lupos acuisse tradatur. . . . Quorum omnium malorum fons cupiditas erat, quae scilicet ex contemptu verae maiestatis erupit."[32]

Various features of Lactantius' career and of the literary quality of his *Institutiones* are of particular relevance to the argument about Jean de Meun's *Roman* that I have attempted to develop in earlier chapters, and two of them—those that link him to Cicero on the one hand, and to Augustine on the other—can be usefully sketched. Lactantius is, in the first place

<hr>

[31] Swift, "Lactantius and the Golden Age," 151.

[32] *Institutions Divines* 5.5.12; 5.6.1; ed. Monat, 1:154, 156.

the Christian Ciceronian *par excellence*. St. Jerome, who bore
the scars on his body that testified to his knowledge of such
things, writes of Lactantius as a "river of Ciceronian elo-
quence."[33] That might be called the beginning of his medieval
reputation, for Jerome is his first biographer. Pico della Mi-
randola, who might be called his last medieval witness, says
this of him: "Quis apud nos non videat esse Ciceronem, sed
Christianum . . . ? quis enim non advertit Lactantium Fir-
mianum aequasse ipsum et forte praecelluisse in eloquendo."[34]
This testimony is a kind of literary criticism, speaking to
Lactantius' Ciceronianism of word and phrase. As a Latin rhet-
orician in an age for which rhetoric and Cicero were so nearly
synonymous as to evade all but the most principled distinction,
Lactantius uses the works of Cicero, and especially the dia-
logues, not so much as models for literary imitation as the
very lexicon of literary language itself. This debt, naturally,
is reflected in matters of substance as well as in matters of
style, *pectus* as well as *lingua*. Lactantius' intellectual repertory
is thoroughly Ciceronian, and if it is true that important recent
work has demonstrated that there is somewhat more to him
than Cicero alone, it has also constructed the backdrop against
which the apologist's essentially Ciceronian profile stands out
in sharpest clarity.[35] Lactantius emerges from these studies
with his old title intact: *Cicero christianus*.

The quality of his literary education renders him a *Cicero*;
the uses to which he puts it reveals him *christianus*. For Lac-
tantius does indeed "use" his literary education—which is the
same as saying that he "uses" specific texts of Cicero, Ovid,

[33] "Lactantius quasi quidam fluvius eloquentiae Tullianae" (Jerome, *Epist.*
lviii [ad Paulinum Presbyterum]).

[34] *De studio divinae atque humanae philosophia* 1.7, as cited in *Divinae In-
stitutiones*, ed. U. Boella (Florence, 1973), 35.

[35] See *Institutions Divines*, ed. Monat, 1:34, in the context of discussing
the important books by A. Wlosok, *Laktanz und die philosophische Gnosis*
(Heidelberg, 1960); and V. Loi, *Lattanzio nella storia del linguaggio e del
pensiero teologico preniceno* (Zürich, 1970).

Vergil, and others—in precisely the ways recommended by
Augustine in the classic pages of the *De doctrina christiana* that
develop the theme of "Egyptian gold." Wherever the truth is
found, it is the Lord's, and to plunder the Egyptians is but
to expropriate the expropriators of divine treasure. The gold
and silver ornaments of an impious cult—the "wisdom" and
the "eloquence" of the ancients—could be and should be brought
from afar to adorn the temple of the true God. I take the
liberty of identifying Lactantius as an Augustinian looter of
Egyptian gold only because Augustine himself has done so:
"Nam quid aliud fecerunt multi boni fideles nostri?" asks
Augustine. "Nonne aspicimus quando auro et argento et ueste
suffarcinatus exierit de Aegypto Cyprianus et doctor suauis-
simus et martyr beatissimus? quanto Lactantius?"[36]

It is not an exaggeration to call the *De doctrina christiana*
the most important single essay on the theory of textual inter-
pretation known to the Latin Middle Ages, and it is hardly
conceivable that writers interested in the nature of language,
the nature of literary style, or the meaning of meaning—to
name but a few of the topics on which it offered authoritative
teaching—would be ignorant of its contents. In particular, its
defense of the uses of Egyptian gold brings together two literary
enterprises sometimes held by critics to be entirely discrete—
the study of the classical authors on the one hand, the study
of the sacred page on the other. For Christian poets of the
vernacular period—and I think here especially of the giants,
Dante, Petrarch, Boccaccio, Jean de Meun, Chaucer—there
was no greater artistic issue than the contemporary uses of
ancient texts. That in the eyes of such men Augustine had in
fact addressed the issue is apparent from the use of the *De
doctrina* in the formal defense of poetry and from Augustine's
arbitration of the tension between humane letters and the
Christian vocation for Petrarch.[37] When Augustine praised

[36] *De doctrina christiana* 2.40.61.

[37] See especially the *Familiares* 10.3, where the example of the Christo-
logical animal allegories echoes *De doctrina christiana* 3.25.36.

Lactantius for his use of classical poetry, he certainly had in mind the *Institutiones*, in which the most conspicuous (not to say ostentatious) vessel of Egyptian gold was the theme of the Golden Age, in the varied use of which Lactantius achieved a particularly virtuoso performance.

Lactantius' studied Ciceronianism joins with what might be called his preemptive Augustinianism on precisely the subject that controls Jean de Meun's introduction of the myth of the Golden Age: the subject of *justice*. In particular, the "obscenity" of Saturn's *coilles* and the "justice" of Saturn's reign are inextricably linked:

> Joutice, qui jadis regnot,   5505
> au tens que Saturnus regne ot,
> cui Jupiter coupa les coilles,
> ses filz, con se fussent andoilles. . . .

The theological connection between the poetic Golden Age and the reign of justice had been definitively established by Lactantius, whose entire fifth book is an essay *De justitia*. In it are preserved a number of the commonplace teachings of the Greco-Roman philosophers, which by happenstance more cruel than any conspiracy have been lost to us in their primary formulations.

Authentic classical teachings concerning justice are in some respects easier to infer than they are to cite. We know that Aristotle's early views on the subject, as codified in the *Protrepticus*, reflect a Platonic doctrine of the unity of being and value.[38] Hence an understanding of the virtue of justice is contingent upon its effectual presence in the investigator, so that to be just is, ultimately, to contemplate the good. We have no reason to suppose that Aristotle ever abandoned this position, though we know that he did develop a much more concrete discussion of justice, one founded in a nuanced analysis

[38] See Mary Clark, "Platonic Justice in Aristotle and Augustine," *Downside Review* 82 (1964): 25.

of human societies and upon a deep meditation on human nature. His ideas were advanced in the dialogue *De justitia*, the loss of which might be easier to bear were it not for the fact that its most conspicuous Latin witnesses have also in part vanished. They were the *Hortensius* and the *De republica* of Cicero. These texts have a special relevance for Jean's poem.

Of the several scholarly articles dealing with the theme of the Golden Age in the *Roman de la Rose*, the most penetrating, in my view, is that of Paul Milan, who set out to test the validity of the fashionable evaluations of Jean de Meun as a deeply original or radical social and political thinker.[39] That reputation was, and is, founded on the statements of various characters in the poem—especially Amis and La Vieille—concerning the nature of Golden Age society: its innocence of legal constraints, the power of princes, and the sophistications of technology. Milan's examination of these views, and particularly the rather pessimistic view toward positive justice that the poem as a whole seems to reflect, discloses their deeply traditional, indeed their commonplace character: "The political and social implications of the Golden Age, modern as they might at first appear, originate in the writings of the Stoic philosophers."[40] Two pillars of Roman *gravitas* were particularly influential in popularizing a widely held theory of justice: Seneca and Cicero. It would be difficult to exaggerate the latter's importance in this respect: "In the fragments of his *De Re Publica* and in his treatise *De Legibus*, Cicero left a nearly complete compendium of the generally accepted political theories of his time."[41] Once again we find Cicero as a silent

[39] Paul B. Milan, "The Golden Age and the Political Theory of Jean de Meun: A Myth in *Rose* Scholarship," *Symposium* 23 (1964): 137-49. In addition to other studies elsewhere cited, there is an article by F.W.A. George, "Jean de Meung and the Myth of the Golden Age," in *The Classical Tradition in French Literature* [Essays presented to R. C. Knight], ed. H. T. Barnwell et al. (privately printed, 1977), 31-39.

[40] Milan, "The Golden Age and the Political Theory of Jean de Meun," 144.

[41] Ibid.

arbiter of ideas central to the *Roman de la Rose*, but in this instance, a peculiarly oblique arbiter.

Two points of antique doctrine concerning justice are of particular significance within the specific context of the dialogue between Reason and the Lover. They concern the organic metaphor of the human body on the one hand, and the relationship between justice and love on the other. That aspect of Aristotelian justice which concerns social groupings is formulated in terms of relationships between one who commands (a king, an elder brother, a husband, etc.) and one who obeys (a subject, a younger brother, a wife, etc.).[42] There is a clear distinction between tyranny and well-ordered hierarchy, and the decisive feature of the latter is the presence of "interior" justice in the commanding partner. What I am calling interior justice concerns the internal hierarchy within all men, that is to say, the relationship between reason and the passions. On the question of this relationship there is a signifcant distinction between Aristotle and the Christians on the one hand, and the Stoics on the other.[43] The early Stoics regarded the passions as absolutely base, proclivities to be annihilated rather than mastered. Aristotle and the Christians speak of "mastery," recognizing within the appetites what is useful and necessary to human life. As Clark puts it, "they are treated by reason as a father would treat his children rather than as a master would treat his slave."[44] We may remember one of Reason's pet terms for the Lover—*beau fils*.

The essence of this interior justice, the necessary foundation of justice in any larger social sphere, is expressed in a commonplace metaphor of the human body, the members of which work in rational concert for the good of the whole. In this context, Clark has drawn attention to a significant passage in

[42] See P. Moraux, *A La Recherche de l'Aristote perdu: Le Dialogue "Sur la Justice"* (Louvain, 1957), 29ff.; cf. Fleming, *The Roman de la Rose*, 152 and n.

[43] Clark, "Platonic Justice in Aristotle and Augustine," 27-28.

[44] Clark, "Platonic Justice in Aristotle and Augustine," 28.

the fourteenth book of the *De civitate Dei*—the locus of our
earlier discussion of the sexual organs—which can suggest the
nearly inevitable way in which Jean de Meun might link *coilles*
and *joutice*:

> Et non credimus ad opus generationis filiorum, si libido
> non fuisset, quae peccato inoboedientiae retributa est, oboe-
> dienter hominibus ad voluntatis nutum similiter ut cetera
> potuisse illa membra servire? Nonne Cicero in libris de re
> publica, cum de imperiorum differentia disputaret et huius
> rei similitudinem ex natura hominis adsumeret, ut filiis dixit
> imperari corporis membris propter oboediendi facilitatem;
> vitiosas vero animi partes ut servos asperiore imperio co-
> herceri?[45]

The unruly members are the very image of that disorder which
denies justice, and we shall not expect to find justice in a brave
new world ruled by the principle of *delit*. "Aristotle and Plato
are in agreement that, if pleasure should be made the end of
appetite, justice would be impossible."[46] That should make
clear the relationship between Amant's love (the sole end of
which is *charnex delit*) and justice, but it does not explain why,
in the *Roman de la Rose*, Reason makes justice subordinate to
love.

That Jean's *Roman* is not without clear organizational prin-
ciples is now generally admitted, but there is a certain breath-
lessness about the poem's propaedeutic flow that can leave the
reader breathless too. It is not unwise or for that matter un-
sporting to pause now and again to remind ourselves where
we are. As a general rule, subjects do not come up at random
in the "Ciceronian" dialogue, at least in those that operate
according to the dialectic that a Marrou has taught us to see
in Augustine; and as readers we have a leisure not always

---

[45] *De civitate Dei* 14.23; the Ciceronian text is directly cited by Augustine
in the *Contra Julianum* 4, 12.61.

[46] Clark, "Platonic Justice in Aristotle and Augustine," 27.

available to the interlocutors themselves to study out their
relevance to the announced topic. The announced topic of the
dialogue between Reason and the Lover is of course love. The
theme of the Golden Age depends upon a subsidiary discussion
of justice, and the question of justice is raised in the dialogue
in a careful way. Thus as we approach the problem of ancient
allegory in his poem—I mean the problem of Jean's figural
use of classical literature—we should be aware that Jean has
in fact already prepared his way for a sophisticated development
of the hermeneutical theme.

The dense passage of the text that we examined in connection
with our consideration of "Carthaginian love" links the dis-
cussion of friendship with that of charity in a most remarkable
way. In that comic but profound passage, the Lover despairs
of finding friendship, and he equates a search for it with three
impossible, vain, or foolish endeavors:

> Puis je voler avec les grues   5393
> voire saillir outre les nues,
> con fist li cignes Socratés?
> N'en quier plus parler, je la tes.
> Ne sui pas de si fol espoir;
> li dieu cuideroient espoir
> que j'assaillisse paradys
> con firent li geant jadis,   5400
> s'en porroie estre foudroiez
> Ne sai se vos le voudroiez,
> si n'en doi je pas estre en doute.

I do not fully understand, perhaps do not understand at all,
the expression "voler avec les grues." Lanly is satisfied with
its metaphoric sense of performing the impossible, and I must
perforce be too, though what might be called the texture of
this part of the poem makes me want to search for some sharp
and specific intertextual point. We have one, certainly, in the
cignes Socratés, for it is a clear allusion, recognized by the poem's
editors, to a story reported by John of Salisbury in his *Poli-*

craticus to the effect that Socrates saw offered on the altar of
Venus a colossal swan, whose neck pierced the heavens and
whose beak touched the stars.[47] The following day Aristides
delivered to him as a pupil his young son Plato, and when
Socrates saw the lad, he realized at once the meaning of his
extraordinary vision. "This is the swan," he said, "that Venus
consecrated to Apollo at the Academy." Since, at an obvious
level of allegory, Socrates' swan is Plato, the Lover is simply
saying in metaphorical fashion that he cannot aspire to wisdom.
Since he gives not a hoot about Socrates himself (presuming
that the rate of exchange is three chickpeas to the hoot), there
is no reason to await his deference toward Socrates' most famous
pupil. There is nothing about clouds in John of Salisbury's
text, except possibly by implication; yet Jean de Meun has
done well to mention them, as they fit in so nicely with a
Boethian analysis of the Lover's condition. In the imagery of
one of Boethius' most famous poems, *Nubibus astris* (I m7), he
is one beclouded. It seems to me very likely, however, that,
as is often the case with Jean's borrowing, the defining context
of the borrowed passage in its original offers elucidation of its
use in the *Roman*.

The story of "Socrates' swan" comes at the end of a lengthy
discussion of dreams, dream images, and the understanding
of figural revelations. This was a popular chapter of the *Po-
licraticus*, and its influence can be traced in various vernacular
texts, including the hilarious "Nun's Priest's Tale" of Chaucer.
Within its context it links a Macrobian distinction of signif-
icant and insignificant dreams with a broader discussion of
allegory or "polysemous" expression. In this regard, its po-
tential ironies for Jean's poem are endearing. The relationship
between Reason and the Lover, like that between Socrates and
Plato, is that of teacher and student, but whereas Plato was
given over by the goddess of love to the god of wisdom, the
Lover rejects the promptings of divine wisdom for servitude

[47] *Policraticus* 2.16; ed. C.J.J. Webb (London, 1909), 1:96.

to the god of Love. The passage in the *Roman* is a kind of thematic prolegomenon to the more developed discussion of words and things, allegory and allegorical meaning, that underscores the Lover's hopeless literalism. All teaching, says Augustine, is concerned either with signs or with things, but sometimes things are signs. For the Lover, the swan is simply a thing, an ornithological curiosity. For Socrates, the wise man, it is a sign. How are we to avoid the pun that Jean has with much labor dragged into his poem? The *cigne* is a *signe*.

The idea of hermeneutical difficulty is what in fact unites the otherwise unlikely collocation of images—the "swan of Socrates" and the vain assault of the giants against the gods of Olympus. The *gigantomachia*, the unwritten epic of Ovid, is widely alluded to in the major classical poets, but for Christian writers its chief significance was as an antique parallel for the story of the Tower of Babel (Gen. 3). Its treatment in the *Eclogue* of Theodulus, a school poem read by everyone who read anything, suggests that the association would have been a commonplace.[48] There is important Augustinian support for the idea, for in his discussion of the confusion of tongues Augustine ascribed the founding of Babylon to the "giant" Nimrod (Gen. 10:10).[49] The Lover's claim is that, unlike the giants of old, he will not aspire beyond his station, his station being, of course, the inability to achieve friendship. But the irony is deeper still, since we find in the passage the clear evidence of Amant's confusion—and Babylon *means* confusion—founded precisely in his inability to understand the language of his interlocutor: "Or me dites donques ainceis / non en latin, mes en françois" (5809–10).

How does all this relate to justice and love? Concerning the Lover's putative inability to achieve friendship, Reason says, parenthetically, "car ausinc bien peut il remaindre / par ton

---

[48] *Ecloga Theoduli*, ed. Osternacher, 35; for other instances, see Eupolemius, *Das Bibelgedicht*, ed. K. Manitius (Weimar, 1973), vol. 1, line 666n.
[49] *De civitate Dei* 16.4.

defaut con par l'autrui" (5406-7), lines that are difficult chiefly because they seem to say so little. There is not much padding in Jean's poem, but there is *some*, and it may not be possible to identify significant thematic content here. Nonetheless, I would suggest that Reason proposes the social nature of friendship and its dependence upon reciprocity. It is possible that friendship would be wanting either through the deficiency of Amant or through that of another (his potential friend). On this account, Reason proposes another kind of love, one that does not depend upon the *fact* of a reciprocal responsiveness but on the *hope* for it and is thus entirely within the volitional control of the Lover. Reason calls this an *amor dou conmun* (love of all men), an expression of the command *amer generaumant* (to love all men generally). What is this love? It is the love stated explicitly in the so-called Golden Rule of Matthew 7:12, a verse here cited by Reason, "Whatsoever you would that men should do to you, do you also to them." In the Christian vocabulary of the Middle Ages, this love was called *charity*.[50] It is not in fact a different love from that of friendship, for friendship is a species of it, as Reason asserts; but it is a more general and inclusive category. Charity is the love of God and the love of one's neighbor for the sake of God. In Augustine's common definition, charity is the "motion of the soul" aspiring to such love, and its debased, inferior analogue is cupidity. The doctrine of charity is the fundamental and unique teaching of the Christian religion. Here, in an emphatic position in the *Roman de la Rose*, Reason recommends it to the Lover in words taken directly from the mouth of the founder of Christianity, Jesus Christ. This leads me to suggest, in the measured and memorable phrase I remember reading somewhere, that the "careful reading of the colloquy between Reason and Amant," which finds that Reason "is limited and inadequate precisely

---

[50] See H. Pétré, *Caritas: Etude sur le vocabulaire latin de la charité chrétienne* (Louvain, 1948).

because she cannot discuss love from a Christian perspective," is not worth three *chiches*.[51]

It leads Reason herself to suggest something slightly different, to wit, that it is because of those who set out to do evil and abandon charity that justice has of necessity been established in the world (5429ff.). Reason here refers to criminal justice, the social redress for crimes against charity (*cest amor*, 5436) such as murder, rape, robbery, and barratry. The Lover in turn asks that Reason render a judgment concerning the relative worth of justice and love. Reason asks *which* love, and the Lover replies, "The one you want me to get involved with" (i.e., charity), for he has no desire to subject his own brand of love to judgment. Reason then proves the superiority of charity to justice for the Lover, who throughout the passage acts out his suitably torpid dialectical role, requiring an *exemplum* before he can construe the meaning of an abstract principle. It is in the final stages of this demonstration that Reason utters the shocking word *coilles*, though the Lover does not have a chance to register a complaint about it until after Reason recalls the story of the corrupt judge Appius, from Livy, a splendid exemplification of the impossibility of positive justice in the absence of interior justice.

This is not aimless meandering on Reason's part, or on Jean's. The *literary* purpose of Reason's scholastic demonstration of the superiority of love to justice is not exhausted by the doctrines adduced. Jean once again seizes the reader by the lapels and demands a recognition of the ambiguities of *amour*. Surely Amant, too, is one who places love above justice—though in a sense that parodies Reason rather than reflects her. When we grasp the connection between social justice and the interior justice of the well-ordered man, we recognize

[51] See Cherniss, "Jean de Meun's *Reson* and Boethius," 683n; and his "Irony and Authority," 230. To be fair, microeconomic analysis does suggest that William Calin's firm assurance that the concept of charity is *nowhere mentioned* in the *Roman de la Rose* ("Defense and Illustration of *Fin' Amor*," p. 36) is worth even less, probably about three *millichiches*.

at once the intrinsic injustice of irrational passion. Amant's acquiescence in, indeed his gratitude for Reason's lesson in civics, is a kind of hollow courtesy without substance. His allegiance is not to the truth of things, but to various kinds of surface elegances, levels of vocabulary, rhetorical competence. We may describe his attitude as "academic," for we shall find him capable of a firm allegiance to most sides of most questions. In this, he somewhat resembles Carneades, the Academic philosopher sent as an Athenian ambassador to the Roman senate in 155 B.C., and a man famous for what might be called a one-man "show" as an orator on the subject of justice.[52] On consecutive days, in audience before Cato the Censor and the great Galba, Carneades first made a brilliant philosophical defense of the necessity of justice to the well-ordered state and then a scintillating and skeptical refutation of his own demonstration. This was good Academic "rhetoric," but it turned the stomach of Cato, who like Augustine after him, was hopelessly interested in the actual truth of things. The tour de force of Carneades' "number" on justice played an important part in Cicero's discussion of justice in the *De republica*, and we find reflections of the Ciceronian texts in Augustine and more than a reflection of them in Lactantius' *Institutiones*, where the story of Carneades occupies a conspicuous position.[53]

The pattern, by now a familiar one, is here particularly articulate. The ideas concerning justice that are advanced in the *Roman de la Rose* are classical commonplaces made famous by Cicero, prominently adopted and subtly "Christianized" by patristic authorities, especially Augustine and Lactantius, and used by Jean de Meun in a way that publicly affirms their classicism and silently acknowledges their Christian character. A certain nexus of Ciceronian texts—the *De legibus*, the *Hortensius*, the *De republica*—looms in the background, visible like

---

[52] See *Institutions Divines*, ed. Monat, 2:198-200.
[53] *De civitate Dei* 19.21; *Institutiones* 5.14, 3ff.

the old ink of a palimpsest through the bolder and more prominent patristic authority of Lactantius and Augustine.[54] These same texts in one way or another prove to be the friendly ghosts that haunt the *Roman de la Rose* as a whole. The first insistent intertextual reference in the poem—it comes as the seventh line of Guillaume's proemium—is to Macrobius' commentary on the *Somnium Scipionis*, one of the books of the *De republica*. Reason's discussion of friendship, dependent as it is on the Christian Ciceronianism of Aelred, alludes to the special meaning of the *Hortensius* for Augustine as celebrated in a famous page of the *Confessions* and as richly exploited for thematic purpose in the *De spiritali amicitia*. And the central repository of medieval "politics," Augustine's *De civitate Dei*, a work whose importance to certain themes in the *Roman de la Rose* has just been once more demonstrated, is a major witness to a Cicero otherwise lost entirely or reduced to a demeaning obscurity.

To Michel Ruch, who has made the most lucid reconstruction of the lost *Hortensius*, we owe as well a most illuminating essay on the literary genre of the work.[55] It is that of the *protreptic*, the literary exhortation and, in particular, the exhortation to philosophy. Though the origins of the protreptic are obscure and debated, its characteristic form in Cicero's time was that of a dialogue debate in which one voice denied the utility, sufficiency, and possibility of "philosophy"—that is, the rational, examined life founded in virtue rather than in the satisfaction of the bodily appetites—and another voice refuted such objections, extolling philosophy as the sole path to true happiness. The introductory and negative critique of philosophy in the protreptic was not academic skepticism, but

[54] Augustine's *De civitate Dei* and Lactantius' *Institutiones* are among the most copious witnesses to the *De republica*. See the tables compiled by E. Heck, *Die Bezeugung von Ciceros Schrift De re publica* (Hildesheim, 1966), 283-86.

[55] M. Ruch, *L'Hortensius de Cicéron: Histoire et reconstruction* (Paris, 1958), esp. 15-25.

a straw man; to knock down the straw man was the propae-
deutic exercise preliminary to a more positive philosophical
contribution.

Cicero makes explicit reference to his *Hortensius* in his extant
works, and it is clear that the lost dialogue is silently recalled
in several of the most famous passages of the *Tusculans*, and
in particular in the rhetorically stunning "hymn" at the be-
ginning of the fifth book. This passage has important echoes,
among other places, in the *Consolatio* of Boethius and the early
dialogues of Augustine.[56] Though Jean no more had at his
disposal the text of the *Hortensius* than do we, it is clear that
he was something of an expert in its chief witness: the classical
repertory of Cicero's extant moral dialogues, Augustine, and
Boethius. The relevance of the protreptic tradition thus re-
membered to the themes of the dialogue between Reason and
the Lover in the *Roman de la Rose* becomes immediately ap-
parent. There is in the first place a clear protreptic element
in Boethius—both in the nature of the dialogue between Boe-
thius and Philosophia, and in the concept of a personified
"guide." Cicero's famous encomium is this: "O vitae philo-
sophia dux, o virtutis indagatrix expultrixque vitiorum"—a
commonplace classicism ossified in the motto of the Phi Beta
Kappa Society.[57] Having traced the very close relationship
between Boethius' Philosophia and Jean de Meun's Reason
we can appreciate the poignancy of Cicero's complaint that
most men ignore philosophy and some even abuse it: "ut a
plerisque neglecta a multis etiam vituperetur."[58] But of great-
est interest of all, perhaps, is the protreptic's anthology of
negative arguments against philosophy.

Philosophy has no antique lineage. The lives of philosophers
refute the possibility of philosophy. Philosophy is too hard to
be obtained. Happiness consists in obtaining all of the one's

---

[56] See ibid., 131.

[57] *Tusculanes* 5.2.5; see the rich commentary of Hildebrech Hommel,
Ciceros Gebetshymnus an die Philosophie (Heidelberg, 1968).

[58] *Tusculanes* 5.2.5.

desires, not in the discipline of philosophy. Philosophy is a kind of folly. Philosophy is impractical. Nature is a sufficient guide for the conduct of a man's life. One is almost tempted to say that what we have lost in Hortensius himself we have found anew in Amant, who says, among other things, that Socrates is not worth the time of day, that he would be a great fool to follow Cicero's example, that carnal pleasure offers rewards infinitely greater than those offered by Reason, and that he can follow no other course than that which his nature dictates. The fundamental meaning of "philosophy" in the *Hortensius* was the rule of the carnal affections by the rational soul.[59] That concept is absolutely fundamental to the *Tusculan Disputations*, to Augustine's *De vera religione*, to Boethius' *Consolatio*—and this is to say that it is absolutely fundamental to the classical Christian view of human nature. Of this *philosophia*, *justitia* is a dependent social manifestation, intimately connected with the rule of reason and the mastery of the passions (especially, we should note, the sexual passion) in individual men and women.

Milan has demonstrated, with an abundance of textual parallels that could be considerably extended still, the deeply Ciceronian nature of the discussion of justice in the *Roman de la Rose*. We risk an unuseful confusion to think of this justice as a "political" category, and there is indeed no reason to think that Jean de Meun is any more capable of political thought in a modern sense than were Cicero or Plato. His doctrine of justice is a moral doctrine.[60] The loss of primal justice is a generalized manifestation of the conduct precisely exemplified by the Lover in the *Roman de la Rose*. If Amant really wants to know why the Golden Age is no more, he should address his own heart.

[59] See D. Turkowaska, *L'Hortensius de Cicéron et le Protreptique* (Warsaw, 1965), 12.

[60] Cf. M. Valente, *L'Ethique stoicienne chez Cicéron* (Paris, 1956), 299: "Notons . . . que, chez Cicéron, le politique n'est jamais loin du moraliste."

4.

Augustinus and Franciscus

I. Somniat iste tamen

The earlier chapters of this book have been concerned with Jean de Meun's literary ancestry and with the commerce between his own poem and certain cardinal texts of classical and Christian antiquity. Many paths lead to the *Roman de la Rose* from that classical literary tradition, from Cicero's Rome and Augustine's Carthage and Boethius' Pavia. To follow them out in their meanderings, often despite their unclear or even intentionally deceptive markings, does not make for easy traveling; but it is an intellectual journey that can contribute significantly to that preparatory education which alone can allow us to read Jean de Meun's poem with confidence and control. The interpretation of the *Roman de la Rose* is a formidable challenge, one calling for assiduous critical application and, perhaps, critical opportunism. We must grasp at what chances present themselves even knowing that some, perhaps most, will prove to be but straws—or straw men. In this final chapter, which from the outset I declare to be speculative, I should like to change directions, to think of Jean's poem not so much in terms of its ancestry as in those of its possible literary posterity, for, as far as the *Roman de la Rose* is concerned, the tracks leading away from the body are just as conspicuous—and as confusingly puzzling—as those leading to it. We can perhaps try to learn something of Jean's mind from his students as well as from his teachers.

Indeed, the fourteenth-century "influence" of the *Roman* may seem to be so massive as to deny utility in matters as delicate and nuanced as those that have been our concern. Without the *Roman*, one might plausibly say, there would be no major poetry in France in the fourteenth century—no Machaut, no Deschamps, no Froissart. Certainly there could have been no Geoffrey Chaucer in England. It would be possible to press the argument further, and the examples further afield. Yet what we seek is not so much evidence of Jean de Meun's undifferentiated "influence" as a poet whose artistic impulses and metabolism are those of Jean de Meun. Our ideal candidate might satisfy several of the following criteria. He would be a *major* poet, and his major subject love, treated in an erotic autobiography, an extended love-fiction. He would be learned, and conspicuously associated with the study and transmission of classical Latin texts. Neither Guillaume de Machaut, for all that he learned from the *Roman*, nor Geoffrey Chaucer, for all the ways in which his career parallels Jean's, precisely fits the bill.

There *is* a fourteenth-century figure whose work was to a conspicuous degree more obviously like that of Jean de Meun than was that of Guillaume de Machaut or Geoffrey Chaucer. He was an indisputably major poet with a truly international reputation. His greatest poem—the only European poem that can rival the *Roman* as an arbiter of the language and psychology of amatory fiction in the later Middle Ages—is an extended erotic autobiography, an elaborate love story whose protagonist is its first-person narrator. Like Jean de Meun, this man was conspicuously learned; and he likewise exhibits his learning in a problematical fusion of classical and Christian formulation. He was a close student of Cicero, and an even closer student of Augustine. We can be more precise and point to text after text that shows his sustained interest in the way in which Augustine was Cicero's Christian mediator. He is, of course, Francis Petrarch. The inquiry of this chapter—a speculative chapter, I repeat—will be to see if we find in Petrarch the evidence, half echo, half response, of an Augustinian's reading of the debate between Reason and the Lover in the *Roman de la Rose*.

A possible relationship between the *Roman* and Petrarch has been no more generally acknowledged than one between the *Roman* and Augustine, though it would be somewhat curious if Petrarch alone of major "secular" fourteenth-century poets proved exempt from its influence. A few lines in the "Triumphus Pudiciae," which seem to introduce Italian versions of several of Guillaume de Lorris' abstractions, have long teased the imaginations of commentators, though I myself do not find in them convincing evidence of familiarity, let alone actual borrowing.[1] L. F. Benedetto, the only scholar to approach the question with determination, correctly concluded that Petrarch certainly knew the *Roman*, and probably knew it pretty well; but his textual demonstrations, which are limited to the *Trionfi*, are not impressive.[2] We are perhaps looking for borrowed lines when we ought to be seeking evidence of other kinds of debts, debts of poetic conception and strategy.

That the question of Petrarch's relationship to the *Roman* has not been vigorously pursued is curious given the topicality of the parallel origins of Italian and French "humanism." I attribute this indolence to the corrupting influence of one great scholar caught for a moment napping—Pierre de Nolhac—and to Petrarch's own posturing.[3] If we believe his own words, Petrarch's *knowledge* of the *Roman* cannot be at doubt, for he describes the poem at some length in a famous letter (*Ep. met.* 3.30), which accompanied a manuscript of it that he sent to Guido Gonzaga. The more interesting literary questions surrounding this bare fact—the extent of his familiarity with the French text, for example, or his own direct poetic response to it—must remain in the realm of surmise. They are obscured

---

[1] See the psychomachic warfare of the personifications ("Triumphus Pudicitie," 76ff.).

[2] L. F. Benedetto, *Il "Roman de la Rose" e la letteratura italiana* (Halle, 1910), 165-71.

[3] See P. de Nolhac, *Pétrarque et l'humanisme*, 2nd ed. (Paris, 1907), 2:228.

from us in part by the tone (perhaps the better word would be pose) taken up by Petrarch. He presents the *Roman de la Rose* as the greatest vernacular poem France has to offer, "France renowned in speech," chiefly to demonstrate its obvious inferiority to the eloquence of Latin, and particularly to the poetry of Vergil, Catullus, Ovid, and Propertius. The attitude is distinctly ambiguous: the *Roman* is the greatest poem of a nation famous for its works of eloquence, but it falls far short of the achievements of "Italy."

What Petrarch says of the content of the *Roman de la Rose* is this:[4]

Scilicet his vulgo recitat sua somnia Gallus   6
Quid zelus, quid possit amor, quid pectus ephebi
Ignis alat, quid ludat anus, quibus artibus amens
Certat amans Veneris, tot sint in limine pestes.
Quis labor atque dolor, requies quae mixta labori   10
Quae risus, gemitusque vites, ut gaudia crebrae
Rara rigent lachrymae, poterat quod latius ergo
Uberiusque dari, fandique capacius arvum?
Somniat iste tamen, dum somnia visa renarrat
Sopitoque nihil vigilans distare videtur.   15

The Gallic poet tells the common folk
The substance of his dreams: what love can do,
And zeal; what fire burns within the heart
Of untried youth; what the false hopes of age,
The craftiness of Venus' maddened lover,
And the dire peril lurking in a glance;
What grief and toil, what rest and toil commingled,

---

[4] *Ep. met.* 3.30; *Opera* (Basel, 1554), 3.1,371. Since there will be no other relevant opportunity in this book to comment on the recent lengthy thesis by P. Badel, *Le Roman de la Rose au xiv* siècle* (Geneva, 1980), which purports to be a study of the "reception" of the *Roman*, I should point out that Petrarch's analysis is nowhere mentioned in it. Badel also ignores the testimony of (among several others) Geoffrey Chaucer. Since Petrarch and Chaucer were, beyond question, the two most important fourteenth-century poets *known* to have "received" the *Roman de la Rose*, we may conclude that (if nothing more) Badel has perhaps not exhausted his announced subject.

What laughter you should shun, and what lament;
How often tears must fall; how rare is joy.
Could there be richer field for eloquence?
And yet he dreams e'en as he tells his dream
And though he wake he is but dreaming still.[5]

Petrarch later uses the facetious phrase "brevis libellus" of the *Roman*, and one theory used to be that he therefore knew only the fragment of Guillaume de Lorris; but Benedetto properly observed that Petrarch's "synopsis" of the *Roman* clearly focuses on Jean de Meun's narrative.[6] The phrase "quid ludat anus" (8) alone is decisive in this regard, pointing as it does to Jean's major development of the "chapter" of La Vieille. Insofar as there is a clear point of view toward the subject matter, it is anything but Ithacan. Petrarch finds the heart of the poem in the Lover's struggles, sighs, and pains. The phrase "requies mixta labori" (10) echoes Reason's oxymoronic definition of love adopted from Alain de Lille. Petrarch's moral attitude toward the Lover is hardly approving or even neutral. There is clear moral condemnation in the phrase "amens amans Veneris" (8-9), or "Venus' maddened lover." The "person" of the second-person singular verb *vites* (11) is the reader. The *Roman* instructs in *what is to be avoided*. In short, Petrarch obviously knew what the *Roman de la Rose* was really about. Given the poem's moral reputation in the fourteenth century, it is of course possible that Petrarch would have known this without knowing very much of its text, but I regard it as doubtful that he would be speaking of a book he had not read in this particular context—the presentation of a book to an important friend and patron.[7]

[5] The translation is that of Ernest H. Wilkins, *Petrarch at Vaucluse* (Chicago, 1958), 39-40.

[6] Benedetto, *Il "Roman de la Rose" e la letteratura italiana*, 167-68.

[7] On Petrarch's somewhat ambiguous attitude toward his patrons at this time, see Ernest H. Wilkins, "On Petrarch's *Accidia* and His Adamantine Chains," *Speculum* 37 (1962): 590-91.

The most interesting lines in Petrarch's account of the poem, perhaps, are those with which he concludes (14-15), and we must return to them in a moment. But we must not in passing overlook those aspects of the mood of Petrarch's epistle that link it to some of the major concerns of the present study. Though its veil of witty irony should forbid us from drawing quick or certain conclusions, it is of considerable interest that Petrarch compares the *Roman* not in the first instance with the *vernacular* works of Italy—although he does eventually make glancing allusion to more "recent" productions—but with the classics of Latin antiquity. Though Italian love poetry could hardly be regarded as a subject on which Petrarch lacked knowledge or a point of view, he implicitly ranges Jean de Meun among the ancients rather than the moderns, chief of whom, of course, was Francis Petrarch. This is either an oblique compliment or an oblique insult.[8] Moreover, Petrarch squarely places Jean de Meun within the tradition that Jean had claimed, with whatever irony and facetiousness, as his own—that of the Latin elegists and love poets.[9] One of Jean's poets of antiquity, obviously borrowed from the controlling text in Ovid's *Amores*, is the mysterious "Gallus." Happily enough, "Gallus" is the

[8] Petrarch does make a passing allusion to the "moderns" in lines 22-23: "Ut sileam reliquos, uel quos antiquior aetas, / Vel quos nostra recens latialibus extulit oris. . . ." It seems to me quite possible that Petrarch's attitude toward the *Roman de la Rose* is colored by the kind of antivernacular prejudices that are apparently evident in his views of Dante. See the stimulating article by Aldo S. Bernardo, "Petrarch's Attitude Toward Dante," *PMLA* 70 (1955): 488-517. My attention was first drawn to some of the concerns of this chapter by a stimulating lecture by John Freccero, later published as "The Fig Tree and the Laurel: Petrarch's Poetics," *Diacritics* 5 (1975): 34-40.

[9] See lines 10477ff. Gallus is named, along with Catullus and Ovid, in 10492. The whole passage, as Lecoy notes, is modeled on the third book of the *Amores*. Concerning the significance of this passage in the *Roman*, see Karl D. Uitti, "From *Clerc* to *Poète*: The Relevance of the *Roman de la Rose* to Machaut's World," *Annals of the New York Academy of Sciences* 314 (1978): 209-216.

name Petrarch is able to use for the narrator of the *Roman de la Rose*. Petrarch, who knew his Ovid, knew Jean's Ovid too.

One effect of placing Jean de Meun within the context of Latin classicism has already been suggested: it conveniently removed him from a possibly competitive position within the arena of vernacular love poetry. Petrarch probably sent the manuscript of the *Roman* to Guido Gonzaga in 1342 or 1343. At that time, the decisive shape of the *Canzoniere* had already emerged—an erotic "history" in the first person, controlled by explicitly Augustinian concepts and built around the Augustinian conflict of the "two loves."[10] The important similarities shared by the *Roman* and the *Canzoniere* are as insistent as the works' formal dissimilarities. They may have been accidental or "conventional," but we can hardly believe that Petrarch was unaware of them. He was *inescapably* aware of them if, as is not unlikely, he knew the Italian "version" of the *Roman de la Rose*, the *Fiore*. The *Fiore* adapts the *Roman de la Rose* to the form of a sonnet sequence, the first example of that important mode of Renaissance love fiction, and the only work in Western literature that could be described as a tolerably convincing formal model for the *Canzoniere* of Petrarch. There are questions of greater interest concerning the *Fiore* than the question of whether Dante had a part in it.

The subject of the *Roman de la Rose* and the *Canzoniere* is one to tempt a comparatist to energetic investigation, but it is not the subject I shall pursue in this chapter, for I would suggest that another work of Petrarch's evidences more sharply his intuitive understanding of Jean de Meun's poetic mind. The last two lines of Petrarch's thumbnail sketch of the *Roman* are these: "Somniat iste tamen, dum somnia visa renarrat / Sopitoque nihil vigilans distare videtur." I believe that I was correct ten years ago when I said that the gist of Petrarch's meaning is that the Lover never really wakes up.[11] That is, he

[10] On this point, see in particular the penetrating study of N. Iliescu, *Il Canzoniere petrarchesco e sant' Agostino* (Rome, 1952).

[11] Fleming, *The Roman de la Rose*, 248.

remains to the end an ironic and opaque narrator. He could, after all, hardly abdicate any claims to authority more forcefully than he does with his formal abjuration of Reason in his final speech. I see now, however, an important implication in Petrarch's phrase, which in my simplicity I earlier overlooked. There seems to be in these two lines an inescapable allusion to Macrobius, and specifically to his characterization of the *insomnium*, the *enypnion* that haunts the sleeper's nights only because it has first haunted his days. Macrobius' phrase is "qualis vigilantem fatigaverat, talem se ingerit dormienti," and the contrast *vigilans/dormiens* is that echoed by Petrarch's *somniare/vigilare*. It is hardly surprising that Petrarch should turn to the categories of the *Somnium Scipionis*, a work alluded to in the opening lines of the *Roman de la Rose*, when he speaks of that poem; but his reference can perhaps help us to see in it what a Ciceronian and an Augustinian saw.

II. CONFESSIONS OR SOLILOQUY?

Ernest Wilkins dated Petrarch's letter to Guido Gonzaga in 1342 or 1343, and this accords with the surmise of other scholars as well.[12] This period of Petrarch's life was a particularly rich one, characterized by intense and diverse industry, public acclaim, and something akin to a private crisis of the spirit. On April 8, 1341, Petrarch had been crowned with the laurel at the Campidoglio, thus gaining that literary *gloria* that was at one level the most obvious and enduring object of his life as a poet. His nearly religious investment in the poetic enterprise is evidenced in several texts of that time, but particularly in his actual "acceptance speech," the *Collatio laureationis*, and in the famous "Canzone of Glory" (119) *Una Donna più bella assai ch'l sole* (1343/1344). The same texts are by no means without their evidences of poetic crisis. The somewhat paradoxical fact is that the *Africa*, upon which, at

---

[12] Wilkins, *Petrarch at Vaucluse*, 39.

least in his own mind, Petrarch's claim to glory was to rest,
languished in uncertainty as the poet sought the direction, or
perhaps the will, to prosecute his intentions. The quest of
glory was complemented by the quest of love, for love pursued
him to the Vaucluse, which was for him after all love's special
battlefield: *Persequendomi Amor al luogo usato* (110). Love and
glory were much in Petrarch's mind and art in those years,
twin appetites ambiguous alike in their vocabulary and their
morality, the ideal subjects of complex and ironic poetry.[13]
We see in the texts of those years much evidence of the driving
force of love and glory: what is less clear is whether Petrarch
thought of himself as the driver or the driven. In the moral
dialogue in which he examines his own state of mind, he
converses thus with his alter ego:

> AUGUSTINE. You are still bound on the left and the right,
> by two adamantine chains. . . .
> FRANCIS. What are they?
> AUGUSTINE. Love and glory.[14]

That book is the *Secretum*, written in its first draft at the
Fontaine de Vaucluse between the autumn of 1342 and the
winter of 1343.[15] The *Secretum* is many things: spiritual au-

---

[13] Wilkins draws attention to the presence of the same themes in the
famous canzone *I' vo pensando*, contemporaneous with the *Secretum*, and sug-
gests that Petrarch's mood was darkened by, among other things, his chaffing
dependence on patronage. See "On Petrarch's *Accidia*," 589-94.

[14] *Secretum*, ed. E. Carrara (Turin, 1977): 111, 113. All citations are from
this standard edition, which first appeared in Francesco Petrarca, *Prose*, ed.
G. Martellotti, P. G. Ricci, E. Carrara, and E. Bianchi (Naples, 1955).
To find the page number in *Prose*, add 20 to the number here cited. English
translations are based on the version of William H. Draper, *Petrarch's Secret*
(London, 1911).

[15] The date for the original composition of the *Secretum* is suggested by a
speech of Augustinus (116), which places the "action" fifteen years after the
first encounter with Laura, on April 16, 1327. The question of the work's
revision is more controversial. See Francisco Rico, "El 'Secretum' de Petrarca:
Composición y Cronología," for a review of opinion. Rico's own opinion is
revised in his *Vida u Obra de Petrarca* (see footnote 30, below).

tobiography, classical dialogue, essay in ascetical theology, and emblem of Petrarch's lifelong quarrel with himself. But it is also, and conspicuously, a debate between Reason and the Lover; and in this respect, I should suggest, it raises again the question left pending since Benedetto's day concerning the extent of Petrarch's understanding and appreciation of Jean de Meun's earlier achievement in the same genre. The evidence we must examine is of course implicit, indirect, and even covert. Though he may have been a slave to his appetites for love and glory, Petrarch was not a man to indenture himself happily to another writer, no matter how much he admired him—not to Cicero, not to Vergil, not even to the greatest of them all, Augustine himself. We shall find in the *Secretum* no plagiarism of the *Roman de la Rose* and no "sources," but nonetheless the *Roman* seems to me to have enabled the *Secretum* in two crucial regards: first, in its "picaresque" narrator, an untutorable foolish lover; second, in its ironic Christian negotiation, through the authority of St. Augustine, of certain classical literary texts.

There is a sense in which the most obvious common denominator between the *Roman de la Rose* and the *Secretum is* Augustine, but Augustine is present in the two books in very different ways. As we have seen, Augustinian concepts, and even specific Augustinian texts, command the critical moments of the debate between Reason and the Lover in Jean de Meun's poem, but they do so in a disguised and at times almost subliminal way. In the *Secretum*, on the other hand, Augustine's presence is immediate, palpable, and nearly overwhelming. It is he who commands the authority of a Philosophia or a Raison, he who has control of the argument, he who begins and ends the book. If the Augustine of the *Roman de la Rose* has been deceptively difficult to detect, the Augustine of the *Secretum* is deceptively obvious. Thus it is that our understanding of the central presence of Augustinian authority within the *Secretum* must begin in a somewhat paradoxical fashion: we must first look beyond the captious idea that the *Secretum* is Augustinian "autobiography" in the mode of the *Confessions*.

The idea that there is a definite and definitive relationship between the *Confessions* and the *Secretum* has been shared by nearly all scholars who have been disposed to take Petrarch's Augustinianism seriously, and this means the very scholars from whom I myself have learned most. The idea is succinctly encapsulated in one of Pietro Gerosa's chapter titles: "The *Confessions* of Petrarch."[16] That an "Augustinian" reading of the *Secretum* should excite such an expectation is hardly surprising. To the extent that it is a work of spiritual autobiography, it must inevitably invite comparison with the medieval model of spiritual autobiography *par excellence*, especially since we know from abundant evidence exterior to this particular text that no other book exercised a more powerful control on Petrarch's thought and art. Furthermore, there are many echoes of the *Confessions* in the *Secretum*, as well as two powerful and explicit citations of Book 8 that draw the sharpest possible comparison between the moral states of Petrarch and the young and carnal Augustine. The first book of the *Secretum* offers us an Augustinus who explicitly claims that, in the agony of conflict that preceded his conversion, he was like Franciscus; and there follows the celebrated exchange about the fig tree and the laurel.[17] In the second book Augustinus accuses Franciscus of desiring chastity without willing it: "Expertus loquor; hoc et michi contigit. Dicebam, 'Da michi castitatem, sed noli modo; differ paululum.' "[18]

It was probably impossible for Petrarch to write on an Augustinian theme without echoing the *Confessions*, a book that had become a part of his very mind and heart. Yet I think we must carefully distinguish between the Augustinianism of the

---

[16] P. P. Gerosa, *Umanesimo cristiano del Petrarca* (Turin, 1966), 82-93: "Le 'Confessioni' del Petrarca." Gerosa's notes contain a rich bibliography of studies devoted to the same idea.

[17] *Secretum*, 22, 24.

[18] Ibid., 80 (*Confessions* 8.7).

Secretum and that of other Petrarchan works. Augustine's *Confessions* can "explain" the letter on the ascent of Mont Ventoux, and probably "explain" the *Canzoniere*, if we mean by "explain" to relate in a direct and controlling manner, whether indicative or ironical. To expect them to "explain" the *Secretum*, however, is a critical mistake that at best presents us with unwelcome and unnecessary difficulties and at worst can lead to a serious misreading. If we come directly from the *Confessions* to the *Secretum*, we must perforce come with "comic" expectations, for the plot of the *Confessions* is conclusively comic. Augustine's history is a history of conversion, of crisis resolved, conflict calmed, and sickness cured. Its moral groundings are tested and secure. Its literary mode is detached and reflective—precisely "confessional," indeed. It is a book written by a middle-aged Catholic bishop about an adolescent Manichee.

How different is the *Secretum*! If the *Confessions* are the memoirs of the retired sea captain, written in the warmth and security of his house overlooking the harbor, the *Secretum* is the daily log of a mariner in the midst of a stormy and dubious voyage. To long for the calming of the waves and for the beacon of a friendly shore is not the same as to have them. In the *Secretum* Franciscus longs for conversion, but "not yet." He recognizes crisis without overcoming it, identifies conflict without resolving it, diagnoses pathology without curing it. The critical expectation of a decisive *likeness* between the two books has actually weakened our perceptions of Petrarch's spirituality and exaggerated further his reputation as a secularist or even a skeptic, for the qualities of the *Confessions* are decisively *absent* from the *Secretum*. Augustine gives us conflict, decisive resolution, definitive conversion. Petrarch gives us conflict, equivocal volition, and rhetorically emphatic indecision. The last speech of his Augustinus begins, as the whole book had begun, in moral deadlock: "We are returning to our ancient quarrel."[19] As a model for Petrarch's "confessions,"

[19] *Secretum*, 194: "In antiquam litem relabimur."

those of Augustine become poignantly ironic. To put this another way, if Petrarch is actually modeling the *Secretum* on the *Confessions*, he seems to do so in a fashion that undercuts Augustine, questions his authority, and removes the focus of psychological scrutiny from the reciprocal drama of penitence and grace to the exploration of Petrarch's personal "hang–ups." All of these claims, and others still, have in fact been made. I think they lack foundation, however, and that the decisive disjunctures between the *Confessions* and the *Secretum* point a quite different lesson. The *Secretum* is so little like the *Confessions* because its primary Augustinian allegiance is to another book and another mode of argument. The moment we make a close examination of questions of literary form, we find several features that, taken together, emphatically deny any tentative claim that the *Confessions* might make as a literary model for the *Secretum*.

Even before such matters are taken into consideration, it is clear enough that the *Confessions* are not the *only* Augustinian text that must occupy our attention. One obvious text of crucial relevance is the *De vera religione*, obvious because of its prominent citation and warm approbation by Franciscus near the end of Book 1.[20] Franciscus there cites Augustine's idea, "which you have spoken of frequently, including in your book *De vera religione*," that the process of spiritual ascent is hampered by the "plague of corporeal images" (*pestis fantasmatum*) that crowd the soul and cloud its vision. In numerous other passages of the *Secretum*, unnoticed by its editors and annotators, Augustinus cites or paraphrases his "own" words from the *De vera religione*, a work that articulates, in the simplest and most catechetical form, the dilemma of Franciscus, his inability to impose volitional spiritual control over the carnal affections that he correctly identifies and disparages: "It is most easy to execrate the flesh, and most difficult not to judge according to it."[21]

[20] Ibid., 46.

[21] "Sed facillimum est exsecrari carnem, difficillimum autem non carnaliter capere" (*De vera religione* 20.40; ed. Pegon, 78).

Thus did the *De vera religione* offer an intellectual entrée to the subject matter of the *Secretum*; and for the "Christian humanist," keen on stressing the continuities between classical philosophy and the philosophy of Christ, it offered much more. The usual view of Petrarch is that he was a man so deeply caught up in conflict that neither his life nor his work can be discussed without major consideration of his own self-conscious "tensions." His moral rhetoric, built as it is around the Pauline conflicts of the two wills, spirit and flesh, does indeed seem to demand such analysis; but I am less certain that the search for a parallel tension at the literary level has been altogether helpful. Typically the question has been cast in terms of a conflict between "classical" and "Christian" elements in his writings—their genres, topics, and styles—and, more especially, in a tension between the Ciceronian and the Augustinian mode. Gerosa wanted to see the mind of Augustine behind the shaping principles of the *Familiares*; but this cannot be, says another critic, for "Petrarch expressly says that he wished to follow the example of Cicero."[22] Here we have a tension, perhaps, but is it one of Petrarch's invention?

We have already seen the tendency of such humanistic Christians as Ambrose, Aelred, and Jean de Meun to impose supertextual Christian freight on Ciceronian design so that it is not always a simple matter to say that a writer is "following Cicero" *tout court*; and we have already examined one particularly crude and therefore unavoidable example of this phenomenon in the *Roman de la Rose*, in a passage in which Reason claims to quote Cicero's *De senectute* but actually quotes St. Paul. There is a conscious artistic manipulation of the texts in such a passage, but not, I think, a tension. The relationship between the text of the *De senectute* and that of the Bible implied in Jean de Meun's lines is in some ways curious, but it is hardly "tense." There is not a dynamic of tension between its

[22] G. Levi, "Pensiero classico e pensiero cristiano nel 'Secretum' e nelle 'Familiari' del Petrarca," *Atene e Roma* 35 (1933): 64; cf. *Familiares* 1.1.32.

classical and its Christian elements, but one of symphony and
accommodation. For Jean de Meun it seems the most natural
thing in the world to "quote" Cicero with the words of Scrip-
ture. It was the effortless reflex of the Augustinian poet and
the Augustinian moralist. How much more obviously was it
the easy habit of Petrarch, a man deeply and systematically
studied in the works of both Cicero and Augustine?

Looking at Petrarch's whole career, we can hardly conclude
that his studied Ciceronianism is not in part a logical and
coherent aspect of his Augustinianism, passionately and to
some extent independently pursued, but nonetheless depend-
ent upon it. Petrarch, tutored by Augustine, looked behind
the Ciceronian rhetoric that any writer could admire to the
philosophical *pectus* known to few. Cicero would be for Petrarch
a great teacher, a great moralist, a great philosopher, who
"even if he was not a Christian, was in other respects a great
and extraordinary man."[23] That phrase is part of Petrarch's
incipit annotation on the first page of his copy of the *De vera
religione* in which he cites, rather as though it had been Au-
gustine's unarticulated epigraph, two sentences from the *Tus-
culans*: "It was because they could frame no mental vision;
everything was brought to the test of eyesight: and indeed it
requires a powerful intellect to abstract the mind from the
senses and separate thought from the force of habit."[24]

In its context this is part of a condemnation of the super-
stitious who, incapable of spiritual experience, substitute for
it the phantoms of a carnal imagination. In the conflict of the
two wills, classically stated by Paul and classically dramatized
by Augustine, Petrarch saw the shape of his own experience
and his own story. It is always exciting to find the evidence

[23] Paris, Bibl. nat. MS lat. 2201, fol. 23v: ". . . etsi non cristianus, in
ceteris tamen magnus et singularis vir. . . ." See Francisco Rico, "Petrarca
y el 'De vera religione,' " *IMU* 17 (1974): 328, and plate 30.1.

[24] Cicero, *Tusculan Disputations*, ed. and trans. J. E. King (Cambridge,
1966), 45: "Nihil enim animo videre poterant, ad oculos omnia referebant.
Magni autem est ingenii sevocare mentem a sensibus et cogitationem ab
consuetudine abducere." (1.16.37-38.)

of a fiction in the making, and that is exactly what we have
in Petrarch's *incipit* annotation to the *De vera religione*, for it
has a clear relationship with the end of Book 1 of the *Secretum*.
There Augustinus tells Franciscus that he undertook the *De
vera religione* on the basis of a word from "your Cicero."

> FRANCIS. O best of Fathers, do not hide from me what that
> word was which gave you the starting-point for so excellent
> a work.
> AUGUSTINE. It was the passage where in a certain book
> Cicero says, by way of expressing his detestation of the errors
> of his time: "They could look at nothing with their mind,
> but judged everything by the sight of their eyes; yet a man
> of any greatness of understanding is known by his detaching
> his thought from objects of sense, and his meditations from
> the ordinary track in which others move." This, then, I
> took as my foundation, and built upon it the work which
> you say has given you pleasure.[25]

The passage is doubly engaging precisely because it *is* fiction.
Augustine cites Cicero literally hundreds of times in his works.
Testard documents about fifty citations from the *Tusculans*
alone.[26] But nowhere does he cite "Petrarch's text," least of
all in the *De vera religione*, which is, in Augustinian terms,
poor in Cicero. There are of course the famous statements,
emblems of Augustine's rare irenic charm, that "the philos-
ophers" (among whom Cicero would rank with Socrates and
Plato in Augustine's eyes) had stopped just short of the Truth,
camping as it were on Truth's threshold; and there is a critique
of sensory experience quite close to that of Cicero in its essential
Platonism. But the undeniable fact is that it is Petrarch who
arranges the marriage of Cicero and Augustine, not Augustine
himself. Petrarch moves from an intuition of literary criti-
cism—the apprehension of a complex intellectual relationship
between the *Tusculans* and the *De vera religione*—to the simple

---

[25] *Secretum*, 46 (*Tusculans* 1.16.37).
[26] See Testard, *Saint Augustin et Cicéron*, 2:133-34.

statement of a fictional "fact," a fact that minimizes if it does not entirely forbid any "conflict" or "tension" between the pagan Cicero and the Christian Augustine. There is a direct generic relationship between *Tusculans* 1.16.37 and the *De vera religione*. Matters are just as simple as that—and as complex!

The *De vera religione* takes us in what I think is the right direction, and that is in the direction of the spiritual profile of the younger Augustine, but in terms of its literary form it is even less promising than the *Confessions* as an actual model for the *Secretum*. In the first place, the *Secretum* is a dialogue. In a prologue notable for a certain artistic self-consciousness, not to say literary coyness, Petrarch draws insistent attention to the dialogue form. He explains that he is writing in the manner of Cicero (*De amicitia* 1.3) when, in order to avoid repetitious recourse to "I said" and "he said," he has chosen instead simply to place the names of the interlocutors (Augustinus, Franciscus) before the words they are imagined to have uttered: "Hunc nempe scribendi morem a Cicerone meo didici; at ipse prius a Platone didicerat."[27] It would be difficult to imagine a more glorious tradition: from Plato to Cicero to Petrarch. Yet that tradition fairly shouts out a name that Petrarch has elliptically omitted: Augustine, the younger Augustine, the author of the dialogues of Cassiciacum. Secondly, the *Secretum* is a soliloquy, that is, a conversation of a single consciousness dramatized by a fictive division among two literary personae. Its dialogue is a double fiction, the one internal, the other exterior. Finally, the *Secretum* is a work in three books. The *De vera religione* shares none of these features. As for the *Confessions*, almost no possibility of literary form is absent from its virtuoso pages, and there are moments in them when the subliminal conversation between the author and his God takes on the vivacity of crafted stage language; yet in no normal sense could it be called a soliloquy. Moreover, the formal structure of the *Confessions*, both in its dispositon into

[27] *Secretum*, 6.

thirteen books and in the rhetorical and intellectual shape of its arguments, differs decisively from that of the *Secretum*.

Yet we have already seen that there is an Augustinian text that is as formally similar to the *Secretum* as the *Confessions* are dissimilar to it. It is the *Soliloquia*, the text that (as I argued in an earlier chapter) was crucial both for the fictive forms of the *Consolatio* and for the long dialogue between Reason and the Lover in the *Roman de la Rose*. The book is a dialogue, though of course also a soliloquy, its speeches divided between Ratio and Augustinus even as in the *Secretum* they are divided between Augustinus and Franciscus. The only inconvenience in this analogy—the fact that the *Soliloquia* form two books rather than three—proves to be more superficial than substantial. As Augustine twice explains in his *Retractations* (1.4.1; 1.5.1), the *Soliloquia* in their two-book form were unfinished. He intended to add to them a third book concerning the immortality of the soul. The rough outline or notes for this essay—he calls it a *commonitorius*—has survived separately as the *De immortalitate animae* in a discursive argument not yet recast in the dialogue form. His remarks about the *De immortalitate animae* in the *Retractations*, indeed, taken with his general description of the *Soliloquia* in the same place, provide an obvious parallel for what Petrarch says about his own *Secretum* at the end of its prologue.[28] The clear implication is that he modeled his own three-book soliloquy on the three-book soliloquy that he correctly found in the *Soliloquia/De immortalitate animae*. Given the seriousness and depth of Petrarch's study of Augustine, we should have little doubt that he was well acquainted with all of Augustine's more important works, or at least those, like the *Soliloquia*, that enjoyed what might be termed extraordinary circulation. In the event we have the explicit testimony of a letter to his brother Gerard (*Fam.* 10.3)

---

[28] *"Secretum* enim *meum* es et diceris; michique in altioribus occupato, ut unumquodque in abdito dictum meministi, in abdito memorabis" (ibid., 6).

in which he counsels him to read the *Vitae Patrum*, the *Dialogues* of Gregory, the *Soliloquies* and *Confessions* of Augustine, and the psalms.[29] The context makes it clear that Petrarch regarded the *Soliloquia* as an ascetic text, one, that is, which intended to move its reader from engagement in the world of inferior loves to contemplation in the realm of spirit.

He has also given his informed reader numerous indications that he should recall the *Soliloquia* as he reads the *Secretum*. Petrarch's first and second books begin with clear echoes of the first and second books of the *Soliloquia*, and a central concept of the *De immortalitate animae* inaugurates the third.[30] We must emend Gerosa's formulation: the *Secretum*, Petrarch's *Soliloquia*. That is, Petrarch's first-person debate between Reason and the Lover points us once again to a controlling text in Augustine that we have already identified in the *Roman de la Rose*. Is this mere coincidence, or the simple manifestation of artistic obeisance to a common inspiration and tradition? These are questions that cannot, perhaps, be finally answered; but the insistent suggestion of Petrarch's book, inferrable from his own orchestration of classical authority, is that he has learned from Jean de Meun.

III. THE DREAMS OF POETS AND THE NIGHTMARES OF CRITICS

We earlier discovered in Jean de Meun's dialogue between Reason and the Lover a pattern of intertextuality in which

[29] *Familiares* 10.3, 56: "Lege Gregorii dyalogum, Augustini soliloquia et scatentes lacrimis confessionum libris . . . ," in *Le Familiari*, ed. V. Rossi (Florence, 1934), 2:299.

[30] Petrarch's general debt to the *Soliloquia* is noted by Francesco Tateo, *Dialogo interiore e polemica ideologica nel "Secretum" del Petrarca* (Florence, 1965), 16, is partly documented in the notes to Carrara's edition of the *Secretum*, and more fully documented by F. Rico, *Vida u Obra de Petrarca, I: Lectura del Secretum* (Padua, 1974). Rico's study is learned and frequently profound; and, to exchange compliments with him, I must say that there is much in it with which I *do* agree. Rico does not consider the *Roman de la Rose* in this book.

ostensible literary authority is actually much indebted to a more covert Augustinian text. The apparent prominence of Boethius in the conception of the character Raison is actually qualified by the anterior achievement of Augustine in the *Soliloquia*. The apparent Ciceronianism of Lady Reason on friendship is crucially increased by the silent Augustinianism of Aelred of Rievaulx. The congruences of Augustine and Cicero on the one hand and Augustine and Boethius on the other are not, I would argue, fortuitous. They reflect the perception, which was no doubt general among medieval humanists, of Augustine's actual debt to Cicero, and of Boethius' to Augustine. In fact, it was probably the conspicuous classicism of the *Soliloquia*, among the book's other attractions, that contributed to its perennial popularity among medieval educators.

The remarkable edition of the *Soliloquia* published by Hanspeter Müller in 1954 has provided us for the first time with a philological commentary of sufficient depth to allow us to gauge the astonishing extent of Augustine's own "Ciceronianism" in that work and to speculate upon its philosophical significance.[31] The debt begins with the first sentence of the book's brief introduction: "Volventi mihi multa ac varia mecum diu, ac per multos dies sedulo quaerenti memetipsum ac bonum meum, quidve mali evitandum esset. . . ." As Müller notes, Augustine is here echoing the famous opening line of what was to be for the Christian Middle Ages and the Renaissance one of Cicero's best-known works, the *De oratore*: "Cogitanti mihi saepenumero et memoria vetera repetenti. . . ."[32]

There are a number of reasons why Augustine might begin his *Soliloquia* with an obvious echo of the beginning of the *De oratore*. In terms of literary form he could hardly have claimed a more appropriate model for what he intended to be *a dialogue in three books*. At this level we may regard Augustine's gesture

[31] *Augustins Soliloquien*, ed. Hanspeter Müller (Bern, 1954), see esp. 59ff.
[32] See *Augustins Soliloquien*, Müller's note, 222.

as deference to Ciceronian *lingua*. But we know that he reverenced *pectus* even more, indeed inestimably more. Augustine's Cicero, like Dante's Vergil, comes astonishingly close to the Wisdom of the eternal Father. He is certainly to be reckoned among those men who, could they but live for one moment in a world now transformed by the grace of Christ, "would, making some small changes of vocabulary and precept, become Christians like the great majority of the Platonists of our own and recent generations."[33] Augustine would likewise have appreciated the close moral affinity between the ethical agenda of the *De oratore*, a work that exalts the capacities of the intellect in the service of the spirit, and his own agenda in the *Soliloquia*.

As for Petrarch, the depth of his interest in the *De oratore* need be in no doubt, for we possess, in Troyes MS 552, the poet's own heavily annotated copy of it.[34] His numerous scholia make clear for us the care with which he had studied the work—following methods explicitly attributed to Augustine in the *Secretum*—and the eloquence with which it addressed his most intimate professional and artistic aspirations.[35] Nonetheless, it has not to my knowledge been pointed out that the very *incipit* of the *Secretum* nods deferentially toward it, and that it does so in a manner of considerable intellectual elegance, by recognizing and acknowledging Augustine's own prior homage to it. The *Secretum* begins as follows:

> Attonito michi quidem et sepissime cogitanti qualiter in hanc vitam intrassem, qualiter ve forem egressurus, contigit

---

[33] *De vera religione* 5.7: "Et paucis mutatis verbis atque sententiis christiani fierent, sicut plerique recentiorum nostrorumque temporum Platonici fecerunt" (ed. Pegon, 34).

[34] See P. Blanc, "Pétrarque lecteur de Cicéron. Les scolies pétrarquiennes du *De Oratore* et de l'Orator," *Studi Petrarcheschi* 9 (1978): 109-166.

[35] "Quod cum intenta tibi ex lectione contigerit, imprime sententiis utilibus (ut incipiens dixeram) certas notas, quibus velu uncis memoria volentes abire contineas" (*Secretum*, 106; cited by Blanc, "Pétrarque lecteur de Cicéron," 111n).

nuper ut non, sicut egros animos solet, somnus opprimeret, sed anxium atque pervigilem mulier quedam inenarrabilis etatis et luminis, formaque non satis ab hominibus intellecta, incertum quibus viis adiisse videretur.[36]

That we have here an echo of the opening phrases of the *Soliloquia* is clear enough.[37] In the midst of introspective reflection appears a personification of authoritative guidance: for Augustine, *Ratio*, for Petrarch, *Veritas*. There is, of course, no such figure of authority in the *De oratore*, which is, so to say, a simple dialogue, not a dialogue set within a vision. Yet Petrarch signals his awareness of the anterior presence of Cicero in Augustine by restoring the specific Ciceronian vocabulary that Augustine has subtly altered. Petrarch restores Cicero's verb *cogere*, which Augustine had changed to *volvere*, and his adverb *sepissime* is a closer echo of Cicero's *saepenumero* than is Augustine's phrase "per multos dies."

Petrarch's Ciceronianism, no less than Augustine's, is a fact of ambiguous implication, yet it is fundamental to his thought no less than to his style. Whatever significance we choose to give to a specific instance of his "use" of Cicero, it would be dangerous to assume that his echoes and borrowings lack artistic intention or intellectual precision. Still less should we doubt that his alert readers would be conscious of the debt and speculative concerning it. Indeed, one of the chief ways that Cicero would be known to the early Renaissance was as he is mediated through Petrarch's pages. Vatican MS Palatino 1820, written in 1394 for one "dominus Iohannes Ludovicus de Lambertatiis, utriusque iuris doctor," contains a broad anthology of Cicero's essays and orations, including the *Catilines*. Giuseppe Billanovich, who has attempted to link the manuscript with Petrarch's own Paduan studium, draws attention to an early marginal notation beside the arresting sentence *Abiit, excessit, evasit, erupit* (*In Cat.* 2.1.1). One Petrarchan

---

[36] *Secretum*, 2.

[37] See, e.g., Rico, *Lectura del Secretum*, 17.

Ciceronian has written "Principium unius epistole Francisci Petrarce in libro sine nomine: *evasisti et cetera*."[38] Of course, to find echoes of Cicero in Petrarch is not quite the same thing as to find premonitions of Petrarch in Cicero. The reader who is disposed to do the latter will find the proemium of the *Secretum* a particularly rich text, one in which Petrarch echoes Cicero's adumbrations of Augustine.

This proemium is, indeed, conspicuously rich in textual interrelationships. Among the authors manifestly present are Vergil, Cicero, Macrobius, and Boethius; among the works, the *Aeneid*, the *Somnium Scipionis* and its commentary, the *De amicitia*, and the *Consolatio Philosophiae*. My speculation is that they are there because among other reasons they were first brought together in a fashion at once strikingly similar to Petrarch's and substantially different from his in the *Roman de la Rose*.

One means of approaching the peculiarly rich and significant "intertextuality" of Petrarch's *Secretum* is through a consideration of its genre. There is little that is simple about the *Secretum*, including the question of its literary kind, and we must be prepared to find that it is many sorts of books at once. It is, of course, something of a spiritual or intellectual autobiography, and it is also a dialogue. Its generic relationships in these regards have been deeply probed by a succession of astute critics. The opening and closing "scenes" of the *Secretum* mark it very clearly as something else as well: a visionary allegory. An Old Girl appears to a first-person narrator. Her silent power controls the dialogue and, we are told, guarantees the authenticity of the content of the vision. All this is familiar enough. The problem arises, of course, from her *silence*. Veritas does not engage Franciscus in dialogue, except for a brief

[38] G. Billanovich, "Petrarca e Cicerone," in *Miscellanea Giovanni Mercati* (Città del Vaticano, 1946), 4:89-90. The Petrarchan allusion is to the incipit of the nineteenth letter of the *Liber sine nomine*; see P. Piur, *Petrarcas 'Buch ohne Namen' und die päpstliche Kurie* (Halle, 1925), 235: "Euasisti, erupisti, enatasti, euolasti."

moment of introductory stage-setting. Rather, she introduces
Augustinus and, like the impresario of a dumb show, retires
to a background of silent and shadowy potency. The interloc-
utors of the dialogue are Augustinus and Franciscus, yet the
dialogue itself is presided over, in rather mysterious fashion,
by Veritas, the Old Girl.

This is, at the very least, an unusual arrangement, and I
am tempted to describe it as unique in the traditions with
which Petrarch shows manifest familiarity. Few critics have,
to my knowledge, recognized the difficulty of accounting for
this visionary mode in terms of its possible relationships with
anterior tradition; and such discussion of the matter as there
has been rather misses the point, in my opinion, since it rests
upon confident but unsubstantial distinctions between a "me-
dieval" and a "Renaissance" spirit in Petrarch. That is, we are
told that Petrarch's preference for Augustinus over the ab-
straction Veritas is a progressive Renaissance touch, the re-
jection of dead medieval allegorical machinery in favor of a
more vibrant historical realism. According to Paul Piehler,
"we are at this point in an age which genuinely felt itself more
comfortable with a living figure rather than an allegorical
abstraction for the *potentia* of its spiritual dialogues."[39] Even
Francisco Rico, our best guide to the *Secretum* and a critic
generous in his appreciation of the complexity of Petrarchan
intention, seems to share this view.[40] I say "even," for I believe
that the view is a superficial one that at once ignores the actual
literary history of the visionary dialogue and avoids the clear
meaning of Petrarch's manipulation of his literary models. In
reading the *Secretum*, it is most useful to learn early what
Franciscus learns only late if indeed at all: that without the
authority of Veritas, the teaching of Augustinus, or of any
mortal man, is nothing worth. The text insists that the use

[39] Paul Piehler, *The Visionary Landscape: A Study in Medieval Allegory* (Lon-
don, 1971), 142.
[40] Rico, *Lectura del Secretum*, 29.

of the human oracle is a condescension to Franciscus' feebleness, but Augustinus also provides, as Socrates has earlier done for Amant, a purely human referent.

The *Secretum* is not a dream, but it is nonetheless a dream vision in the sense that its literary strategies have been defined by the repertory of what might be called medieval literary "somnology." I refer, of course, to the technical terminology of dreams that Macrobius advances in his commentary to the *Somnium Scipionis*, a vocabulary that was to become the authoritative if somewhat fuzzy lexicon of visionary poetry for a thousand years and more, and one that claimed authority not merely for poets, but for physicians, moralists, and cosmologists as well.[41] We may note briefly in passing—to return to the fact in a moment—that there is abundant evidence that Petrarch was meditating deeply on Cicero's *Somnium* in the early 1340s; and of course, Macrobius' commentary claims conspicuous authority in the very opening lines of the *Roman de la Rose*. What is perhaps of particular interest is that in the *Secretum*, as in the *Roman de la Rose*, Macrobian authority is sometimes honored and sometimes studiedly denied.

In Macrobius' famous five-fold classification of dream experience, two of the categories—the *insomnium* and the *visum* (of which the exemplary types are, respectively, the erotic dream and the hypnogogic delusion)—are dismissed as valueless for moral education.[42] The three others, however, all do have moral and educational authority. They are the *oraculum*, in which an imposing authority appears to the dreamer and instructs him; the *visio*, a narrative dream of verisimilar char-

---

[41] For evidence of its widespread authority, see P. Courcelle, "La Postérité chrétienne du *Songe de Scipion*," *REL* 36 (1958): 205-234; and H. Silvestre, "Note sur la survie de Macrobe au moyen âge," *Classica et Mediaevalia* 24 (1963): 170-80.

[42] Macrobius, *Commentarii in Somnium Scipionis*, ed. J. Willis (Leipzig, 1963), 8ff. This is the edition cited throughout. English versions are based on the excellent translation by William H. Stahl, *Commentary on the Dream of Scipio* (New York, 1952).

acter truthfully predictive of things to come; and the *somnium*
proper, roughly speaking, an enigmatic dream requiring al-
legorical interpretation before its meaning can be grasped.
Macrobius does not describe the *somnium*'s nature because, he
says, there is no one who is not familiar with it: it is apparently
what we normally think of when we think of dreams. The
somnium itself displays five subcategories, depending upon
whether it be *proprium, alienum, commune, publicum,* or *generale*,
that is, whether its protagonist be the dreamer himself, or
another person, or the dreamer himself acting together with
others, and whether its arena be local and specific (as a par-
ticular city) or extraterrestrial. Neither the categories of dreams
themselves taken generally nor of the *somnium* in particular are
exclusive, and in fact the *Somnium Scipionis*, according to Ma-
crobius, includes elements of the *oraculum*, the *visio*, and the
somnium; and of the *somnium*, it exemplifies all five kinds. The
promiscuity of dream-genres can sometimes be confusing in
medieval poems, but it can also be artistically effective. Part
of the wit of the *Roman de la Rose* is that it advances simul-
taneous and unresolved claims to be both a *somnium* and an
insomnium, a work requiring allegorical explication and a work
unworthy of it. I shall return to this important point in a
moment.

The specific literary patterns that most insistently claim our
attention in the context of the *Secretum* are, of course, those
associated with the *oraculum*. Macrobius' definition of the *ora-
culum* is as follows: "Et est oraculum quidem cum in somnis
parens vel alia sancta gravisve persona seu sacerdos vel etiam
deus aperte aventurum quid aut non eventurum, faciendum
vitandumve denuntiat."[43] This definition is entirely adequate
for Cicero's text and for other classical *oracula* that Macrobius
no doubt had in mind, but it is palpably inadequate in one
crucial particular as a description of the very numerous body
of medieval *Christian* Latin texts that use or play off against

---

[43] *Somnium Scipionis*, ed. Willis, 10.

the oracular mode. The trouble lies in the phrase "vel etiam deus." It was natural for a pagan grammarian, attempting to generalize on the basis of texts familiar to him, to say that the oracular authority might be an imposing personage or "even a god." It is equally natural that his Christian contemporaries, who, after all, daily trumpeted the demise of the "lying gods" whom he had in mind, would themselves seek other and more reliable oracles. Thus it is that if we look at the modes of oracular vision in medieval literature, we find that Macrobius' definition fails to touch by far the greater number. Leaving aside a number of texts in which the pagan gods actually did survive—as, for example, the wonderfully witty *Rota Veneris* of Boncompagno—we can easily enough find two distinct types based on two obvious models. In the first, the apparitional authority is an historical personage, a man. In the second and far more numerous class, the apparitional authority is a philosophical or moral or psychological abstraction, a woman. Without for the moment concerning ourselves with the complex literary relationships that link these modes with antique philosophical traditions, we can easily enough identify the two most conspicuous models. They are the *Somnium Scipionis* itself, in which the visionary authority is a great figure from Roman history, Scipio Africanus, and the *Consolatio Philosophiae* of Boethius, in which that authority is Lady Philosophy, the allegorical personification of an abstract noun in the feminine gender.

We have already seen in the first chapter of this book that the personification of Philosophy or Wisdom in antique Platonic tradition could involve one kind of literary apotheosis, and it seems obvious enough that the apparitional ladies of medieval Christian oracles—whether they be called Philosophy, Truth, Phronesis, or Holy Church—are quasi-divinities, "insofar as the law of Christ allows." Although the fact is in my opinion inadequately explained by the imagined conflict of the medieval and the Renaissance "spirit," we may safely say that the personified abstraction is the distinctively Christian

form of the oracle, both the logical accommodation of and
perhaps the explicit rejection of Macrobius' phrase "vel etiam
deus." It is, in a certain sense, a kind of literary expropriation,
a movement from ideas that medieval Christians typically thought
of as "old" to ones they thought were "new." The phenomenon
is evidence of a supertextual imposition upon the categories
of Macrobius.

Charles Dahlberg has taught us to appreciate the extent of
Macrobius' unifying presence in the *Roman de la Rose*.[44] The
Somnium Scipionis is directly cited in Guillaume's opening lines,
and its final line is Jean de Meun's final line. In the more than
twenty thousand intervening lines Macrobian topics occur and
recur. We cannot know Guillaume de Lorris' mind on this
matter, lacking his specific rhetorical plan for an ending to
his poem; but Jean's attraction to Macrobius seems to have an
easy explanation. From one point of view, indeed, Macrobius
is the very mirror of an intertextual author, and the *Commentary*
the image of the intertextual book. Macrobius' work is entirely
contingent, in a formal sense, on Cicero, yet it generates a
powerful independent authority. Looked at from the other end,
Cicero depends upon Macrobius, who has provided the clarified
amber in which the most eloquent witness of the *De republica*
is preserved intact, a jewelled relic of a vanished masterpiece.
The analogous relationship of Jean de Meun and Guillaume
de Lorris is not an exact one, but it is significant.

I have been criticized for insisting that the *Roman de la Rose*
is, in its content, an *insomnium*.[45] Yet even after the reflection
always due to thoughtful reprimand I must persevere in my
opinion. Macrobius gives as his first example of the *insomnium*
that of "the lover who dreams of possessing his sweetheart or
of losing her." The poem that Jean de Meun inherited began
with the dreamer's deep anxiety over the loss of his beloved

[44] Charles Dahlberg, "Macrobius and the Unity of the *Roman de la Rose*,"
SP 58 (1961): 573-82.
[45] See, e.g., Friedman in *RPh* 28 (1975): 743ff.

and ends with the raucous celebration of possessing her. *That
is insomnium*. I am encouraged in my possibly obdurate view
by Petrarch: "Somniat iste tamen, dum somnia visa renarrat /
Sopitoque nihil vigilans distare videtur." "And though he wake
he is but dreaming still"; *that* is *insomnium*. I certainly must
give ground to my critics in acknowledging more explicitly
than I have before that the poem repeatedly insists (as Rupert
Pickens has nicely shown) that the dream experience is a sig-
nificant one, a "true" one, one that merits and demands inter-
pretation.[46] According to Macrobius, the *insomnium* is "un-
worthy of interpretation"; yet the whole nightmare of the rose
demands that all of its readers, and not a few of its own dream-
characters, be self-conscious exegetes. In short, we have an
unmistakable nightmare making unmistakable claims to the
kind of allegorical significance nightmares are not supposed to
have.

That the irresolution is intentional and artistic seems en-
tirely likely. I think that it was part of Guillaume's plan, and
I am certain that it was part of Jean's, both to posit the classical
authority of Macrobius and to supersede it in certain particulars
with another and a higher. In this regard, Jean shows his own
hand most clearly, perhaps, in the tragicomic allusions to the
castration of Saturn. As we noted briefly in an earlier chapter,
Lady Reason's demonstration of allegorical language—centered
on the example of the *coilles* of Saturn, cut off by his son
Jupiter—involves the explicit, even ostentatious cashiering of
Macrobius.[47] In the *Commentary* Macrobius distinguishes among
literary types between the *fabula* and the *narratio fabulosa*. The
fabula is simply a fiction: "the very word acknowledges their
falsity."[48] *Fabulae* can be vain or moral, but they make no

[46] Rupert T. Pickens, " 'Somnium' and Interpretation in Guillaume de
Lorris," *Symposium* 28 (1974): 175-86.

[47] This has been noticed by David Jeffrey Baker, "Allegory and Exegesis
in Jean de Meun's *Roman de la Rose*" (Ph.D. diss., Yale, 1978), 80. I do
not share Baker's view of the significance of the phenomenon.

[48] *Somnium Scipionis* 1.2.7; ed. Willis, 5; Stahl, *Commentary*, 84.

claim to literary truth either in setting or plot. The *narratio
fabulosa*, on the other hand, "rests on the solid foundation of
truth, which is treated in the fictitious style."[49] The *fabula* is
in general not suitable for elevated discourse—Macrobius calls
it "philosophical" discourse—but there is also a class of *nar-
rationes fabulosae* of similar unworthiness: "The presentation of
the plot involves matters that are base and unworthy of di-
vinities and are monstrosities of some sort (as, for example,
gods caught in adultery, Saturn's cutting off the privy parts of
his father Caelus and himself thrown into chains by his son
and successor)."[50]

There is a pattern here. Macrobius teaches that erotic dreams
are intellectually vacuous, "unworthy of interpretation"; Jean
creates an erotic dream of arresting dimensions and repeatedly
insists that we study out its significance. Macrobius denies the
suitability for moral literature of stories of the gods taken in
adultery or the castration of a god; Jean uses the former to
make an important moral point and the latter to offer a par-
adigm of allegory itself. The supererogation of Macrobius in
the *Roman de la Rose* is decisive yet tactful; he is venerated as
a classical authority who had much to teach, yet less than he
once did. The figure within the poem who continues to main-
tain what might be called a Macrobian hermeneutic is, of
course, the Lover himself. *He* will have no part in a poetics of
the privy. But in this, as in so many other things, he is guided
by canons made obsolete by the advent of grace.

IV. Dreams that Lovers Make

One of the puzzles of the *Secretum* comes early in the book,
in the brief and sole speech of Veritas to Franciscus: "I am
that Lady whom you have depicted in your poem *Africa* with

---

[49] *Somnium Scipionis* 1.2.9; ed. Willis, 5; Stahl, *Commentary*, 85. It is
significant that in the second book of the *Secretum* (132) Augustinus defends
Vergil's use of a *narratio fabulosa* in the story of Dido.

[50] Stahl, *Commentary*, 85.

a rare art and skill, and for whom, like another Amphion of
Thebes, you have with poetic hands built a fair and glorious
Palace in the far West on Atlas's lofty peak."[51] At these words,
Franciscus recognizes that the woman must be Veritas: "I
remembered how I had described her abode on the heights of
Atlas." The reason all this is puzzling, of course, is that there
is no such passage in the *Africa* as it has come down to us. The
reference is either an enigmatic invention, or a testimony to
a poem that no longer exists. There is further evidence more
curious still. The second part of the third book of the *Secretum*
deals with the second "adamantine chain," *gloria*. Augustinus
attacks the composition of the *Africa* as a vainglorious pursuit
and advances a theory of true glory, the "shade of virtue,"
clearly dependent on Cicero in general and on the *Somnium
Scipionis* in particular. What is curious is that the doctrine
preached by Augustinus in the *Secretum*, directed in good meas-
ure against the project of the *Africa*, would seem to be indis-
tinguishable from that preached by Scipio Africanus in the
Africa as we have it.

   This evidence is ambiguous, not to say cryptic, but it has
been plausibly explained in a brilliant if speculative study by
Enrico Fenzi.[52] Not all of the suggestions of Fenzi's rich anal-
ysis are relevant to my own argument, but several of his most
original suggestions bear directly upon it. He posits a cycle
of composition in which Petrarch worked intensively on the
Africa, left it unfinished for a protracted period during which,
among other things, he wrote the *Secretum*, and then returned
to the *Africa*. The "new" *Africa*, significantly revised and sig-
nificantly augmented, was a poem very different from that at
which he had labored so intensively during the second half of
1341. It was transformed in terms of poetic conception and
moral vision alike. The "Palace of Truth" on Mount Atlas was

---

[51] *Secretum*, 2.

[52] E. Fenzi, "Dall' 'Africa' al 'Secretum': Nuove Ipotesi sul 'Sogno di
Scipione' e sulla composizione del poema," in *Il Petrarca ad Arquà*, ed.
G. Billanovich and G. Frasso (Padua, 1975), 61-115.

excised, presumably along with numerous other set pieces. But
more importantly, argues Fenzi, the poem was morally trans-
formed by a deep meditation on the vanity of human wishes
attendant upon the spiritual crisis evidenced by, and to some
extent described in, the *Secretum*. The new *Africa* has as its
first emphatic, major episode the dream of Scipio Africanus,
and Fenzi speculates that it reflects a crucial intellectual con-
frontation of Petrarch's period of trial: a confrontation with
the *Somnium Scipionis* of Cicero, which now became the artic-
ulate moral basis for the doctrine of glory advanced in the
poem—the doctrine enunciated in the *Secretum* by another elo-
quent African, Augustine of Hippo. If Fenzi's speculations are
correct—as I believe them essentially to be—they throw con-
siderable light on the *Secretum* as well as on the *Africa*. We
look in vain for a dramatic conversion of Franciscus in the
Secretum. Perhaps we are searching in the wrong book. The
evidence may lie in the *Africa*, or rather in the silence of blank
leaves that lie between the *Africa* as we know it and the poem
that is the object of the reproaches of Augustinus.

My linking of the two Africans, Scipio and Augustinus, is
not mere captiousness. It will have escaped no careful reader
of Petrarch that there is in his mind a mysterious, poetic
kinship between his two great heroes, almost as though he
believed that Scipio was an antique type of the great Father.
Like Scipio, Augustine combines Roman civility with impos-
ing moral presence. When Augustinus appears in the visionary
proemium of the *Secretum*, Franciscus is in no real doubt as to
who stands before him. Augustinus is clearly signaled by his
Roman eloquence and his African garb—"habitus afer sed
facundia romana."[53] The "typological" habit of mind was,
indeed, an intellectual trait that Petrarch shared with Augus-
tine, who in his *Confessions* had gone to some pains to draw
out the analogies between his own Carthaginian youth and the
African adventures of the *Aeneid*. Just as the sacraments of the

[53] *Secretum*, 4.

Faith were greater than the ancient types that foreshadowed them, so also was Augustine greater than Scipio, even though we have no epic *Augustiniad* to prove it. What we do have—in the *Secretum*—is the graceful submission of the oracular Scipio to the oracular Augustinus. Scipio is, to be sure, in no way decreased by this capitulation. It is arguable, indeed, that he is morally augmented by it. But the categories of the *Somnium Scipionis* are infiltrated by an Augustinian supertext. To put this another way, the authority of Cicero's pagan commentator, Macrobius, yields to the higher authority of his Christian commentator, Augustine.

Few medieval writers can have been so keenly aware of the obligations, or the invitations, of literary model; and the opening lines of the *Secretum* are particularly dense with acknowledgments, not in every case decorously unified, of classical and Christian traditions. In them we see underscored, as we have earlier in the pages of Jean de Meun, the poetic and moral relationships of the old and the new wisdoms. Petrarch at once claims a place for his "secret" dialogue in the tradition of pre-Christian classicism and recognizes the moral and literary superiority of the newer, Christian mode. Oracular expectation is, as it were, divided between the characters Veritas and Augustinus. Petrarch's "control," if Fenzi is right, was certainly the *Somnium Scipionis*, yet it is dealt with in a surprising fashion. In several crucial matters Petrarch turns his back on Cicero and Macrobius in order to follow Augustine and Boethius. This is hardly the work of a "Renaissance" classicist determined to reject medieval sterility.

Veritas and Augustinus, grammatical abstraction and apparently historical man, rather uncomfortably occupy the same allegorical space. Jean de Meun shows no compunction about this sort of thing—Reason chats happily with Amant, a fictive abstraction, about Conrad of Sicily, a real man. All three have been transfigured, *not* reduced, into exemplary ideas. Petrarch will not suffer Veritas a speaking part in the dialogue proper, but not, I would suggest, because of a "Renaissance" disdain for abstract ideas. In the *Secretum* Augustinus is every bit as much an "idea" as is Veritas. One Frenchman who clearly knows what Petrarch is about—though he makes a poor show of it when he tries his own hand at it—is Honoré Bovet, whose *oracula* attempt to imitate Petrarch in their visionary apparatus. Their literary mediocrity is no impediment to their testimony on this account. Bovet had close connections with Avignon, and his subject is the Great Schism. He is certainly a spiritual cousin of Petrarch and, though of a younger generation, may well have known him personally. His general familiarity with the *Secretum* as well as his intelligent understanding of what Petrarch was doing with earlier texts in it, seems obvious from his own work.

In *L'Apparicion Maistre Jehan de Meun* "Augustinus" has become Jean de Meun himself. Bovet, meditating in the garden of the Tournelle, a house that had once belonged to Jean, sees the apparition of the poet before him: "ou je me fu mis tout seul ou quignet du jardin, prins telle ymaginacioun qu'elle me tint tant longuement que, se je m'endory, soit en bonne heure. Mais vecy venir un grant cler bien fourré de menu ver. . . ."[54] The *quignet du jardin* is a good touch, nodding as it does ambiguously toward the eighth book of the *Confessions* and the *Roman de la Rose*; and the most explicit ancestry of the passage, looking back to the *Soliloquia* through the prologue of the *Secretum*, becomes even more arresting when we read it alongside Bovet's other vision on the same theme, the Latin *Somnium super materia scismatis*. Here Bovet plays off against the *Secretum* in a different way, by introducing his allegorical abstraction (the Church as Old Girl) by means of an historical authority (St. Augustine, of course): "Grabato jacens, super jactura scismatis nunc currentis, mane festo luminosi doctoris Beatissimi Augustini, mens mea anguste commota est cogi-

[54] *L'Apparicion Maistre Jehan de Meun et le Somnium super materia Scismatis d'Honoré Bonet*, ed. I. Arnold (Paris, 1926), 5. It is now generally believed that this author's name was Bovet.

tare. Quae michi cogitatio unam speciosissimam dominam presentavit. . . ."[55]

To return to the *Secretum*, there is a rich ambiguity about Veritas, whose Christianity, if it is there at all, is as silent and reserved as Lady Philosophy's. Her shadowy diffidence in the *Secretum* will seem all the stranger the more clearly we recognize her family resemblance to Lady Reason. Nearly all the familiar "topics" are there—the preternatural feminine beauty, the unworldly antiquity and luminosity, the awesome visage, the radiant eyes. We are surely in the presence of a latter-day Philosophia or Raison. Yet Petrarch gives us other unmistakable signals that Veritas is not merely the literary companion of Augustinus, the guarantor of his wisdom and the underwriter of his authority in the *Secretum*, but is an actual Augustinian concept. She is the Veritas of the Cassiciacum dialogues—Platonic wisdom given flesh in Christ, one of whose scriptural names is Veritas (John 14:6)—and when she speaks, we shall hear echoes of an Augustinian Christology. Her first words to Franciscus, the first words spoken in the *Secretum*, are strange words: "Noli trepidare, neu te species nova perturbet."[56]

That we have here an echo of the angelic reassurance to the witnesses of Christ's birth ("Nolite timere" [Luke 2:10]) is hardly surprising. The biblical text itself is probably influenced by "classical" oracular expectation. But there is more: "neu te species nova perturbet." In one of his many rich studies of the literary posterity of Augustine's *Confessions*, Pierre Courcelle notes with surprise that such a keen reader of the book as Petrarch appears never to make a specific reference to the famous "lyric of regret" in Book 10, the "Sero te amavi."[57] Yet I should suggest that it is precisely this famous passage

[55] *Somnium*, ed. Arnold, 69.

[56] *Secretum*, 2.

[57] P. Courcelle, "Le Thème du regret: 'Sero te amavi, pulcritudo!' " *REL* 38 (1960): 287.

to which Veritas makes a veiled allusion with the remarkable phrase "nova species."

Augustine's word, *pulchritudo*, lacks the ambiguity of Petrarch's *species*. The translators who have rendered *species* as "beauty" are of course correct, but the word also means form, appearance, manifestation.[58] Veritas, as an oracular lady in the classical mode, is like Augustine's God and Boethius' Philosophia—both old and new—"pulchritudo tam antiqua et tam nova." That she is characterized by a "nova species" is actually less surprising than that the "nova species" is not paralleled by an "antiqua species." Actually it is, for Veritas will presently explain, "I am that Lady whom you have depicted in your poem *Africa.* . . . Be not afraid, then, to listen and to look upon the face of her who, as your finely-wrought allegory proves, has been well known to you from of old [*pridem*]."[59] As I understand this line anew in the light of Fenzi's hypothesis, I take it to be an acknowledgment of the new plan for the *Africa* taking shape in Petrarch's mind. The "old" *species*, the *pulchritudo antiqua*, was that Truth who dwelt like a goddess of old in a poetic palace built on the slopes of Mount Atlas. But God does not dwell in houses built by hand. The new *species* is that inward guarantor of truth whose silent presence confirms the authority of the Augustinian autopsy of Franciscus' love in the *Secretum*.

Although Veritas can claim priority over Augustinus in terms both of her narrative appearance and of literary authority, our analysis of Petrarch's manipulations of the oracular mode begins most directly with a consideration of Augustinus. According to Macrobius, the oracular authority might be "parens vel alia sancta gravisve persona seu sacerdos vel etiam deus."

----

[58] Petrarch may have used the word *species* in part for its particular Augustinian reverberations. Although he does not use it in the lyrical *Sero te amavi*, it is Augustine's favorite word for "beauty." It appears twenty-six times in the *De vera religione* alone, usually with punning intent. See the learned note, "Species, forma," in Pegon's edition, 486-88.

[59] *Secretum*, 2.

Augustine is certainly a spiritual "father," and he is frequently so addressed by Franciscus throughout the *Secretum*. Neither his sanctity nor his gravity (among Petrarch's adjectives describing him are "grave" and "sober") are in question; and he is, of course, a *sacerdos*. What he is pointedly not, as we shall see, is *vel etiam deus*, but in nearly all other senses he satisfies the Macrobian criteria splendidly. This is hardly accidental, for he is in a very specific sense Scipio Africanus *redivivus*, or rather a supertextual version of Scipio. The Scipio of Cicero is addressed as "pater sanctissime atque optume."[60] Augustinus is "pater glorisissimus"—a term of the greatest possible interest given the importance of *gloria* to the third book of the *Secretum*—and "pater optime."[61]

Yet Augustinus remains an insistently *human* oracle, not a divine one. Indeed, he is introduced into the dialogue by the divine Veritas precisely because he, like Franciscus, is a mortal man: "I would that some human voice speak to the ears of this mortal man. He will better bear to hear truth so."[62] His authority is, ultimately, guaranteed only by the silent presence of personified Truth, a point made by Franciscus at the end of the third book when he thanks her by saying to Augustinus, "Had She turned away her face from us we should have wandered in darkness; your discourse had then contained no sure truth, neither would my understanding have embraced it."[63]

The literary strategies in play here are quite complex, but their ironic effect is that in seeming to undercut or delimit the authority of Augustinus, they actually aggrandize it. There is in the first place a Petrarchan obeisance to the "historical" Augustine of the *De vera religione*, a work without which the *Secretum* could not have been written and without which it cannot be understood. There, in an early chapter (10.20), Augustine suggests the germ of the twinned oracle, at once

---

[60] *Somnium Scipionis*, ed. Willis, 157.
[61] *Secretum*, 4, 46.
[62] Ibid., 6.
[63] Ibid., 192.

human and superhuman, by claiming that God teaches the truth to men of good will "with the help of good angels and certain men."[64] In the same passage he goes on to say that the truth taught by individual men is always subject to the authority of the Church: "What you recognize as true, that hold, and attribute it to the Catholic Church. What is false reject, and forgive it me, who am a mere man."[65]

Thus Truth will indeed instruct Franciscus, but she will do so through the agency of a *vox humana*. Franciscus, who has made an idol of a human woman, might yet be rescued by the intervention of a human man. I argued that the greeting of Veritas to Franciscus makes allusion both to the birth of Christ and to the Augustinian lyric *Sero te amavi*. That is quite a lot for a single sentence, but there is more to come. That Franciscus knows what to expect of an oracle, as well as what he is not getting when one appears, is obvious from his own first speech of reply: "When I heard her thus speak, though my fear still clung about me, with trembling voice I made reply in Vergil's words: 'O quam te memorem, virgo? namque haud tibi vultus mortalis, nec vox hominem sonat.' "[66] These are, of course, the words of Aeneas, spoken to his mother who appears, unrecognized by him, to utter the urgent commands of an oracle. Petrarch doubtless uses them for many reasons. One reason would be his own awareness of Augustine's habitual Christianization of Vergilian oracle in the *Confessions*, where he wittily uses the phrase *errores Aeneae* (the wanderings of Aeneas, the mistakes of Aeneas) to play off against his own *errores*.[67] The failure to recognize his own mother is Aeneas'

---

[64] *De vera religione* 10.20; ed. Pegon, 50; "per bonos angelos et quoslibet homines adjuvante."

[65] *De vera religione* 10.20; ed. Pegon, 50, 52: "Quae vera esse perspexeris tene, et Ecclesiae catholicae tribue; quae falsa, respue, et mihi qui homo sum ignosce." See further Antonio Castelli, "Suggerimenti di una lettura del Secretum di Francesco Petrarca," *Rassengna di Scienze Filosofiche*, (1969), 112.

[66] *Secretum*, 2 (*Aeneid* 1.327-28).

[67] See O'Meara, "Augustine the Artist and the *Aeneid*," 257-58.

first error in the poem. But Petrarch also cites the lines from
Vergil for what they do *not* say. His quotation cuts the hex-
ameter short. The concluding phrase of line 328, suppressed
by Petrarch, is "o dea certe!" The visionary authority of Pe-
trarch's baptised *oraculum* is not to be *etiam deus* as Macrobius
would allow, let alone *dea certe*, but rather God/Veritas, the
Truth. And though the voice of Veritas has not a human ring
(*nec vox hominem sonat*), she nonetheless has as her mouthpiece
the human voice (*vox humana*) of St. Augustine. We must wait
for his third book to discover what else Petrarch has in mind.

Augustine's consistent doctrine, variously exposed in the
differing forms of the Cassiciacum dialogues yet unchanging
in its fundamentals, is that the guarantor of what is true is
Truth Himself, speaking not with tongue and vocal chords
but in the silence of the heart. His most astonishing statement
of this doctrine, perhaps, comes in the concluding section of
the *De magistro*, where he proves that the only one who teaches
us anything true is the indwelling Christ; but its best-known
formulation is probably that of the *Soliloquia*, where anything
true is demonstrated to depend upon the priority of Truth
itself. Hence it must be that ratio, with or without its per-
sonifying capital letter, cannot alone be the guarantor of what
is true, only the means by which what is true is known. Truth
is different from, and above, reason.[68] This doctrine can help
us understand the strange doubling of authority in the visionary
figures of Veritas and Augustinus, in which the *potentia* of
Ratio/Philosophia/Raison has been subjugated to the silent
censor Veritas.

There have been few poets in literary history more conscious
than Petrarch of the challenge of literary authority and the
"anxiety of influence." Augustine he read deeply and contin-
uously throughout his long scholarly career. He considered
him to be the greatest genius in the history of Latinity and

---

[68] See the lucid explanation of this doctrine in C. Boyer, *L'Idée de la Vérité
dans la philosophie de saint Augustin* (Paris, 1920), 64ff.

thought his literary achievement would never again be matched.[69]
The claim that he read Boethius "not once but a thousand
times" we may regard as possibly hyperbolic; but we shall
hardly doubt that he knew what was in the *Consolatio*.[70] Even
in the absence of explicit testimony it would seem to me an
obvious probability that he understood that relationship be-
tween the *Consolatio* and Augustine's dialogues that we ex-
plored in an earlier chapter. One Augustinian disciple would
hardly mistake the inspiration of another, and he surely rec-
ognized in his fellow student the doctrine of their common
master. There is a lovely phrase in his famous description of
Pavia, written for his friend Boccaccio, in which he speaks of
the happy justice by which Boethius had found a common
tomb with Augustine: "You would say that Boethius had
followed the track of St. Augustine: in his life in his inspi-
ration, and particularly in the books he wrote on the Trinity,
and in death with his corpse and his tomb."[71] The creative
articulation of this perception that we find in the structure of
the *Secretum*, in which the literary model of Boethius' Philo-
sophia is at once honored and referred back to her superior
"original" in Augustine, has but one analogue known to me.
It is Jean de Meun's dialogue between Reason and the Lover
in the *Roman de la Rose*, acknowledged by Petrarch as the
greatest poem of the French language in a verse essay written
in France during the very years of his deep concentration on
the *Secretum*. I can conclude only, if tentatively, that we here
find the evidence of an unusually intelligent reading of the
Roman. Like many and perhaps most of Petrarch's literary
"borrowings," this one would involve a degree of masterful
reformulation that would allow him to seem more the creditor
than the debtor; yet I cannot think that the *Secretum* would be

[69] *Seniles* 17.2.

[70] *Familiares* 22, 2.12: "Legi apud Virgilium apud Flaccum apud Seve-
rinum apud Tullium; nec semel legi sed milies."

[71] *Seniles* 5.1: "Putes Augustini uestigia Seuerinum sequi, ut uiuentem
ingenio et libris his praesertim, quos post illum de Trinitate composuit."

as it is were if not for Jean de Meun. If this speculation is valid, it makes a point of some interest to literary history, though not the point I hope to make in this chapter. We are still trying to learn to read the *Roman de la Rose* of Jean de Meun.

In the battle of wits and words in book three of the *Secretum*, the most decisive words are almost always those of classical authors: Seneca, Terence, Ovid, and above all Cicero. Time and again in this book Petrarch takes up a classical text only to turn it against that part of himself we can identify in Franciscus, either through its powerful use by Augustinus or its comic abuse by Franciscus. An example of the latter, and a fine one, arises out of the book's sticking point—whether there is an unworthy element in Franciscus' love for Laura. Throughout this lengthy passage there are numerous parallels with aspects of Jean de Meun's dialogue between Reason and the Lover, as Franciscus, like Amant before him, conspicuously demonstrates that he is a poor *logicien*. For example, he defends the *quality* of his love in terms of its object. Since Laura is good, his love for her cannot be bad. To love a whore as he loves Laura would be wrong, but her virtue guarantees the virtuousness of his love. We may presumably apply the same defense to the dirty old men who importuned Susannah. A man may cut himself with his own knife, or sin with his own wife, as Chaucer's Parson remembers, and as his Merchant forgets. Franciscus does not, of course, stick to this argument, nor to any argument; he shifts to new ground, or rather sand, as swiftly as Augustinus scoops the old from under him. His final position is, quite simply, that even if he is wrong, he wants to be wrong. Amant, in the *Roman de la Rose*, says that he must follow his passionate obsession even if it leads him to hell, and even though he knows it is madness. Franciscus says something strikingly similar, but he does so in the words of Cicero: "You are wasting your labor. Whoever asserts that view of love I shall never believe him. And I will rest on

Cicero's saying 'If I err here I err willingly, and I shall never consent to part with this error as long as I live.' "[72]

Now this is a genuine Ciceronian citation, from the twenty-third chapter of the *De senectute*. But as Augustinus is quick to point out, Cicero is there testifying to his belief in the *immortality of the soul*. That Franciscus should thus abuse this powerful Ciceronian text in his third book of the *Secretum*—which schematically corresponds to the "third book" of Augustine's *Soliloquia*, that is, the *De immortalitate animi*—is at once witty and trenchant. The whole point about Franciscus' love for Laura, viewed from the point of view of Augustinus, is that it forbids him the proper contemplation of the implication of his own mortality and the immortality of his soul. As in the *Roman de la Rose*, moral error is linked to intellectual error exemplified as the failure to perceive the meaning of an ancient text:[73] "But you see what will be the consequences of the error in which you stand; it will precipitate your soul into all manner of folly, when shame and fear, even reason, that now acts as some check on passion, and the knowledge of truth itself shall all have disappeared."[74] We may wish to recall the special configuration in the *Roman de la Rose* of Honte, Paour, and their "mother," Reason. Throughout this third book, the antierotic testimony of the *Tusculans*, grounded in its conception of the governing role of Reason in the ordering of the soul, is powerfully brought to bear on the illness shared by Amant and Franciscus.

A second example of the power of classical texts to inform the dialogue, this one Vergilian, comes a page or two later in Augustinus' indictment of Franciscus as an idolator—another idea, of course, prominent in Jean de Meun. Franciscus has

---

[72] *Secretum*, 114 (*De senectute* 23.85).

[73] The artistic equation of carnality and intellectual error is a recurrent theme in Augustine's major writings, and in the *Confessions* in particular. See L. F. Pizzolato, *Le 'Confessioni' de Sant' Agostino: Da Biografia a 'confessio'* (Milan, 1968), 87.

[74] *Secretum*, 114.

been forced into the position—a position he cannot long main-
tain—that in loving Laura he is "not infatuated with any crea-
ture that is mortal," meaning that he loves Laura's soul.[75] He
continues by praising her extravagantly and by applying to
her imagined death the noble statement of Laelius concerning
Scipio Africanus, "It is her goodness that I loved, and that is
not dead."[76] Augustinus in no way impugns the actual virtue
of Laura—his quarrel is with the manner of Franciscus' love—
so he is willing to grant the most exalted claims that can be
made concerning her. "Sing the praises of your darling lady
as much as you will, and I will gainsay nothing; make of her
a queen, a saint, or even a goddess." "Mulierculam tuam
quantalibet laude cumules licebit; nichil enim adversabor: sit
regina, sit sancta, sit

> 'dea certe
> an Phebi soror, an nimpharum sanguinis una.' "[77]

This Vergilian citation (*Aeneid* 1.328-329) is devastating, for
it picks up, in mid-line, the first poetic citation in the *Secretum*,
in the proemium, when Veritas appears to Franciscus. As
Aeneas was unable to recognize the divinity of his own mother,
so also did Franciscus stop short of seeing the divinity of
Veritas, *quedam mulier* in his eyes. By the same token, implies
Augustinus, does he impose a vision of divinity upon one who
is wholly human, not merely a *mulier* but a *muliercula*.[78]

The propaedeutic of sweet reasonableness in the *Secretum* is
not precisely that of Petrarch's dialogues on Fortune, where a
personified Ratio takes up the argument in her own voice, but
it surely shares a tradition of the education of the "lover" as

[75] Ibid., 120.

[76] Ibid.

[77] Ibid., 122 (*Aeneid* 1.328-29).

[78] There is evidence here of the all too realistic misogynism of Augustinus.
The word *muliercula* is not an innocent diminutive, as its sole scriptural
appearance (II Tim. 3:6) makes clear. The Authorized translation is "silly
woman."

we find it exemplified in the *Soliloquia*, the *Consolatio*, and the
Roman de la Rose. Petrarch is more of a classicist than Augustine
and Boethius—they are instead classical authors writing in a
still continuous tradition—and than Jean de Meun, who is a
vernacular popularizer, and whom he may well have disdained
for that very reason. This means that Petrarch's anti-erotic
doctrines are more conspicuously and more explicitly based in
classical texts. For his purpose there could be no more powerful
indictment of unreasonable love than that in the fourth book
of the *Tusculans*, and he himself uses the Ciceronian texts
powerfully:

> AUGUSTINE. I might reply to you with a word of Cicero
> and tell you, "You are talking of putting boundary lines on
> vice itself."
> FRANCIS. Not in vice, but in love.
> AUGUSTINE. But in that very passage he was speaking of
> love. Do you remember where it occurs?
> FRANCIS. Do I remember indeed. Of course I have read it
> in the *Tusculans*. But he was speaking of men's common
> love. Mine is one by itself.

That, as Augustinus is quick to point out, is what they all
say; "for true it is that in all the passions, and most of all in
this, every man interprets his own case favorably."[79]

Yet the fact that this is *Christian* doctrine hardly needs a
ratification further than that it comes from the lips of the
greatest doctor of the Latin Church; that for all its classicism
it is strikingly *medieval* doctrine is likewise inescapable. Au-
gustine, and Augustine's Cicero, are strangely expert in the
symptomology of "courtly love."

> AUGUSTINE. Therefore Cicero was right when he wrote that
> "Of all the passions of the soul, assuredly the most violent
> is love," and he must have been very certain of his ground
> when he added that "assuredly"—he who in four books

[79] *Secretum*, 128; cf. *Tusculans* 4.18, 41.

shows he was aware of how Plato's Academy doubted everything.

FRANCIS. I have often noticed that reference, and wondered that of the passions he should call this the most violent of all.

AUGUSTINE. Your surprise would have vanished if you had not lost your powers of memory. But I must recall you by a short admonition of a recollection of its many evils. Think what you were when that plague seized upon your soul; how suddenly you fell to bemoaning, and came to such a pitch of wretchedness that you felt a morbid pleasure in feeding on tears and sighs. Passing sleepless nights, and murmuring ever the name of your beloved, scorning everything, hating life, desiring death, with a melancholy love for being alone. . . .[80]

These are the symptoms of a Troilus or an Aurelius or of any "courtly lover," the amorous torments laid on Amant by the god of Love in Guillaume's *Roman*.[81]

In one very funny exchange Franciscus asks Augustinus if he has time to listen to a brief encomium of the sole mistress of his heart, and Augustinus, by now tiring of this sort of thing, replies rather testily that he does not. He does so by citing a well-known line from Vergil's eighth eclogue: "qui amant ipsi sibi somnia fingunt" (do I not know that "those who love fabricate dreams for themselves?")[82] That is a serviceable account of the first-person fiction of the *Roman de la Rose*, and certainly of Petrarch's own description of that poem:

> Scilicet hic vulgo recitat sua somnia Gallus. . .
> Somnait iste tamen, dum somnia visa renarrat
> Sopitoque nihil vigilans distare videtur.

---

[80] *Secretum*, 134, 136; cf. *Tusculans* 4.35, 75. Augustinus here refers with a nice familiarity to "Cicero noster."

[81] Most, if not all Franciscus' symptoms, are included in Amours' summary of the erotic law, lines 2213ff.

[82] *Secretum*, 122 (Vergil, *Bucol.* 8.108).

There is another place in which Petrarch toys with Vergil's line about lovers' dreams. In the fifth book of the *Africa* the pitiful Massinissa, caught between his degrading, treasonous, and irrational passion for Sophinisba and the unyielding demands of civic virtue embodied in Scipio, wallows in a frenzy as fine as that of any courtly lover of medieval romance. Lying alone in his bed, tormented with erotic desire, he tries repeatedly but without apparent self-fulfillment to make love to the bed sheets, then dreams a waking dream of love and death wherein Sophinisba, poisoned by his own hand, will mate again with him in Tartarus.[83] It is a scene of great emotional violence and extravagance; but if it stops short of the comic, it is only because of that discomfort any reader must feel when faced with the tragedy, or the embarrassment, of the presence of stark, raving madness. "Mad" is the very word Massinissa himself uses when, coming for a moment to his senses, he dismisses the folly of his dreams: "Somnia sunt que fingis amans, et faleris amens."[84] Rico says that Petrarch here "cites or evokes" Vergil.[85] An obvious echo it is, certainly, but it reorders and alters Vergil's sense to give voice not merely to moral truism but to some specific implications of "heroic" love within an actual social context: "These are the dreams that thou, a maddended lover, makest and mistakest." The lover, the dreams, and their making—all this Petrarch takes from Vergil. The explicit madness is his own contribution. Mas-

[83] We may compare the young Massinissa's plight with that of Guillaume's Amant, to whom Amours enjoins masturbational reveries (2421ff.) all the more painful for the consciousness of their purely hallucinatory nature. That these are "dreams" is underscored by the striking couplet "En la pensee delitable / ou il n'a que mençonge et fable" (2433-34), which of course significantly echoes the opening couplet of the poem. The phrase "pensee delitable" is a precise French translation of "cogitatio delectabilis," a commonplace term in thirteenth-century theological discussions of the "stages of sin."

[84] *Africa* 5.680; ed. N. Festa (Florence, 1926), 128.

[85] Rico, *Lectura del Secretum*, 289n. Cf. A. Noferi, *L'Esperienza poetica del Petrarca* (Florence, 1962), 264-65.

sinissa is *amens* as well as *amans*. This is the same phrase he uses of Jean de Meun's mad Lover in his verse epistle on the *Roman de la Rose*.

The central irony of the *Roman de la Rose* is the irony of an unwaking dreamer, the ineducable narrator. There is a similar irony in the *Secretum*. Franciscus knows all the "right" arguments; indeed, he supplies many of them against his own more foolish self. But the dialectic of the third dialogue does not lead to clear conversion. It ends, instead, in impasse. Franciscus wants to be whole, but still does not entirely will to be whole: "Da mihi castitatem, sed noli modo." The pattern of this irony is certainly present, in potentiality, in the meandering dialectic of the *Tusculans*, and more obviously, in the Cassiciacum dialogues—dialogues sufficiently guarded in their final moral point of view to have excited an enduring and credible scholarly controversy as to whether Augustine was a Christian or a pagan neoplatonist when he wrote them. The pattern is somewhat clearer yet in the *Consolatio Philosophiae*, in the studied imbecilities of the narrator "Boethius," and in the dramatic exasperations of his teacher Philosophia. But only in the *Roman de la Rose* of Jean de Meun, among works anterior to Petrarch, do we find a major and extended drama of an obtusely, persistently, and invincibly wrong-headed "I."[86] The Lover's values are squarely at odds with those of the privileged authority within the poem, Reason, and the nature of their conflict has been focused by authorial manipulation upon certain Ciceronian and Augustinian texts. This is a complex and ambitious literary creation, and sufficiently distinctive that its presence in Petrarch's *Secretum* must excite our speculation and hypothesis.

[86] Two provocative attempts to deal with some of the complexities of the first-person narration in the poem are E. B. Vitz, "The *I* of the *Roman de la Rose*," *Genre* 6 (1973): 49-75; and Dahlberg, "First Person and Personification in the *Roman de la Rose*," 37-58. Dahlberg in particular has a number of excellent observations about the use of the first-person voice in Augustine's *Confessions*.

It is possible, of course, that Petrarch has stumbled onto Jean's path by accident, led like Jean before him by certain commanding texts of their shared humanistic tradition. On the whole, however, this strikes me as unlikely. Along with all of us, Petrarch ran afoul of the seven deadly sins, and like many great poets before and after him, he suffered much from *amor* and *gloria*. Nevertheless, he is not much of a stumbler, at least not when it comes to knowing what is in the books he read and wrote. He might never admit to himself, and still less to us his readers, that vulgar Gallus has much to teach not merely about love, but how to write about love. Here, however, in marked contrast to the final page of the *Secretum*, it may not be Franciscus who has the final word.

AFTERWORD

"True wit is Nature to advantage dressed," says Pope, "what oft was thought but ne'er so well expressed." Jean de Meun is a great poet but hardly a great thinker. We may doubt that many, if any, of the ideas in his poem are original with him, and the most important of them are in fact the commonplaces of a moral tradition already ancient in late classical antiquity. Jean's cleverness, his mental agility, indeed what we must finally recognize for what it is as his intellectual brilliance, is more clearly demonstrated by his poetic manner than by his poetic matter.

Those scholars who have studied Jean de Meun's commerce with his antique "sources" have drawn attention to the remarkable fashion in which he characteristically enriches his classical borrowing with increments of his own poetic imagination. Langlois was satisfied to call this phenomenon "development" of a source, and in many instances Jean's mode of development is to translate a few words into many. Eric Hicks draws attention to a specific instance from the "chapter of Amis" in which the Jaloux translates some lines from Juvenal's sixth satire in the course of an antimatrimonial diatribe.[1] "Must Postumus take a wife?" asks Juvenal. Can he not instead hang himself, leap from a high window, or throw himself from the bridge? Juvenal suggests the idea of hanging with a single use of the word *restis*, "rope": "Ferre potes dominam salvis tot restibus ullam?" Jean "develops" Juvenal's fine understatement into a lexically rich image: "Ne peuz tu trover a vandre / ou harz ou cordes ou chevestres?" (8708-9). There is loss as well

[1] Eric C. Hicks, "Le Visage de l'Antiquité dans le *Roman de la Rose*" (Ph.D. diss., Yale, 1965), 258-59; the relevant passage in Juvenal's sixth satire is at lines 28ff.

as gain in this procedure, and some might well think more
loss; but the independence and self-confidence of Jean's practice
of *translatio*, when applied to the larger narrative movements
of his poem, gives the *Roman de la Rose* its essential and ine-
luctable originality.

Paul Renucci, in a nice book title, called Dante "the disciple
and the judge of the Greco-Roman world." His phrase captures
a general truth about "medieval humanism," one particularly
relevant to Jean de Meun's literary classicism. Jean's eclectic
reading among the ancient authors is everywhere guided by
the practical concerns of the Christian moralist. Much of his
classical education must have come to him prepackaged, as it
had to a large extent even for some of the more learned Latin
humanists of the twelfth century, in the form of epitomes,
digests, and anthologies—practical books put together by
practical men with practical educational aims in mind. From
his favorite Christian authors—Boethius and Alain de Lille—
he took both individual ornaments of Egyptian gold and the
bold but tested strategies of his dialogue form and his
mythographic plot. In this and much else his considerable
originality operates within a strictly delimited arena: the li-
brary of major works of Christian classicism by other "disciples
and judges" of the ancient world. Like them he habitually
subjects his acknowledged pagan masters to a confident Chris-
tian correction when necessary.

The act of judgment, subtle and even subliminal in the
most interesting instances, can be quite coarse when need be.
Lady Reason, wishing to use the lamentable career of the
Emperor Nero for her exemplary purposes, turns with a con-
fident censoriousness to the impeachable authority of Seuton-
ius:

Et dit li livres anciens,   6425
diz *des .xii. Cesariens*,
ou sa mort trovons en escrit,
si con Suctonius l'escrit,

qui la loi crestiene apele
fause religion novele   6429
et malfesant, ainsint la nome
(vez ci mot de desloial home!) . . .

Here we may find the disciple nearly eclipsed by the judge.
In the broader strategies of Jean's classicism in the *Roman de
la Rose*, his judgment of "old books," though just as confident,
is much less insistently censorious. Much of his poetic mean-
ing, and of our poetic understanding, depends upon fine ad-
judications and subtle nuances, as in the differences between
Ciceronian and Aelredian friendship.

In the dialogue between Reason and the Lover, Jean de
Meun has created an ironic Christian protreptic. The dialogue's
structure, its principal themes, and its moral intentions derive
from a clearly definable classical tradition that had become, in
Christian antiquity, subtly transformed to Christian purpose.
Jean's "Reason and the Lover" is of course conspicuously related
to this ancient tradition, but its most remarkable poetic qual-
ities reflect Jean's uses of its literary history, his keen awareness
of the poetic possibilities inherent in the transformation of old
wisdom to new, of the philosophy of the philosophers to the
philosophy of Christ.

For Jean de Meun, a learned Latin Christian of the thirteenth
century, the tradition was principally defined by the names of
three great *auctores* of Latinity: Cicero, Augustine, and Boe-
thius. His own education in the tradition involved both trans-
lation and transformation. He became the translator of Boe-
thius, who had been the transformer of Augustine, who had
been the transformer of Cicero. Jean was also the translator of
Aelred of Rievaulx, the Augustinian transformer of Cicero. He
obviously knew the most important positive relations of the
tradition, and he probably grasped its more subtle and elegant
linkages: the hint of Boethian consolation in the final *levatio*
with which the *Tusculan Disputations* end, the complex vo-
cabulary of Ciceronian interiority that signals Augustine's strategy

in the first sentence of the *Soliloquia*, the comic potential latent
in the figure of the opaque interlocutor of the mind's dialogue
with itself.

The liberation of this comic energy is perhaps Jean's most
original contribution as (again perhaps) Petrarch may have
realized. One common bond linking works as diverse as the
Academica and the *De oratore*, the *Contra academicos* and the *De
ordine*, the *Consolatio* and the *Contra Eutychen*, is the proposition
that man, *rational* man, is capable of discovering and knowing
truth. In the philosophical tradition summarized by Cicero,
the epistemological claim was inextricably involved with a
moral doctrine: that the rational soul must reign over the
passions of the flesh, the worst of which (as Augustinus re-
minded Franciscus) is "love." The Christian Paul spoke of a
law of God in his "mind" and a law of sin in his "members."
Augustine called this second law *concupiscentia*; the members
over which it ruled were especially those that, whether they
be called *coilles* and *viz* or *escharpe* and *bourdon*, govern Jean de
Meun's Lover. There is little that is new in the protreptic
machinery of "Reason and the Lover" except for one thing:
the obdurate willfulness and ineducability of Reason's inter-
locutor. In the dialectical brilliance of his delineation of Amant's
dialectical torpor lies Jean's considerable comic achievement.
Jean de Meun does not in fact "overthrow," "undercut," or
"limit" the powers of Reason; but he does shake the body of
the protreptic dialogue until we hear the bones rattle.

My own *Reason and the Lover* has been an attempt to place
a particularly important part of the *Roman de la Rose* within
the specific literary traditions that most clearly claimed Jean
de Meun's close attentions, whether as disciple or as judge.
The defense of Lady Reason was a preliminary step necessary
to this enterprise, though the implications of her rehabilitation
are in many ways greater for those vast stretches of Jean's poem
from which the Lover forever banishes her than for the dialogue
that has been the focus of my book. The three great classical
writers who dominate Jean's view of the moral dialogue of

Latin Antiquity—Cicero, Augustine, Boethius—would force themselves upon any serious examination of the literary genre of our material; but Jean has used them in a fashion that goes far beyond what we usually speak of as generic models or the exploitation of sources. I have tried to show with specific examples based in a more detailed examination of poetic language than has often been granted to Jean's poem that "Reason and the Lover" has been built not so much on a foundation of the ancient dialogue "in the Ciceronian mode" as out of the very energies released by its subtle but decisive christianization. Parts of my argument I regard as positive demonstration, other parts reasonable speculation; and I have tried to be explicit in distinguishing between the two.

There is one final matter. "Reason and the Lover" composes less than a fifth of Jean's whole contribution to the *Roman de la Rose*. It is a particularly important part of the poem—in the emphasis of its initial position, in the cleverness of its continuities and discontinuities with the poem of Guillaume de Lorris, and in its moral and thematic preparation of the major chapters from which Reason is banished—and this importance recommends its special study. I am hardly unaware, however, of the need for a comprehensive understanding of the *Roman de la Rose* founded in a careful and detailed analysis of *all* of its parts. Many of the more important implications of "Reason and the Lover" for the rest of Jean's poem strike me as rather obvious, but I am silent concerning them pending the leisure and the inclination to submit them to the test of new researches. For now it is perhaps enough to contemplate the Lover's sad condition; suffering *grans douleurs* at Reason's arrival (4192), he is left *pensis et morne* at her final departure (7200). From this day's dialectic he has been left no richer; with him we must wait to see what another's brings. *Sufficit diei malitia sua.*

INDEX

LIBRARY OF CONGRESS CATALOGING IN PUBLICATION DATA

Fleming, John V.
  Reason and the lover

  Includes bibliographical references and index.
    1. Roman de la Rose. 2. Jean, de Meun, d. 1305?—Criticism and interpre-
tation. 3. Jean, de Meun, d. 1305?—Sources. 4. Dialogue. 5. Reason in literature.
6. Love in literature. I. Title.
PQ1528.F49 1984   841'.1   83-42557
ISBN 0-691-06578-0

GPSR Authorized Representative: Easy Access System Europe - Mustamäe tee
50, 10621 Tallinn, Estonia, gpsr.requests@easproject.com